DEATHLY WIND

Published by Sapere Books.

11 Bank Chambers, Hornsey, London, N8 7NN,
United Kingdom

saperebooks.com

ISBN: 978-1-912546-15-2

Keith Moray is represented by Isabel Atherton at Creative
Authors.

DEATHLY WIND

Inspector Torquil McKinnon Mystery Book Two

Keith Moray

SAPERE
BOOKS

To Lyla Grace,
welcome to the world

PROLOGUE

The assassin edged closer, sliding forward on his belly through the sand of the machair, gradually steering a course between the thick tufts of coarse grass and clumps of yellow-blossomed gorse. It was slow going, but he was prepared to take as long as it needed to get in position in order to carry out the execution crisply and cleanly.

It was an unexpectedly hot day with hardly a cloud in the cobalt blue sky. A day to soak up the sun, or so his targets might have imagined when they found the isolated strip of beach. The parents were snoozing while the two youngsters frolicked in the shallows.

Quite the little family group, he thought, with a sneer of contempt. He adjusted the silencer on the barrel of his Steyr-Mannlicher rifle and slid it through a clump of tall coarse grass, resting it on the bipod and squinting through the Leupold 'scope to take a bead on the father.

The youngsters were making a lot of contented noise, yet despite that, perhaps due to some sixth sense their mother suddenly shot up, her beautiful eyes wide with alarm.

She opened her mouth as if to cry out, but the assassin shifted his aim with unerring speed and squeezed the trigger. There was a dull popping noise, at variance with the effect of the bullet as it smashed into her throat, hurling her back against the sand to thrash wildly as her life began to ebb swiftly away.

The youngsters looked up, suddenly fearful and panicking. The father, awakened by the spray of blood across his face shot upright, his eyes sweeping round to fix the assassin. For one so big he moved surprisingly fast, instinctively trying to protect his family. But he was not fast enough. The assassin coolly aimed and fired, another popping noise belying the power of the bullet that bored its way between the eyes, exiting almost instantly from the occiput in a spray of blood and brain pulp.

Then the assassin was on his feet, the blood lust taking over. The youngsters were cowering, edging backwards from the bodies of their parents and the expanding pools of blood soaking into the sand. He had no compassion, no pity. He dispatched them both with a shot to the head.

He smiled contentedly as he looked up at the bright blue sky. It was the sort of day that made one feel good to be alive, he reflected. Especially when a commission like this one had been so easy and so pleasurable.

Five minutes later, he had dragged the parents' bodies up onto the machair and was just returning for the youngsters when he heard the motor of a boat approaching from the other side of one of the small islands. He hesitated for a moment then ducked down and made his way back to his sniper's position in the tall grass of the machair.

PC Ewan McPhee had set off on his round of the West Uist waters early that day and he was hungry. He came round the small island in the West Uist Police *Seaspray* catamaran and slowed down to coast towards the beach. He intended to snatch a break and have a cup of tea from his flask.

But then he saw the bodies and the blood soaking into the sand.

He cruised into the shallows, cut the engine and jumped over the side, running towards them. And, as he squatted beside them, he felt an overwhelming wave of nausea come over him.

He doubled up and began retching.

He never heard the soft footfalls coming towards him from the machair, and he never felt the blow that sent him flying face down beside the dead bodies.

CHAPTER ONE

The Reverend Lachlan McKinnon, known throughout West Uist as the Padre, was in a subdued mood, just as he had been for the last three days. For twenty-four hours following the discovery of the West Uist Police *Seaspray* catamaran, drifting empty like a latter-day *Mary Celeste*, he had hoped that they would find Ewan McPhee alive. On the second day, as hope started to peter out he had prayed fervently that the big police constable, the hammer-throwing champion of the Western Isles, would have somehow kept himself afloat on the sea until he was rescued. First thing that morning he had simply prayed that they would find the constable's body before too long, so that Jessie McPhee, his elderly mother, would be able to get on with her grief.

And then there was poor old Gordon MacDonald. His had been a sad and lonely way to die, but at least he could be put to rest. He ran over the notes that he had made in readiness for the funeral then tossed them on the desk and sat drumming his fingers on the surface for a moment. Finally, with a sigh, he got up and put on his West Uist Tweed jacket that was hanging on the back of his study door. He glanced in the mirror, adjusted his clerical collar a mite and ran his hand through the mane of white hair that permanently defied both brush and comb. He pushed his horn-rimmed spectacles higher up on his nose and reached for his golf bag that leaned in readiness beside the bookcase.

Life had to go on, as he told everyone. And golf was one of his ways of coping; apart from giving his bagpipes a good airing. Yet with his nephew, the local police inspector, Torquil

McKinnon, still away on a protracted leave of absence after his own recent personal tragedy, the pipes held little attraction for him.

A few moments later, with his golf bag slung over his shoulder and his first pipe of the morning newly lit and clenched between his teeth, he let himself out of the front door of the house and scrunched his way down the gravel path to the wrought-iron gate, then crossed the road and mounted the stile that led directly onto the ten-acre plot of undulating dunes and machair that he and several local worthies had converted and transformed into the St Ninian's Golf Course.

There was a fine early morning mist, and under its cover a few terns were dive-bombing some of the sheep that grazed freely over the coarse grass fairways of the links. He stopped on top of the stile and removed the spectacles that had already misted up. When he replaced them and dismounted he saw that three men were standing by the first tee.

'*Latha math*! Good morning!' Lachlan greeted them. 'If you are already playing don't let me hold you up.' He glanced at his watch. 'Not many start this early at St Ninian's.'

'It is the Reverend McKinnon, isn't it?' replied the eldest of the trio, in an unmistakable Glaswegian accent. 'See, I heard that you usually have an early round and I wanted to try out this famous golf links of yours. Maybe we could have a game?'

He was an olive-skinned, well-built man in his mid-forties, of medium height, with cropped black hair and a small, slightly upturned nose. Neat though it was, however, it seemed a tad smaller than one would have expected from his overall bone structure. That and a certain tautness of the skin on his face suggested to the Padre that at some time he had submitted himself to the skill of the cosmetic surgeon.

A bit of a peacock; a preening peacock, the Padre silently concluded.

'I'm Jock McArdle,' the man went on, assuming that the Padre had accepted his invitation. He extended a muscular hand bedecked with expensive thick gold rings. 'I've just moved into —'

'You've just moved into Dunshiffin Castle,' Lachlan interjected with the affable welcoming smile of the clergyman. 'Which makes you the new laird of Dunshiffin. I heard that you bought the estate a fortnight ago, Mr McArdle, and intended paying you a visit as soon as you took up residence, but I am afraid that we have had a few upsets on West Uist lately.' He shook hands and suppressed a wince at the power of the other's grip. He assumed that it was the habitual grasp of a hard-bitten entrepreneur, designed to indicate dominance. He duly ignored it, having long since refused to feel intimidated by anyone.

'No worries, Reverend, I only arrived four days ago. I've had to tie up a lot of business before I could move in. But I'll be living at the castle most of the time. I have big plans for the place.'

The Padre smiled unenthusiastically. 'Are you all three playing this morning?' he asked, his eye hovering over the single professional-spec leather bag and the two men standing a pace behind Jock McArdle.

'Naw, Reverend, it's just me,' Jock McArdle returned with a grin. 'These are two of my employees that I've brought from Glasgow. I thought that a bit of good clean sea air would be good for their health. Isn't that right, boys?'

'It's a bit deathly if ye ask me,' returned the one holding the golf bag. 'There's no night life. Just a handful of pubs.'

Jock McArdle guffawed. 'This is Liam Sartori, Reverend. As ye can see, he's a wee bit lippy, but he's a good lad.'

The Padre shook hands, his practised pastoral smile belying the shrewd appraisal that he had made of the two young men. Liam Sartori was a tall, well-built and excessively tanned fellow, probably the result of a sunbed rather than the sun's rays, the Padre reflected. Possibly a third or fourth generation Glasgow Italian. His clothes were casual and brashly expensive. A gold medallion hung from a heavy gold chain on the front of a red, white and blue sports shirt. He was unsure whether Jock McArdle's criterion of goodness matched his own.

'And this is Danny Reid,' Jock McArdle said, introducing the other young man who was in the process of opening a cigarette packet and offering it to Liam Sartori. 'See, he's the quiet one.'

'I'm the thinking one, Reverend,' said Danny Reid, clipping the cigarette in his lips and shaking Lachlan's hand.

He was a shade shorter than his associate, possibly a touch under six foot, well-muscled, with a tattoo of a claymore on his right forearm and at least six body piercings that the Padre could count on lips, ears, eyebrows and nose. Like his associate he had a medallion on a thick gold chain. His blond hair was spiky and most probably the result of peroxide. Lachlan watched as he lit their cigarettes with a gaudy Zippo lighter.

'I can only manage nine holes, I'm afraid,' Lachlan said. 'I have a funeral to conduct in a couple of hours.'

'Nine holes would be excellent,' returned Jock McArdle, enthusiastically. 'But see, would I be insulting your cloth if I suggested a wager?'

The Padre struck a light to his pipe, then replaced his box of Swan Vestas in his jacket pocket. 'A small wager always adds a frisson to a game, so I don't see why not. Match play or Stableford?'

'I prefer simple match play, Reverend. Winner takes all.'

The Padre blew a thin stream of smoke from the side of his mouth and nodded. It fitted with his assessment of the Glaswegian. The new laird was clearly a man confident in his own abilities. 'Shall we say five pounds for the winner? What's your handicap, Mr McArdle?'

'Fourteen.'

'And mine's a rather shaky eight. Exactly one eighth of my age. So, that means I give you three shots over the nine holes. That will be at the second, the fifth and the ninth.'

Jock McArdle nodded to Liam Sartori who unzipped a side pocket of the golf bag and extracted a box of Dunlop 65 balls, and a tee, then pulled out a Callaway driver. 'You'll be needing the big one, boss,' he said with a confident grin.

The Padre puffed thoughtfully on his pipe and pulled out his two iron, the club he favoured for the tricky first drive, especially when the wind was gusting as it tended to do on the first three holes.

'I'm thinking that you will enjoy the course, Mr McArdle. It isn't exactly the Old Course at St Andrews, but it's a good test of golf. Nature designed it with the Corlins on one side and the North Atlantic Ocean on the other, and we just added a few refinements. It has six holes dotted about the sand dunes of the machair, with three tees for each one, so you can either play a straight eighteen, or, when it is quiet, string any number of combinations together. The fairways are mowed once a week, the sheep nibble the green to billiard-table smoothness and the bunkers have been excavated by generations of rabbits. Watch out for the gorse and the thistles; think your way round and you'll be all right.'

He puffed his pipe again and nodded at the honesty box hanging from the fence. 'And, of course, the green fee is pretty reasonable.'

Jock McArdle grinned and nodded to Danny Reid, who drew out a roll of money and peeled off a five pound note. 'Is this safe here, Minister?' Danny Reid asked incredulously as he deposited it in the box.

The Padre pointed to the nearby roof of the church. 'This is West Uist, Mr Reid. St Ninian's Golf Course is beside church land. Who would steal from the church?'

Liam Sartori sneered, 'I'm willing to bet that you've never been to my part of Glasgow, Minister.'

Jock McArdle eyed the yardage marker by the side of the first tee, then the two iron in the Padre's hand. He handed his driver back to Liam Sartori and pulled out his own two iron. 'Aye, golf is a thinking game, Reverend. A careful game.' He grinned, a curious half smile with no humour in it. 'You'll find that I am always careful. It's a good policy in my book.'

Jock McArdle was a bandit off a handicap of fourteen, Lachlan decided, after they had played three holes and he found himself three holes down. Or rather, he was a 'bandit chief', on account of the fact that his two boys seemed to take it in turns to caddy and to find their boss's ball, a task that they seemed to achieve with miraculous skill. Indeed, knowing the extent of the gorse and thistle patches on the undulating dunes as well as he did, the Padre was almost certain that twice the ball had been discovered at least twenty yards further on than it should have and, on both occasions, had seemed to fortuitously find a nice flat piece of fairway.

'You play well for a fourteen handicapper, Mr McArdle,' the Padre said, as they walked onto the fifth tee. 'And your two *finders* have done sterling work this morning.'

'I like to win at everything I do, Reverend. That's why I've been successful in business. That's how I came to buy the Dunshiffin estate.'

The Padre pulled a dilapidated pouch out of a side pocket of his jacket and began stuffing tobacco into his battered old briar pipe. 'Am I right in sensing that you have something more than golf on your mind this morning, Mr McArdle?'

'You're a shrewd man, Lachlan,' returned Jock McArdle with an ingratiating grin. 'Do you mind if I call you, Lachlan?'

The priest shrugged. 'Most people on West Uist just call me Padre.'

'OK then. Padre. I'm not the sort of guy who beats about the bush.' He nodded to his two boys and raised his voice: 'You two go and have a smoke over by that pot bunker. But keep your eyes open. I'll be driving over your heads in a minute, so mind and duck.' When they were out of earshot he went on, 'Do you know how I came to buy the Dunshiffin estate, Padre?'

Lachlan had won the last hole and gained back the honour to drive first. He shoved a tee into the ground and perched his ball on top. 'I was aware of the liquidation of Angus MacLeod Enterprises after the death of the last laird of Dunshiffin, Angus MacLeod.'

'I picked the estate up for a song. Two and a half million, if you want to know.' His mouth twisted in a curiously self-satisfied way. 'That's not bad for a lad who started selling cones and wafers from a fourth-hand ice-cream van. I built up the biggest confectionary business in Midlothian over the last twenty years. And I have plans. Padre. Big plans.' He bent and picked up a few blades of grass and threw them into the air where they were caught in the breeze and wafted sideways. 'The wind is not too bad here, is it?'

'No, the Corlins give us a bit of shelter.'

'But it is really windy on the west of the island, isn't it? Especially over by the Wee Kingdom.' He seemed to puff up his chest. 'You know that as the owner of the Dunshiffin estate,' he beamed and corrected himself, '— or as you rightly said, as the new *laird*, I own all the land on the Wee Kingdom.'

The Padre stiffened a tad. 'Aye, you own it all right, but there are crofters there. They lease the land from the estate.'

'Exactly. See Padre, I'm their new landlord.'

'And you are thinking of erecting windmills on some of your land?'

Jock McArdle tossed his head back and laughed. 'So you know all about the wind farm idea?'

'Mr McArdle, I've been the minister on West Uist for thirty-five years. People have been talking about introducing wind farms in the Hebrides for a decade. They are almost a reality on Lewis already. It's only our remoteness on West Uist that has prevented talk of them coming here. That and the cost.'

'I am an entrepreneur, Padre. I have no ties to the energy department, or the electricity boards. I see an opportunity to generate a lot of electricity on this windy island, enough to supply every family and every business at a fraction of the cost. And where better than to start up a wee wind farm than on the Wee Kingdom? The most westerly point of the most westerly island. The wind is roaring in from the sea; it's a power source just waiting to be tapped.'

'I doubt if you'll have much support. They're unsightly things and we are proud of our wildlife on the island.'

Jock McArdle shrugged. 'There is little evidence about it affecting wildlife, Padre,' he said dismissively. 'In any case, I'm used to resistance. It doesn't worry me.'

The Padre glanced at his watch. 'I have to give you a shot at this hole, so I'd best nail this drive down the middle.' And taking his trusty three-wood from the bag, he did just that.

For the next four holes, the Padre watched his opponent's ball like a hawk and himself played with grim determination. Despite the strokes he had to give away, by the time they had reached the ninth green they were all square on aggregate.

'How many of these windmills are you thinking of having?'

'I'd be starting small. Just two or three to see how it goes, then who knows? My boffins tell me that twenty-five would produce a sizeable amount of power. That would be my target in the first year.'

The Padre stared aghast at him. 'You cannot be serious! There is no room. And you would need to be building pylons to carry the electricity.'

The Glaswegian nodded. 'I know all that, Padre. I have had it all researched. I have the means to invest and I have the permission to go ahead. I've had my lawyers check with everyone that matters — the Land Court, the Crofters Commission — you name it, I have had it checked and double-checked.'

'But you don't have the crofters' permission. They'll never agree to this.'

Jock McArdle smiled. It was a strange crooked smile that seemed to be formed by two very different halves of his face. One side was all innocence while the other was cunning personified. 'Technically, I don't need their permission, Padre. The original deeds that go with the Dunshiffin estate are quite clear: it is my land to do with as I please.' He looked at their two balls, comparing the distance of each from the hole. 'I'm on in three and you're there for two. With my stroke that makes us all square. And it looks like it's me to putt first.' He lined up his putt and struck the ball, cursing as it slipped a yard past the hole. 'I'm going to begin with the MacDonald croft. I have a couple of boys on their way to West Uist now with the components for a couple of wind-testing towers.'

The Padre eyed his opponent askance. 'This funeral that I have to take, did you know that it was Gordon MacDonald's?'

Jock McArdle nodded as he lined up his return putt. 'Aye, I knew that, Padre. I never knew the man myself so I won't be going to his funeral.' He tapped the putt and grinned with satisfaction as it rattled into the cup. 'A five, net four. You have a putt for the match.' His two boys smirked and lit fresh cigarettes.

As the Padre lined up his five-foot putt, McArdle remarked casually, 'Of course, as the new laird, I thought it my duty to attend the wake after the funeral.'

If the remark had been intended to make the Padre miss the putt, it did not succeed. Lachlan struck the ball smoothly and it disappeared into the cup with a satisfying rattle. The Padre retrieved it and held out his hand. 'My game, I think.' After shaking hands he pulled out his pipe from his top pocket and struck a match to it. 'I am thinking that is your right, Mr McArdle, but perhaps you should go easy on the wind-farm information.'

Jock McArdle again gave his curious half smile. 'I was hoping that maybe you could smooth the way a little. See, Padre, I am a good man to have on your side. I am always grateful for help shown to me.'

Liam Sartori smirked and was rewarded with an elbow in the side from Danny Reid.

'I'm thinking that you will find that the folk of West Uist make up their own minds, Mr McArdle.'

The Glaswegian gave a wry smile and gestured meaningfully

at Danny Reid. 'Well, it was good to play and talk with you anyway, Padre. And so I owe you five pounds. That's one thing that you should know about me: I always pay my debts — in full.'

The Padre smiled as he accepted a five pound note from the roll of notes that the be-pierced Danny Reid peeled from the roll that he produced with the dexterity of a conjurer.

'Well, let's just hope that you don't run up too many debts on West Uist, Mr McArdle. West Uist folk are pretty keen at calling in debts themselves.'

CHAPTER TWO

The Wee Kingdom was almost another island of the archipelago that formed West Uist. It was a roughly star-shaped peninsula with steep sea cliffs, home to thousands of fulmars and gannets, facing the Atlantic Ocean on its north-west coastline. Gradually the terrain descended to sea level at its most westerly point, where three successive basalt stacks jutted out of the sea. On the top of the last one was the ruins of the old West Uist lighthouse and the derelict shell of the keeper's cottage. Moving inland, the machair gave way to lush undulating hills and gullies surrounding the small central freshwater Loch Linne. To its inhabitants, this oft-times wind- and sandstorm-swept islet was heaven on earth.

The name, the Wee Kingdom, had been coined back in 1746 by the families that farmed the islet after the Jacobite laird, Donal MacLeod had granted the land in perpetuity to them and their descendants and heirs in gratitude for the sanctuary they had given the fugitive Bonnie Prince Charlie during the five days that he had stayed on the island while waiting for a French vessel to take him to safety. It had been the sighting of a heavily armed English frigate by Cameron MacNeil, the lighthouse-keeper, that resulted in the change of plan to move the prince back to South Uist from whence Flora MacDonald helped to take him over the sea to Skye and thence to freedom.

An automatic beacon on the cliff tops above had rendered the old venerated lighthouse obsolete in the mid-1950s, and it remained a ruin, accumulating a veneer of guano from generations of seabirds.

There were six smallholdings on the Wee Kingdom, each lived in and worked by a person or family, who had inherited it from a forebear or patron in keeping with the original dictates of Donal MacLeod's grant. Essentially, only six holdings were ever to be worked on the Wee Kingdom, the lease for each depending upon a peppercorn rent paid to the current laird in goods manufactured on the Wee Kingdom by the holders themselves. Effectively, the holdings pre-dated the crofting system by a full fifty years.

All six crofts were granted the right to use the natural resources of the islet of the Wee Kingdom and the surrounding waters up to a good stone's throw off the coast, including the same area around the three stacks and the lighthouse. And well stocked it all was. In days gone by the crofters had taken the eggs and birds from the cliff-faces, just as their distant neighbours, the St Kildans, had done for centuries. Like them, they cut and burned peat, farmed Soay sheep and kept a few cattle, goats, ducks and geese. They grew crops of potatoes, cabbages, turnips and beetroots on the traditional *feannagan*, or 'lazy beds' that had been artificially built up in long swathes and fertilized with innumerable barrowloads of seaweed over two and a half centuries. They each operated a treadle loom, using their own wool and traditional methods to produce the famous West Uist Tweed that was bought and sold down the west coast of Scotland. And in the shallow southern waters between the causeway and the edge of an underwater shelf they collected edible seaweeds for cattle fodder and fertilizer, and farmed the rich oyster bed, using their own boats and ten-foot long oyster tongs to rake up the valuable delicacies that were in much demand on West Uist and the other Western Isles. All in all the Wee Kingdom Community was a throw-back to the old days. Although each croft was worked as a separate enterprise, they still co-operated, shared and bartered; and they produced West Uist Tweed, pâté and oysters which were marketed under the label of the Wee Kingdom Community. All profits were poured back into the community and used or shared in equal measures. It was a system that had worked successfully for two and a half centuries.

An unmetalled road that was in a continual state of disrepair had been constructed across the causeway, wide enough for a single vehicle. It was just after noon when the Padre zipped across on his Ariel Red Hunter, the classic motorcycle that was his trademark, as he followed the wake party led by Rhona McIvor's erratically swerving minibus and a motley assortment of cars, vans and wagons. The state of Rhona's battered minibus was testimony to her propensity to bump car fenders, roadside rocks, gates and harbour walls. Her corner-taking was renowned and most people were aware that her vision had been progressively deteriorating to the point where she should not be driving, yet no one had so far had the temerity to suggest it to her.

The cortege followed the minibus up the rough pockmarked road to Wind's Eye, the late Gordon MacDonald's croft, then parked up amid the pens and outhouses and disembarked. Inside the austere thatched cottage with its mixed smells of seaweed, brewing yeast, turnips and stale tobacco, Rhona had already set out a spread of sandwiches, beer and whisky.

There were about a dozen mourners standing awkwardly in the low-ceilinged main room that had served the old crofter as a sitting-room, kitchen and workroom. The old thatched cottage, which had been built on the site of one of the old medieval 'black houses' reflected the late crofter's personality and had never been renovated or added to, as had most of the

23

other Wee Kingdom dwellings. Fishing nets and rods were stacked in a corner; a large brewing bin took up space beside the plain porcelain sink and on a shelf lay a well-thumbed King James Bible, the only book in the cottage.

'He was a religious man in his own way, Padre,' Rhona said, as she lifted a tray of glasses, a whisky bottle, a jug of beer and a jug of water. As she did so, Lachlan noticed how pale she suddenly looked. He also noticed the slight intake of breath, as if she had experienced a spasm of pain.

'I'll take that, Rhona,' he said, reaching for the tray, his manner brooking no argument. 'Is it the angina again?'

A thin smile came to Rhona McIvor's face. She nodded and pushed her thick-lensed wire-framed spectacles back on the bridge of her nose. She was a slim woman of about his own age he guessed, since it was not a statistic the remarkable Rhona ever cared to divulge. Lachlan remembered when she had taken her croft some twenty odd years before. Back then she had been a glamorous redheaded woman of the world. A freelance investigative journalist and a prize-winning cookery-book writer, she had come to the Wee Kingdom upon inheriting her holding, having made the decision to retire from the rat race forever. And that she had done, immersing herself in the crofting traditions and lifestyle of her forebears. 'It's a paradise, Padre,' she had told him one Saturday morning many years ago when he called in on one of his pastoral visits to the residents of the Wee Kingdom. 'No telephones, no deadlines, no editors breathing down your neck. You just have to put bread on the table and wool on the backs of the rich folk of Inverness.' He remembered her peal of laughter, as she then set about shearing a sheep, a cigarette in an ebony holder clasped between her small pearly teeth. In her dungarees and Wellingtons she made an impressive, if incongruous, sight.

The Padre had looked at her concernedly, but was relieved to see the pained expression quickly disappear. She was dressed in a smart trouser suit, her once tumbling Titian locks now iron grey, pulled back in a pony-tail that exposed her intellectual brow and the long neck that had attracted so many would-be suitors over the years. It was widely believed that she had had several lovers since she came to live on West Uist, yet neither she nor they ever broadcast the fact. Discretion seemed to be a guiding principle in Rhona's life.

'Aye, this angina is a bugger, Padre,' she said with a twinkle in her eye as she produced her trade-mark ebony cigarette holder from her shoulder bag and slipped a fresh cigarette into it. Lighting it with a small silver petrol lighter she blew out a stream of blue smoke. 'These things will be the death of me, I suppose.' Then she sighed. 'But we all have to go some day. Gordon was only a couple of years older than me, you know?'

'You'll go on forever, Rhona,' said the Padre.

'God, I hope not,' she returned, picking up a couple of plates of sandwiches. 'Look, you do the drinks and I'll feed the hoards.' Saying which she was off, a trail of smoke following in her wake.

Lachlan turned and went over to the two McKinleys standing by the merrily burning peat fire. Father and son, they worked Sea's Edge, the most westerly croft on the Wee Kingdom. As he held the tray and muttered a few words about the funeral he let them help themselves. Unconsciously, he found himself appraising them.

Alistair McKinley was a smallish wiry man in his mid-fifties with the gnarled and wrinkled skin of a man used to the elements. He was bearded with short cropped hair and an almost perpetual scowl on his face. He helped himself to a whisky from the tray while his son, Kenneth, took a glass of beer. In contrast to his father he was tall and broad-shouldered, his eyes blue like his dead mother's. His expression was not as severe as his father's scowl, yet there was about him a suggestion of unease, as if he was anxious to be off somewhere. Lachlan had seen that look so often among the young islanders as they began to hanker after some of the comforts, luxuries and attractions of civilized life. He wondered if the younger McKinley would soon announce to his father that he was going to cut loose.

'Is the croft going well?' the Padre asked Alistair.

'Passable, Padre. Passable.' The older crofter flashed a look at his son. 'It would be better if we were more focused.'

Kenneth McKinley shook his head slightly. He was twenty-two, but looked five years older. 'Och, we're doing fine. Father. We just need to ask —'

'We need to be patient, Kenneth,' Alistair said curtly. He sipped his whisky, and then turned back to Lachlan. 'You best see to the others, Padre.'

Lachlan nodded, quite unperturbed by the other's curtness, since he was renowned for it throughout West Uist, just as his father and grandfather before him had been. He went over to a trio, two young women and a man, standing by the door. Katrina Tulloch, the local vet was chatting with the two newest crofters, Megan Munro and Nial Urquart.

'Anyone for a dram?' he ventured. 'To see old Gordon off.'

A pretty girl in her mid-twenties with finely chiselled features and spiky blonde hair smiled and took a glass of water. 'I'd love to have a beer, Padre, but I'm afraid I am still on duty. A vet is always on the go in the Hebrides, you know.'

'Like a minister, eh Katrina?' said Lachlan, giving her a wink. 'I doubt if the sheep will notice the smell of beer. They never seemed to mind your uncle when he had the practice.'

'I'll have a glass of water as well, thank you, Padre,' said Megan Munro who was about the same age as Katrina. Unlike the other mourners, Megan had come in her work clothes, a beanie hat pulled down over her auburn hair, and almost over her earlobes from which dangled large hooped ear-rings. Despite her lack of make-up and grooming she still had the looks and curves that would make many men turn their heads. Her features were only slightly marred by a certain sternness of expression that seemed fastened around her mouth. 'I don't approve of alcohol,' she said firmly. 'I don't know why everyone thinks they should drink at funerals. I think it's a sad occasion.'

The Padre was about to say something when Nial Urquart, her partner, chipped in. 'That's a bit harsh, Megan. Gordon was a neighbour and we're all sad to see him go, especially the way he did, but it is natural to have a little party. Give him a send-off so to speak.' He nodded at Lachlan. 'That was a beautiful funeral service, Padre.'

Lachlan smiled, noticing that two pink patches had formed on Megan Munro's cheeks; a mix of ire and embarrassment, he thought. Although the couple had only lived on their croft for six months, he had already had enough contact with her to form an opinion on her character. She was strong-willed, passionate about animals and the environment, and moderately outspoken.

'This is a community, Nial,' she said, arms hanging rigidly at her sides. 'Poor old Gordon died in this cottage and no one noticed for two days — and that's us included.' She looked about the room melodramatically, then asked, 'And just where are the rest of the Wee Kingdom residents? Where is Vincent Gilfillan? Where are the Morrisons? They should be here now.'

'Vincent was at the funeral, Megan,' said Lachlan, turning to dispense drinks to a party of mourners, consisting of various tradesmen and shopkeepers from Kyleshiffin, who had known the deceased crofter for decades.

'But why isn't he here now?' he heard Megan persist. 'This is a time when a community should pull together.'

The Padre smiled to himself as he heard Nial remonstrate with her. Lachlan quite liked the young Scottish Bird Protection officer, and thought that he had taken on a challenge when he moved into Megan Munro's holding with her. The word was, of course, that she had seduced him after one of the public protest meetings she had organized after the announcement that there was to be a cull of the hedgehogs on the island. Nial Urquart was there to lend strength to the argument that the hedgehogs were devastating the seabird population by stealing eggs. However she did it, whether by art, craft or sexuality Lachlan did not know, but he had moved in with her and now he helped her to run her croft.

'Would you listen to her, the wee madam,' Rhona whispered in his ear, as she met him back at the big table where she was picking up another salver of sandwiches. 'She's only been a crofter for six months and she's telling everyone where they should be. She's really put old Alistair's back up with her hedgehog sanctuary and all her vegetarian propaganda.'

'Alistair has been appointed in charge of the hedgehog culling, hasn't he?' Lachlan asked in a half whisper.

'That's right, and a fine to-do they had over it. And there's another war brewing over the way he slaughters the livestock. And she's already made it clear to me that she doesn't think we should be making pâté from the duck livers.'

Lachlan frowned. 'But he's been doing it for years. He's a trained butcher, isn't he? And the Wee Kingdom pâté sells all over the islands.'

Rhona shook her head as she screwed another cigarette into her ebony holder and lit it. 'But that doesn't cut any ice with Megan. She thinks we should all turn vegetarian.' She sipped a whisky. 'I doubt that she will last long as a crofter. We never had any trouble with her great uncle, Hector Munro. He'd be turning in his grave at the way she carries on. And that poor Nial.' She shook her head sympathetically.

'Where is Vincent, by the way?' Lachlan asked.

'On his way to Benbecula. Oh it's quite legitimate. He talked to me after the funeral. He has to be there to meet the tweed buyer. It's normally Geordie Morrison's job, but he's gone off somewhere and taken the whole family with him.'

The smell of tobacco had given the Padre a craving and he pulled out his cracked old briar from his breast pocket and filled it. 'But it's still school time. He surely can't have taken wee Gregor and Flora away with him?'

'Och, Geordie is a law unto himself. Sallie Morrison has just about given up. He gets a bee in his bonnet about going off looking for whales or something, and just tells her that it'll be educational for the children. And off they go. They'll be back in due course.'

'So they don't know about Gordon's death?'

'No, they'll be devastated when they find out, but we have no idea where they are just now.'

Lachlan struck a light to his pipe and picked up a glass of beer. He was about to take a sip when Megan Munro's raised voice carried across the room and caused all heads to turn.

'But you're a vet, Katrina! You can't condone the killing of innocent hedgehogs.'

'Megan, we've been through all this before,' Katrina returned, patiently. 'The hedgehog population is getting out of control.'

'It's no good, Katrina,' came Nial Urquart's voice. 'Megan just won't accept that point. She doesn't like birds; she's just into cute little hedgehogs, hence her Mistress Prickle-back Sanctuary.'

'I might have known you'd bring it round to your precious birds,' said Megan, heatedly.

'It's not that simple, Megan,' Nial returned. 'The golden eagles up in the Corlins may take a lot of eggs and young seabirds, but not as many eggs as the hedgehogs. In any case they are a protected species, unlike the hedgehogs. Here the hedgehogs are regarded as vermin.'

Megan was about to reply, when the McKinleys joined the discussion. 'They're vermin right enough,' said Alistair, his beard bristling. 'But so are those eagles in my opinion.'

Katrina Tulloch looked aghast. 'You can't be serious, Alistair? The golden eagles are a national asset. We're lucky that they are nesting on West Uist again.'

'Not when they take our young lambs,' cut in Kenneth McKinley.

Katrina shook her head and smiled at him. 'I think you'll find that's a superstition, Kenneth. Eagles don't take lambs.'

Kenneth stood up straight. 'Don't patronize me. You may be a vet, but I've lived on Sea Edge all my life and I've seen them.' And suddenly his eyes widened and he pointed out of the window at the majestic sight of a golden eagle in the distance flapping its way towards the Corlins. 'If I only had a rifle now, I'd get that one.'

'And you'd end up in jail,' Nial Urquart returned. 'They're beautiful birds and as Katrina says, they are protected.'

Megan Munro had been seething for a few moments. 'That's everyone's answer to everything here, isn't it? Kill it! Shoot it! Well, you won't touch any of the animals in my sanctuary. If you do I'll have the police on to you straight away.'

'The police!' Kenneth exclaimed with a sarcastic tone. 'If you can find a police officer on the island, you'll be lucky. They all seem to be disappearing faster than smoke around here.'

Katrina Tulloch spun to face him, her eyes registering disbelief mixed with ire. 'Kenneth McKinley! You — you insensitive oaf!' She snapped her glass down on a window ledge, swung her bag onto her shoulder and with an involuntary sob, ran for the door.

Lachlan was about to go after her, but Rhona stopped him with a hand on his arm. 'Let her be, Lachlan,' she said, as the silence that had momentarily followed Katrina's exit was immediately broken by a cacophony of raised voices.

'Maybe we ought to break it up,' the Padre whispered to Rhona. 'It looks as if there's going to be a civil war in the Wee Kingdom.'

But before they had time to move, there was a loud rap on the door which was shoved open to reveal Jock McArdle and his two boys. Lachlan noticed that they were all dressed as they had been that morning, except that Jock McArdle was now wearing a pair of wire-framed spectacles and a black blazer on top of his golf clothes.

'Correction, Padre,' said Rhona, suddenly stiffening. 'It might be the start of World War Three. Unless I am mistaken, this is the new laird.'

Jock McArdle stood nodding his head at the assembled mourners and took off his wire-framed spectacles. 'It's a sad day. A lassie just ran past us as we came in. Greeting her eyes out she was.' He pulled out a handkerchief and swiftly and noisily blew his nose, then, 'For those of you who don't know me, and I think that is probably you all except for the Padre there, I am Jock McArdle.' He paused for a moment, then added emphatically, 'I am the new laird of Dunshiffin.'

Rhona was the first to say anything. 'You will have come to pay your respects to Gordon MacDonald. That's good of you, Laird. Would you and your sons like a drink?'

Jock McArdle stared at her in bemusement for a moment as his two minders smirked. He shook his head. 'Oh no, these are my boys, but not my sons,' he replied cryptically. 'But a drink would be good, thank you. And I thought that this would be a good time to meet my tenants. A good opportunity to let you know a few of my ideas.'

The Padre, being used to organizing groups, introduced everyone while Rhona poured drinks.

'We are not all here, though,' Rhona said, as she lit another cigarette. 'Vincent Gilfillan is doing business on behalf of the Wee Kingdom Community in Benbecula and the Morrison family have gone — off somewhere. You will be meeting them in due course, I am thinking.'

'What about Gordon MacDonald's croft, Laird?' Kenneth McKinley asked.

Alistair McKinley gave his son a poke in the ribs. 'My son has pre-empted me, Mr McArdle. I was going to make an appointment to see you. We have some business I need to ask you about.'

Jock McArdle shoved his hands into his golf trousers and stood facing the old crofter. 'Ask away. I am here now.'

Alistair McKinley cleared his throat. 'Could my son here take on the lease for the Wind's Eye croft? Gordon MacDonald died without issue and it is traditional that the holding —'

'No!' the new laird replied emphatically. 'He cannot take it on.'

'And why not?' Kenneth McKinley demanded, heatedly.

'The holding will not be re-leased.'

Rhona McIvor removed her cigarette holder from her mouth. 'You are not serious! The Wee Kingdom Community has always had the right to pass on the holdings to family or appointed heirs.'

'I am rescinding that right,' the laird replied, removing a hand from his pocket and languidly taking his glass of whisky from Liam Sartori. 'It will not be the case in the future.'

'Are you sure that is legal, Mr McArdle?' the Padre put in.

'Oh, it is absolutely legal, I assure you, Padre,' McArdle returned, his eyes glinting behind his spectacles. 'I have had my lawyers check over the original agreement. If any of the holders had ever taken the trouble to research it they would have seen that it was written up in such a way as to give the laird the right to do whatever he wanted with the land, subject to certain minor restrictions.'

'Lairds! I knew this would happen!' barked Kenneth McKinley. He made for the door, but found his way barred by Liam Sartori and Danny Reid. He squared up to them. 'Out of my way! Now!'

Neither seemed inclined to move, the same challenging grin having appeared on each of the two minders' faces.

'Let him pass,' McArdle barked. Then once the younger McKinley had stomped out, he turned back to the assembly. 'I will be putting up several wind installations on this croft in the next few days.' He grinned patronizingly. 'It will be good for the whole island, you'll see it will.'

Rhona had been standing beside the Padre, her face getting whiter and whiter as anger seethed inside her. 'We'll not permit this. We will fight you.'

'That is not recommended, Rhona,' he replied smugly.

'You'll not break up the Wee Kingdom Community. If you do, it will be over my dead body.'

Liam Sartori sniggered.

Rhona saw him and made to cross the room towards him. 'You young whelp! I'll teach you —' She had taken two steps then suddenly halted, clutching at her chest before collapsing on the floor.

Lachlan was by her side instantly, feeling for a pulse. His face was like thunder as he turned and rattled out the order, 'Somebody call Dr McLelland. Now!'

CHAPTER THREE

The Macbeth ferry *The Laird o' the Isles* slowly loomed out of the morning mist and manoeuvred into the crescent-shaped harbour of Kyleshiffin. As the great landing doors slowly and noisily descended to allow the walking passengers to disembark before the inevitable cavalcade of traffic, Sergeant Morag Driscoll blew into her hands and stamped her feet. She felt cold and shivery, and not just because of the outside temperature. She was waiting for her boss, Inspector Torquil McKinnon, to return to the island after his extended leave. And she did not relish the news that she had to give him.

'Morag! I thought I would find you here,' came the Padre's booming voice. She turned to see Torquil's uncle hurrying along the harbour to join her, his mane of white hair blown awry.

'Lachlan, have you been on that motorbike of yours without a helmet again?' she chided him with a smile. 'You know full well it's against the law.'

'Och Morag Driscoll, I was in a hurry to meet Torquil. He's been away a good long while, you know.'

'I know, Padre, and I was just teasing.' Her face became serious again. 'How is Rhona?'

Lachlan clicked his tongue. 'As well as can be expected. Doctor McLelland has her trussed up with wires all over the place and a monitor that bleeps every second. There's a no-smoking policy in the cottage hospital and she's threatening to discharge herself because of that alone. She hasn't had a cigarette since the wake yesterday. That's an age and a half for Rhona.'

'Was it a heart attack, then?'

He nodded. 'Her third. She's going to have to take it steady from now on.'

'Not easy when you work a croft in the Wee Kingdom.'

'Not easy when your name is Rhona McIvor, you mean.'

'It sounds as if the new laird of Dunshiffin Castle is causing quite a stir in the Wee Kingdom. There are a lot of rumours going around.'

They moved aside as a stream of walking passengers disembarked from the ferry, fully expecting that Torquil would be among the motorcyclists that were usually permitted off ahead of the heavier vehicles. After the foot passengers, half-a-dozen motorcyclists rode down the gangway with much gunning of engines, but there was no Torquil. Instead, a large container lorry edged off.

'I wonder if he isn't coming after all,' mused the Padre.

Morag bit her lip. 'I hope he comes soon, or I'm in a fix. There's only me and the Drummond twins to run the show, and they're only special constables.'

'Aye, and they have their fishing business to run,' the Padre agreed.

The container lorry stopped and the driver wound his window down. 'Excuse me, darling,' he called to Morag. 'Are you with the police?'

Morag smiled up at the man, a large fairly good-looking man with a pony-tail and tattoos on hefty forearms. She understood his question since the West Uist division of the Hebridean constabulary had a fairly liberal attitude towards uniform. She was dressed in jeans and trainers, the only indication that she was in the force being the blue Arran pullover with three small white stripes on the right sleeve. 'Right this minute, I am the police. What can I do for you?'

The man nodded at a swarthy, surly-looking youth wearing a red baseball cap sitting in the cab beside him. 'Me and the young 'un here need to find a place called the Wee Kingdom. We've got a consignment for the Laird of Dunshiffin.' He grinned and winked at her, adding, 'It's the first of many. I'll be coming here fairly regularly, you ken.'

Morag was a pretty, thirty-something, single mother of three. She recognized the man's unsubtle meaning and treated it with the contempt she thought it deserved. 'Follow the road past Loch Hynish, then turn left at the big T junction. The Wee Kingdom is signposted from there. Watch out for the sheep by the roadsides and don't exceed the speed limit at any time. My colleagues are out with the mobile speed cameras today and we always prosecute.'

His charm, having failed to impress her, evaporated, the smile vanished from his face. He muttered a remark to the silent youth beside him then looked back at Morag, tapped his forehead and started off again.

'That was a wee bit harsh, was it not, Sergeant Driscoll?' said Lachlan with mock severity. Then before she could reply he pointed to the side of the lorry as it passed. It bore a large picture depicting a row of windmills linked by lightning bolts. Underneath in red lettering were the words: NATURE'S OWN ENERGY.

'So it's really going to happen, is it?' Morag asked. 'The new laird is going to build a wind farm.'

A stream of cars followed the lorry off, drowning out the Padre's reply. Then came a familiar noise as Torquil's Royal Enfield Bullet gunned its way down the ramp towards them. He was wearing his usual goggles and Cromwell helmet and looked tanned and healthy, despite several days' growth of stubble. He swung the classic motorbike up onto the harbour road and dismounted. He swept Morag off her feet in a warm hug and then pumped his uncle's hand.

'I'm so glad that you two are here to meet me.'

'Torquil, we need to —' began Morag.

'I've been with the Tartan Army in Belgium,' Torquil went on. 'There were about a dozen of us with our pipes,' he said, pointing to the pannier on the Bullet, from whence his travel sticker-covered bagpipe case was protruding. 'The football wasn't up to much, but that Roi Baudouin stadium in Brussels is something else. And the Belgians just love the kilts and the pipes. It was just the break that I needed.'

'Torquil, Morag has —'

'And then I caught the ferry from Zeebrugge back to Rosyth and just tootled up the East coast. I even managed to take in a couple of Highland Games Days.'

He clapped his uncle on the shoulder. 'I won a pibroch cup at Strathpeffer and a Strathspey at Dornoch.'

He looked at them. 'I've had lots of time to think things over and I've made a decision: I'm leaving the force.'

Morag and the Padre stared at each other in astonishment.

'But you can't leave, Torquil!' Morag exclaimed.

Her inspector put an arm about her shoulder. 'I know, we've been through a lot together, Morag. But it will all be for the best. After Fiona's death I need to move on. I want you to be happy for me. And I —'

The Padre grabbed his nephew's wrist and held it firm. 'Torquil, hold your breath for a minute and listen to Morag.'

Torquil turned to his sergeant and raised an eyebrow quizzically. Then he realized how pained she looked. He felt a shiver of dread run up and down his spine.

'Torquil you can't leave,' said Morag, her voice quaking. 'Ewan is missing! He's gone!'

Torquil stared from one to the other, his dark, handsome features registering bewilderment. 'Gone? Gone where?'

The Padre put a hand on his shoulder. 'This is the fourth day since he disappeared.' He took a deep breath; then, 'We think he's drowned.'

Ten minutes later in his office in the Kyleshiffin Police Station off Kirk Wynd, with a mug of hot, sweet tea in front of him, Torquil listened in shocked amazement as Morag recounted all that they knew about Ewan's disappearance.

'He was on the morning round of the islands and due back at ten o'clock, but he never showed up. The Drummond twins were out fishing and found the *Seaspray* drifting beyond the Cruadalach isles at about two in the afternoon.'

'And Ewan?'

Morag shook her head. 'There was no sign of him. The boat was just drifting and had run out of fuel.' Her normally unflappable visage was showing signs of strain. Tears were forming in the corners of her eyes. 'We think that he must have tumbled overboard.'

Torquil rubbed his eyes and sighed. 'It's not possible, Morag. Ewan McPhee, the Western Isles hammer-throwing champion, who's been a strong swimmer since he was a lad — there's no way that he could have just fallen overboard. And even if he had, he would have pulled himself back on board, no bother.'

'We've agonized over all that ourselves, Torquil,' the Padre pointed out. 'But if the boat had been moving fast —'

'And he may not have been well, Torquil,' said Morag. 'There was blood on the side of the catamaran.'

Torquil eyed her quizzically. 'You think he may have banged his head and fallen overboard?'

'No. I think he may have had one of his nose-bleeds. You know how prone he is to them when he's stressed.'

'And how squeamish he is,' the Padre added.

Morag went on, 'The Drummonds notified me immediately and they tried to retrace the route of the *Seaspray*, but they could only guess at the direction he had taken. I called out the coast-guard helicopter from Benbecula and the RAF at Macrahanish despatched two Sea Kings — they spent two days looking for his body. They combed the whole area but found no trace of him. And you know full well that's what usually happens. We are waiting day by day to hear about the body washing up somewhere along the coast or on one of the islands.'

Torquil picked up his mug of tea and began pacing the room. He sipped it, thinking of the many gallons of stewed tea that Ewan had made him over the years. 'I just can't believe it. He was my friend.'

'He was a good friend to all of us, Torquil,' Morag said. 'The Drummonds are both cut up about it and even Calum Steele has been writing sentimental pieces in the *Chronicle* about him.' She stood up and put a hand on his shoulder. 'Now do you see why you can't go resigning? I need you, Torquil.'

He turned and smiled down at her. Like Ewan McPhee, Morag was a good friend, as well as being his sergeant. He noticed how tired and drained she looked. And how much weight she had lost, although now he realized that it must have been from worry. He gave her a big hug. 'Och, of course I won't leave, Morag — for now anyway.' He released her, then asked, 'How is Jessie?'

The Padre struck a light to his pipe despite the prominent No Smoking notices scattered all over the station. 'She's struggling, Torquil. But she's a tough old lady. She lost her husband in a fishing-boat accident when Ewan was only five, so it's bound to be stirring up old wounds.' He sighed. 'But until the Fatal Accident Enquiry, whenever that is, we can do nothing.'

'Poor Ewan, he'd been through the mill, hadn't he?' Torquil said. 'What with that last relationship and everything.'

'A relationship may have had something to do with this, Piper,' said Morag, using the name that Torquil was often known by throughout the island. 'You know how involved Ewan can get? Well, I think he had fallen head over heels. His mind hasn't been on the job for days. The trouble was, I don't think the lassie knew exactly how much he felt for her.'

'Who is she?' Torquil queried.

'Katrina Tulloch — the new vet.'

Torquil nodded his head as he put the face to the name. 'Old Tam Tulloch's niece. I met her a couple of times before I left. She's a bonnie lassie, right enough.'

The Padre blew smoke ceiling-wards. 'Actually, I think she did know he liked her, Morag. She was upset yesterday at Gordon MacDonald's wake. She left in a hurry after Kenneth McKinley said something to her about there not being many police officers left on West Uist.'

'Gordon MacDonald is dead?' Torquil repeated.

'Aye, from a stroke. That was Ralph McLelland's opinion, and he'd been Gordon's GP for years. He'd been dead for a couple of days before he was found. Rhona McIvor discovered him when he didn't show up to help her with the geese.' He shook his head. 'And now poor Rhona is in the cottage hospital herself after having another heart attack.' He told Torquil about the events at the wake.

'So the new laird, this Jock McArdle, is really going to set up a wind farm?' Torquil asked in disbelief. 'Here on West Uist? There will be an outcry.'

'Morag and I just saw the first one,' said the Padre. 'That lorry that just came off before you looked as if it was carrying the components for a windmill.'

'I can't believe that all this has happened since I went away,' said Torquil with a sad shake of the head. 'Especially Ewan ...'

'We're all trying to get our heads round it, laddie,' agreed the Padre.

At that very moment Katrina Tulloch, the veterinary surgeon in question, was not feeling at all caring towards one of her patients. She had been feeling tense and on edge ever since Ewan had disappeared. She knew perfectly well that the big constable had fallen for her, but over the last couple of weeks he had seemed to be preoccupied with something and his attitude towards her had been slightly strained, as if he was suspicious of her.

God! How do I get myself in such emotional messes? she mentally chided herself. Without any active encouragement she seemed to have had at least three men fawning over her since she had taken over her uncle's practice. And she had felt torn and confused to say the least. Which of them did she really want? Dammit, it was all so bloody —

Her wandering attention was brought back to bear on the large dog that had begun to snarl at her again.

'Zimba has always been a wee bit protective of his bottom,' explained the dog's owner, Annie McConville, one of Kyleshiffin's renowned eccentrics. She ran a dog sanctuary that covered the whole of the Western Isles, and she was an almost daily visitor at both the local police station, where she would lodge complaints about local ordinances, and the local veterinary practice with at least one of her many canine charges. Zimba was a large Alsatian who had developed a limp over the preceding week which had done nothing for his somewhat mercurial disposition.

'I think I'll have to take him in for a general anaesthetic, Miss McConville,' Katrina said, edging backwards, peeling off her latex rubber gloves as she did so. 'Zimba isn't going to let me near enough to examine that abscess.'

'Oh, so it is an abscess that he has? And there was me thinking it was just a bad case of worms again. He sits down and pulls himself along to scratch his bottom a lot.'

Katrina smiled uncertainly, scarcely believing that Annie McConville hadn't seen the abscess as large as a duck's egg to the left of the Alsatian's anus. Attempting to examine the brute had almost cost her a couple of fingers.

'I'll make an appointment then shall I, Miss Tulloch?' Annie asked, alternately stroking the Alsatian and tugging on the chain leash to encourage him off the examination table.

'Just see Jennie at the reception and we'll get him in tonight. He'll need an operation tomorrow.'

The Alsatian jumped down and yowled with pain.

'See, he's not liking that proposition,' said Annie.

And while Katrina sprayed the table with disinfectant and then washed her hands in preparation for her next client, she mused that in many ways human medicine seemed preferable to veterinary work.

'Hi, Katrina,' came a familiar male voice.

She spun round at once, her face registering surprised joy, which was quickly suppressed by professional bedside manner. 'Oh, Nial,' she said, on recognizing the Scottish Bird Protection officer-cum-smallholder. He was holding a cage containing a young fulmar. 'You sounded just like someone else.'

Nial Urquart pressed his lips together. 'I'm, sorry, Katrina. You mean Ewan McPhee, don't you?'

Katrina shook her head and smiled dismissively. 'Forget it. What can I do for you? A wounded fulmar is it?'

The bird protection officer nodded and laid the cage on the table. He undid the front grille and, reaching in gingerly, removed the bird.

'Just hold her on the table while I give her the once over,' Katrina said. She swiftly and skilfully assessed her patient. 'She's been lucky,' she announced. 'She's got a pretty bloodstained wing, but the wound is superficial. No bone damage that I can find.' She looked up at him, instantly aware that his eyes had been roving appreciatively over her upper torso. She pretended not to notice, instead asking, 'What was it, an eagle?'

'It was one of the golden eagles from up in the Corlins. I saw it swoop on her in mid-flight, and just failed to keep hold. I saw her fall and the eagle just flew on and took the next fulmar it spotted. The last I saw it was heading back towards its eyrie in the Corlins.'

'You really love those eagles, don't you?'

He nodded enthusiastically. 'They are majestic creatures, Katrina.' He put the fulmar back in its cage, then turned to her with a smile. 'I love all beautiful creatures.'

Katrina chose to ignore the flattery, if flattery was intended. Instead, she continued conversationally, 'I'm heading up to the Wee Kingdom after I finish surgery here. I've got to go and see Alistair McKinley's sheep. He's worried that a couple might have a touch of foot rot.' There was silence for a moment, then she asked, 'Any news of Rhona?'

'I've just been to the cottage hospital. She was really out of it, with morphine I guess. She just came round enough to ask me to get her some cigarettes, then she fell asleep again. I don't know if she actually realized that it was me. That set-to with the new laird didn't help one iota.' He gritted his teeth. 'The bastard! Him and his two Glaswegian lackies.'

'Yes,' Katrina agreed. 'He's got a lot to answer for if he caused Rhona to have a heart attack.'

Nial picked up the bird cage and prepared to leave. Then, almost as an afterthought, he plucked a couple of leaflets from a side pocket of his waterproof jacket. 'Could I leave a few of these in your waiting-room? They're for a protest meeting against the wind farm.'

Katrina looked at him with concern. 'Be careful, Nial. The new laird doesn't sound as if he's the sort that it is wise to cross.'

The bird protection officer grinned. 'I didn't know you cared.'

'It's Morag I'm worried about,' she lied.

It was after lunch before Katrina could get out to the Wee Kingdom to see Alistair McKinley's sheep. It was misty for one thing. For another the causeway across to the little islet was blocked by a large container lorry that could only just get across, by literally edging its way inch by inch, each move directed by a swarthy well-built youth in a red baseball hat. After waiting behind it for quarter of an hour, she zipped past in her battered old Mini-van, ignoring the wolf whistles from the driver and his mate as they pulled into the side of the road prior to negotiating the pock-marked drive up to Wind's Eye croft.

As Katrina expected, she found the old crofter working away at his hand loom in one of the outhouses, outside which Shep, his nervous but friendly old collie stood guard. After a cursory bark, the collie advanced with tail wagging at half-mast. Katrina patted him, stroked his head then entered the outhouse. 'You never stop, do you, Alistair?' she said admiringly.

'Time is money, Vet,' he returned, barely looking up to acknowledge her entry. 'Just let me finish off this bit of weaving, and then I'll be with you.'

Katrina watched admiringly for a few minutes as he operated the foot treadles which raised the heddles to open a shed for the shuttle, which was thrown across when he pulled a string with his right hand. That done, he swung the sley back and forth, gradually transforming a seemingly impossibly complicated arrangement of threads of yarn into the famous patterned West Uist cloth. There was something almost hypnotic about the pleasing rattle-tattle noise of the most basic technology.

'It really is a cottage industry in every sense, isn't it?' she commented. 'West Uist Tweed is sold all over the west of Scotland, yet I guess few buyers in the fancy shops realize that it is all made by hand in the crofts of the Wee Kingdom.'

'Aye, that's right. We don't have the market of the Harris Tweed, of course, but we have our own style. All of the crofters contribute and we all aim to make our quota each month. It's the way it has always been.'

'And will it always be done like this?'

Alistair finished and tapped the shuttle, 'I have my doubts. Especially if that new laird has anything to do with it.' He looked as if he was about to spit, but thought better of it. 'Windmills!' he exclaimed in exasperation. 'He's just sent poor Rhona into hospital and as for my Kenneth —'

'He's sent Kenneth where?'

The old crofter turned sharp penetrating eyes on her. 'Are you interested in Kenneth, Katrina? I saw he got your blood up yesterday at the wake.'

Despite herself, Katrina flushed. 'I interrupted you. What do you mean, am I interested in Kenneth?'

'Are you just being polite when you ask where he is, or are you interested in my son?'

Katrina smiled and gently shook her head. 'I think we are talking at cross purposes here, Alistair. I had heard that Rhona had been sent to hospital and I somehow thought you meant that Kenneth had gone too. And to answer your question — your very direct question — I am not interested in Kenneth as a boyfriend. He's a good-looking lad, but he's ... a lot younger than me.'

'Not all that much, lassie. He's twenty-two now.' Still the penetrating eyes fixed on her. 'And he likes you, you ken.'

Katrina pursed her lips and folded her arms across her chest. 'OK, how can I say this,' she said pensively. 'I am interested in —' She hesitated and bit her lip. 'I was interested in someone else.'

'Young McPhee, the policeman?'

Katrina stared at him for a moment, saying nothing. Then she glanced at her watch. 'Maybe I could see those sheep you're worried about.'

Alistair shrugged and stood up. 'This way then,' he said. At the door he stopped and looked at her pointedly. 'But look, lassie, I think you need to be realistic. It's been days since the accident. I doubt that we'll ever see Ewan McPhee again.'

The mists had rolled down from the tops of the Corlins making the ascent perilous. Yet the assassin was as sure-footed as a mountain goat. Or rather, he usually was. Having slept rough overnight, he had only eaten snails, a few worms and taken a goodly few drams of whisky from his flask. The combination had slightly numbed his senses and he was aware that he had taken one or two chances that he would not normally have taken. Even so, he shinned up the almost sheer slope of the crag that levelled to a small shelf in a little less than half an hour. He pulled himself over the jutting overhang and, after resting for a moment or two to get his breath, he stood up and adjusted his rucksack. The mist swirled around him making it hard to see more than an outline of the upward crag, atop of which he knew rested the eyrie.

'It's illegal to steal golden eagle eggs, you know,' said the voice from out of the mist.

He started despite himself, his hand reaching over his shoulder for the rifle in its shoulder bag. Then he regained his composure, and he laughed. 'It is also illegal to kill eagles, but I am going to.'

The figure came out of the mist. 'No, you will not! You will restrict yourself to the tasks I give you. And there will be no more killing.'

He scowled angrily. 'I take orders from no one.'

'What did you do with the bodies anyway?'

'I ... disposed of them.'

He swung his rucksack off and delved inside, pulling out a small thermos flask. He tossed it over and watched with amusement as the other raised it and gently shook it. Their eyes locked, then, 'Are they iced?'

'Just as you said.'

He watched as the lid was unscrewed and some crushed ice

was allowed to escape before a polythene bag fell out into the waiting hand. He half-expected a reaction upon seeing the gory contents, but there was none. Instead: 'And what about the policeman?'

He sneered, 'I already told you.'

'You were lying.'

His eyes narrowed, then he bit his lip. 'He got in the way.'

'You fool!'

'Never call me that!' he snapped, swinging the rifle bag off his shoulder and undoing the press studs to withdraw the weapon. 'I did what I had to do and that's that. And maybe now I should be the one to give orders.'

They both heard the sound of flapping wings followed by the characteristic chirping noise as the eagle returned to its nest.

The assassin screwed on the silencer on the barrel of his Steyr-Mannlicher rifle.

'What did you do with —?'

'With him?' He laughed. 'That's my wee secret. Now get out of my way. I've got another job to do.'

'I won't let you this time.'

'Don't try to stop me.' He put the rifle to his shoulder and squinted through the mist in the direction of the last screech. 'Come to me, birdie!' he said, his voice dropping almost to a whisper.

'I said — no!'

'Shut up!' he hissed.

The mists swirled and he thought he saw a shape flit across the Leupold 'scope. He swung the weapon, squeezed the trigger and there was a popping as the report was muffled by the silencer. Looking up he scowled and took a step backwards towards the ledge to get a better view upwards.

He had no time to deflect the blow. He felt a thump on the side of his head, a searing pain in his face — and then he was falling backwards, the rifle slipping from his hands as he clawed futilely at space. His scream rang out and died upon the moment of impact on the rocks below.

The other stared down, only dimly conscious of the flap of retreating wings.

CHAPTER FOUR

Megan Munro's libido was always at its best in the early morning. As a self-styled neo-pagan, she believed that it was because she felt closest to the earth when her mother-earth force awakened and demanded satiation. Regardless of morning breath, overnight perspiration or flattened hair, the need was there, like a powerful itch. And the means of assuaging it was also there in the form of Nial, always eager to please, and to be pleasured by her.

Afterwards they lay side by side, heart rates gradually recovering, thoughts turning from the carnal to the more mundane business of the day ahead. And as usual it was Megan who threw back the duvet and ran naked to the bathroom to brush teeth and perform ablutions before hitting the kitchen to make that first post-coital cup of tea.

Nial took a few sips then lay back dozing contentedly. Morning sex with Megan had been a revelation. It lifted him to heights of delirium then plummeted him into pleasant somnolence. She was like an enchantress, he mused, as he rolled over and burrowed further under the duvet. In many ways she liked to project a simple persona. She eschewed make-up, avoided alcohol, tobacco and drugs. She dressed simply and made no secret of her beliefs and opinions. She was vegetarian — on moral grounds — a former animal rights campaigner — as was he — and a paid up member of the Green Party. Yet in the bedroom, or any other room where the fancy took her for that matter, she was primal passion itself. Yes, that was it, he thought, passion the key to her personality. She was passionate in everything that she thought or did.

Animals seemed to come first with her, even more so than they did with himself. But especially those blasted hedgehogs of hers. He grinned through his semi-conscious haze as he pictured her now, buff naked, running through the dew, to check the runs of her 'Mistress Prickleback Sanctuary'. The islanders all thought that she was a nutter of course, with her New Age ideas, her views on animal rights and her obsession with the West Uist hedgehog population. To him she was more than that. She was a wonderful, eccentric nymphomaniac that he was happy to live with — for now. As to whether he would want to spend the rest of his life with her, however, was another matter. But, as he inhaled the scent of her body on the bedding, he felt the stirring of a fresh erection. And because she was not physically there, his mind spiralled off in another direction, conjuring up an image of that other woman whom he found so attractive. He grinned as he thought how wonderful it would be ...

Megan's scream broke through his reverie and he shot out of bed, stopping only long enough to pull on a pair of underpants. The kitchen door was open and through it he saw her slowly walking up the path, as naked as she was born, her face contorted in horror as she stared at her outstretched, bloodstained hands.

Her eyes slowly rose to meet his and she screamed again.

The Padre was busily stirring a porridge pot on the Aga while a couple of herrings in oatmeal sizzled in a pan when Torquil slinked into the kitchen in a towelling dressing-gown and bare feet.

He was a tall, dark-haired young man of twenty-eight, handsome in the opinion of many an island lass, albeit with a slightly hawk-like profile that he himself disliked. Despite his exhaustion after all his recent travel, he had slept poorly, because his mind refused to stop thinking about Ewan, his friend as well as his constable. He had showered and shaved off his accumulated stubble, much to his uncle's approval.

'That's better, laddie,' he said, lifting the porridge pot and taking it over to the table. 'You look more like an inspector now and less like a tramp.'

Torquil grinned and ran the back of his hand over his freshly shaved chin. 'And there was me toying with the idea of letting the beard grow.' He took his seat and sniffed the air appreciatively. 'I must say, I had dreams about having a good West Uist herring while I was away.'

'Porridge first though, eh,' said Lachlan, ladling out two bowls. He smiled at his nephew, then, 'It's good to be having you home, laddie. I just wish it could be under happier circumstances.'

'Like it was before we lost Ewan?'

The Padre nodded. 'And before we lost Fiona.'

Torquil sighed. 'It was losing Fiona that made me take time off. I thought I had it all sussed. That's why I'm thinking of leaving the force.' He sprinkled a little salt on his porridge. 'But I'll have to put my plans on hold for a while. The Procurator Fiscal will need to be consulted, and a Fatal Accident Enquiry is likely.'

'I keep hoping that we'll find the lad's body. There's nothing worse than knowing somebody's drowned, but not being able to pay your respects properly. I've been praying every day that we'll find him washed up on some shore.'

Torquil shivered despite himself and reached for the previous day's copy of the *West Uist Chronicle* that his uncle had been reading as he prepared the breakfast.

53

'Calum Steele has written a fine piece about Ewan,' Lachlan said. 'He's written a review of all of Ewan's sporting achievements since he was a boy at the school. I doubt if his hammer record will ever be beaten.'

Torquil scanned the two-page article, then jabbed at a photograph of a row of windmills. 'Calum is taking up cudgels about windmills, I see. A regular Don Quixote, eh?'

The Padre raised his eyes heavenwards. 'Windmills indeed! Here on West Uist.'

'But there has been talk of wind power in the Hebrides for years. Why are you against it, Lachlan?'

'I'm not, in principle. I don't much like the new laird of Dunshiffin though.'

'That's not like you. You usually give everyone the benefit of the doubt. What have you got against the man?'

The Padre shook his head disdainfully. 'He cheats at golf for one thing. You can tell a lot about someone's character by the way they play golf.'

'Ah, the hallowed game,' Torquil said with a grin.

'Aye, laddie, you may laugh, but it takes a lot — ' Then seeing his nephew's grin growing wider he shook his head. 'Suffice it to say that despite his cheating I took a fiver off him and put it straight into the *Say No to Windfarms'* kitty.'

Torquil finished his porridge and sat back. 'So what exactly is the laird proposing?'

'We don't know precisely yet, beyond the fact that he's already ordered the first one and is having it set up on Wind's Eye, Gordon MacDonald's croft on the Wee Kingdom. From what he said the other day I don't think he's planning to let anyone work the croft in the future.'

'But I thought the crofters had a right to transfer their crofts to family or close friends if they had no offspring.'

'That's what everyone thought, but it doesn't look to be the case. The laird has looked into it.' Lachlan finished his own porridge then stood up and went over to the Aga where he had left the herrings at the side of the simmering plate. Transferring them to plates he returned to the table. 'Och! And I don't like the way he's taken on the title of 'laird.' He's a puffed up Glaswegian —'

'A Glaswegian what?'

'I don't know exactly, Torquil. But I suspect that he's a bully as well as a cheat. And I cannot abide a cheat.' He sighed as he poured tea for them both. 'The trouble is that I have seen his like before and I fear what may happen in the future. I am concerned about Rhona McIvor and the other crofters. I don't like to take issue with the Good Book, but the fact is that the meek do not seem to inherit the earth. It is the bully-boys who do, and they are the ones who seem to know how to hang on to things.' He started on his herring with gusto.

'What is his background?'

'Bakery, I think. He calls himself an ice-cream and confectionary millionaire, but that's a bit suspicious if you ask me. You know about the ice-cream wars in Glasgow back in the eighties? Well, he's got a couple of heavies that he refers to as his boys with him.'

'Sounds like I should check out his background.'

The Padre buttered an oatcake. 'It would do no harm to let him know that we have law here on West Uist.'

Torquil nodded. 'Maybe I'll take Ewan —' He stopped, realizing that he had momentarily forgotten that he would never be able to take Ewan on official business again. He hit the side of his head with his fist and scowled. 'Maybe I'll take the Drummond lads with me.'

The Padre smiled sympathetically and nodded. 'Aye, they are

good lads and will not be intimidated by any number of Glasgow heavies.' He sipped his tea then nodded reflectively. 'So tell me, what were you planning to do if you left the force?'

Torquil leaned back and stretched his legs under the table. He nodded towards the open kitchen door where a half-stripped carburettor from one of their classic motorcycles could be seen leaking oil onto an old newspaper. The whole hallway was similarly littered with bike parts and repair equipment. 'Mend motorcycles maybe,' he said with a grin. 'Or perhaps something to do with music and the pipes. Teaching maybe, or even set up a business.'

'A piping business here on West Uist? You would starve, laddie! There's only really you and I who play the pipes on the island.'

Torquil grinned. 'The internet, uncle. Technology has changed the world. If you set up a decent website and do your homework you can soon have customers all over the world. And you'd be surprised how many people are interested in piping now. The Tartan Army showed me that. People love the Scottish football fans and their pipers.'

'But you've put the idea on the back burner? You're not going to leave the force? Morag really needs you right now.'

Torquil stood up and stretched. 'Aye, I'm staying put for now. But later on, who knows.'

Nial Urquart stared transfixed at the blood on Megan's hands and at the way her jaw trembled as she shifted her attention from them to him. But no words came, instead she screamed again, startling him into motion. He ran to her and gingerly put an arm about her shoulders, but she shrugged him off, her eyes wide with horror.

'It's awful!' she exclaimed. 'The body! It's been —'

She did not finish, but suddenly bent double and vomited.

Nial patted her back, feeling uncertain how he could best comfort her. Then, as she continued to retch, he decided that action was the best course. 'I'll take a look, Megan,' he said. He ran down the path and passed the outhouses, beyond which were the hedgehog runs and the tiny sheds filled with straw that were used to house Megan's prickly waifs and strays.

The body was lying in between two of the runs, covered in blood and with deep lacerations from which the vital fluid had oozed. It looked as if it had literally dropped from the sky. And indeed, looking at its position between the runs, he assumed that must have been exactly what had happened.

He steeled himself and bent over the body of the dead hedgehog and pictured what had happened. He was sure that he had witnessed something similar the day before. The golden eagle swooping on the flock of fulmars, catching one, then dropping it and nonchalantly taking the next with barely a break in its flight. And now, in his mind's eye, he saw the great bird swooping down from above, having spotted the hedgehog run. Grabbing one in its two-inch talons, rising, then dropping it and returning for the next unfortunate hedgehog that had not scurried to the safety of the small sheds, and flying off with it to the eyrie up in the Corlins. A natural killer, it wouldn't have given a second's thought to the exsanguinated hedgehog that it had left behind.

'You're a bit of a butterfingers, aren't you!' he mused with a grin.

He heard Megan behind him and instantly the grin on his face disappeared.

'I ... I thought it was still alive,' she sobbed. 'I picked it up — ' She looked down at her bloodstained hands, still held well away from her naked body. 'They're evil, Nial. They're murderers. They enjoy killing.'

He was worried by the glazed stare in her eye. She was bordering on the hysterical. He stood to put himself between her and the sight of the dead hedgehog. 'Come on, let's get you into a bath then I'll make you a good strong cup of chamomile tea.'

'You'll bury it, won't you?'

He put an arm about her shoulder and shepherded her back to the cottage. 'I'll do it while you are having a bath,' he assured her.

'We have to get them, Nial. Kenneth McKinley was right. They're vermin! Vermin!'

Vincent Gilfillan stood at the end of Rhona McIvor's bed in the four-bedded unit of the Kyleshiffin cottage hospital. The fact that she was the only patient seemed oddly poignant, as if her health was particularly precarious. Tears threatened to form in the corners of his eyes as he looked down at the middle-aged woman who meant more to him than his own mother. This is all wrong, he thought. It shouldn't be happening this way. Not to Rhona. Although she was twenty years older than him, he loved her dearly.

He shuddered as he looked at the wavy green trace on the oscilloscope of the heart monitor, at the wires attached to her chest and the intravenous line that ran into the back of her heavily bandaged left wrist. There seemed to be flowers, fruit and Get-Well cards everywhere. He looked at his own modest collection of freesias and let out a disdainful puff of air through tight lips. It was enough to wake the dozing Rhona. She turned her head and saw him, her eyes momentarily opening wide in alarm. It was not the sort of reaction that he was used to from Rhona. She reached for her spectacles on the

58

cabinet and put them on. Then, recognizing him, 'Vincent,' she said dreamily, almost with relief as if she had woken from a troubled sleep. She held out a hand to him. 'You startled me.'

He took her hand and pressed it to his lips. 'Rhona, I'm sorry,' he mumbled apologetically. 'I heard as soon as I came off the ferry. I should have been here.'

'For what?' she said with a smile. She reached up and stroked his wiry black beard that had recently begun to display a peppering of silver hairs. 'Would you have stopped this old ticker of mine from having a heart attack?'

He shrugged awkwardly, indicating a particularly large bouquet of red roses that dominated the display. 'It looks like someone has sent the contents of Betty Hanson's florist shop.'

Rhona pushed herself up against the bank of pillows and harrumphed. 'They're from the new laird, Mr Fine And Dandy Jock McArdle. A peace offering, I think. Did you hear what happened?'

Vincent sat down on the side of the bed and handed her his Get Well card. 'I saw Morag Driscoll on Harbour Street. She told me about his plan to put up windmills on Gordon MacDonald's croft.'

'And I told him it would be over my dead body,' Rhona said, with a shake of her head as she opened the card and smiled at the picture of an old goat in bed. She perched it on the bedside cabinet alongside the others. 'And then one of his toadies sniggered and I saw red. I was about to give him a good skelp on the side of his head — and then I ended up in here.'

Vincent's jaw muscles tightened. 'I think I'll be having a word with this lad then. He sounds as if he needs teaching a lesson.'

Rhona noticed the way his fist opened and closed. 'You'll do no such thing. I can fight my own battles and I'll not have you getting into trouble with the likes of him. It's not your battle.'

'It sounds as if it is a battle for all of us on the Wee Kingdom. What have the others said about it?'

Rhona pouted. 'Nial Urquart was round yesterday and he said that Megan was upset, of course. And they've had a bee in their bonnet about the wind farm threat anyway for a while. This has just sort of focused everything a bit.' She bit her lip. 'God, I could murder a cigarette!' She looked at him pleadingly. 'You couldn't sneak in a pack for me, could you?'

'More than my life is worth. And it's time you were stopping anyway.'

'Ach! It's too late for me now.' She made to fold her arms, but being unable to do so because of the heavily bound wrist with its drip-line she swore volubly.

'I see that you can't be too ill then,' came Alastair McKinley's voice from the end of the unit. He came forward, nodded to Vincent and bent to kiss Rhona on the cheek. 'That was some fleg you gave us yesterday, Rhona. You'll not be planning another, I'm hoping.'

Rhona scowled, then looked worried. 'Will you manage my goats?'

'Everything is taken care of,' said Alistair. 'All the animals are fed, the crops are doing well and the weaving will get done as and when we've time.'

Rhona gave a smile of resignation. 'Of course, like always, the Wee Kingdom folk will pull together.'

Vincent put a hand on Alistair's shoulder. 'Will you point out the young fool that caused all this to me?'

'Vincent!' Rhona exclaimed. 'I've told you already.'

'Of course I will,' Alistair said, ignoring Rhona's look of exasperation for a moment. 'But I'm thinking that you might need to stand in line if you're contemplating violence. Kenneth went off in one of his huffs and you know what a temper he has. He didn't come home last night. He does that when he's working himself up about something. And he's been doing that a lot lately.' He shoved his hands deep into his pockets and stared at the floor for a few moments, as if deep in his own thoughts. Then he added, 'And as for that mad woman —'

'Alistair! I've told you before about calling Megan Munro names! We have to be united in the Wee Kingdom.'

'Ach, well, she is mad,' replied Alistair. 'Her and her hedgehogs. I don't know what she gets up to sometimes, but I heard her screaming away this morning. Her man dropped another of those flyers of his on my doormat, but didn't stop long enough to talk to me. No manners!'

'What flyer was this?' Vincent asked.

'This meeting he's been on about for a while. The anti-windmill thing this afternoon. I suppose under the circumstances we should be there, don't you?'

Rhona sat forward. 'Of course, the pair of you should go and represent our interests. But don't do anything silly. No violence, or any of that nonsense.'

Vincent smiled and clicked his tongue. 'This coming from the woman who was going to give that lad a "good skelp" herself!'

CHAPTER FIVE

No one on the island of West Uist had ever known Jesmond's first name. He was not a local man, but had come to the island to serve Fergus MacLeod as a footman in the 1950s when he was about sixteen. The household at Dunshiffin Castle had been trimmed right back with the last laird, Angus MacLeod, but Jesmond had worked loyally for his master and had come to be associated with the very fabric of the building. Indeed, when Jock McArdle had purchased the estate, he found to his delight that he had also retained the services of a butler.

The elderly retainer seemed to have all the qualities one could have wished for in a butler. He was old, lean as a rake and so straight that he could well have had such an instrument thrust up the back of his ever present white jacket. He had a slightly bulbous nose speckled at the sides with tiny red veins, suggestive of a partiality for the castle brandy, and a comb-over that perpetually threatened to fall back whenever he bowed. And the deferential bow was something that he had down to a fine art. All in all, Jock McArdle couldn't have been happier with him.

But the feeling was not reciprocated by Jesmond. He had been a loyal butler to the MacLeods for fifty years. And in his book, being loyal to the laird meant being loyal to the estate and all that the estate represented. He did not like the new laird's two heavies from Glasgow. He did not particularly like the new laird himself, whom he thought to be boorish and bullying. He did not approve of the laird's plans for the development of the estate, such as he had overheard while serving dinner or port to him and the two heavies whom he seemed to dote on as if they were his own sons. But more than any of that, he did not approve of Jock McArdle's two pet Rottweilers. Nasty-tempered buggers, he thought them, leaving hairs all over the place, skidding on the polished floors and barking whenever a fly landed. His nerves were shot to pieces, but he judged that it was too soon in the relationship with the new laird to protest about them.

He came into the billiard-room where the laird was playing snooker with Liam and Danny. The air was thick with tobacco smoke and he eyed with disdain Liam's habit of leaving a cigarette-end balanced on the edge of the billiard table while he took a shot.

Dallas and Tulsa, the two Rottweilers, lay sprawled on the mat in the window bay, both growling menacingly at his entry.

'This note was dropped through the letterbox, Mr McArdle,' he said, executing his bow and proffering the envelope on his little silver salver.

Jock picked it up and tore the envelope open. As he read it his eyes widened and anger lines appeared between his eyebrows. 'Did you see who left this?' he demanded.

Jesmond had moved a crystal ashtray from the side table onto the edge of the billiard table, beside Liam's cigarette-end. 'No, sir, it was lying on the mat. But as you can see, it was hand-delivered rather than mail-delivered.'

'What's it say, boss?' Liam asked.

In response, Jock tossed the single sheet of paper down on the table for them to see. Upon it, with words cut out of a newspaper, was the message:

THERE IS A WIND OF DISCONTENT
NO WINDMILLS
WE'RE WATCHING YOU

Liam laughed his strange laugh. 'Is that someone trying to frighten you, boss? That's a good one that is. That's original.'

'Shut it, Liam!' snapped Danny, indicating Jesmond with a slight motion of his eyes.

'Should I call the police, Mr McArdle?' Jesmond asked.

'Naw, pal,' replied the laird. 'I don't think we need bother anyone about this. See, it'll just be kids playing a joke. Don't worry about it.' He patted Jesmond's arm and picked up a Moroccan leather cigar ease and tapped out a Montecristo Corona. He clipped the end and winked at the butler. 'We'll be OK, pal. Thanks.'

When Jesmond left, Danny asked, 'What do you really think, boss? Is somebody playing silly buggers?'

Jock struck a light and puffed the cigar into life, 'They'd better bloody not be, lad. These island yokels don't know what trouble really is.' He glanced at his Rolex watch. 'See, it's almost time for that windmill meeting. You two had better get there in order to ... represent my interests.'

Liam laid down his cue and picked up his cigarette. He took a deep inhalation on it and smiled at his employer. 'We'll do you proud, boss.'

'You do that. As for me, I'm going to take the girls for a walk.'

The Duncan Institute was packed and the meeting was in full swing when Torquil arrived. The Padre had suggested that it would be a good idea for him to be there to get a flavour of the strength of local opinion about the wind farm issue.

Nial Urquart and Megan Munro were sitting behind a long table on the dais, together with Miss Bella Melville, the local retired schoolmistress who had educated most of the local people on West Uist between the ages of twenty and fifty. She was a sprightly looking seventy-something woman dressed in tweeds and a rust-coloured shawl. A tubby fellow of Torquil's age with a double chin and lank hair, wearing a yellow anorak was standing in the front row of the audience addressing a question to the committee. In his hands he held an A5 spiral notebook with a pencil poised above it.

'As you are all aware,' he said, 'the *West Uist Chronicle* has been running a series of articles on the pros and cons of wind energy for the last month. The SNWF committee say that windmills are injurious to wildlife, but could you give us any evidence that this will be a problem on West Uist?'

Torquil grinned. Calum Steele, the editor-in-chief, and in fact the only reporter on the *Chronicle* was one of his oldest friends. They had been classmates together and both shared a healthy respect for Miss Bella Melville. As Torquil anticipated, their old teacher came out on the attack.

'Calum Steele, you are fishing for a quote. You were always a nosy boy at school. That's why I told you to become a journalist —' Calum swallowed hard and two red patches began to form on his cheeks as general laughter went round the hall. '— and you already know about the damage that windmills do to bird populations. I sent you a paper about the European experience, which you quoted in an article last week.' She glowered at him, daring him to refute her statement. 'You know and I know that it will be just the same here on West Uist if these things are allowed to be erected.'

Calum raised his hand again. 'Yes, but — er — how do you know it will be the same?'

Miss Melville sighed and shook her head in exasperation. 'Nial, will you illuminate the *Chronicle* editor?'

Nial stood up and grinned. 'Absolutely, Miss Melville. The problem relates to location. If wind farms are based near the coast then there is a significant danger to seabirds. And, of course, on West Uist, we have an incredibly diverse seabird population. As the local Scottish Bird Protection Officer, I have been surveying the coastal birds for the better part of a year. We have fulmars, puffins, shags, oyster- catchers —'

Calum raised a hand. 'Excuse me for interrupting, but these are all common birds, are they not? What about our other birds, the protected species? The golden eagles, for example?'

Nial suddenly looked uncomfortable. 'They would be at risk too. They are master predators and will take any food they can. If they were hunting near windmills, they might be in danger of flying into the arms.'

'A good riddance, too!' exclaimed Alistair McKinley. 'They take young sheep.'

Nial smiled humorously. 'That is a myth, Alistair.'

'They kill hedgehogs!' Megan Munro piped up. 'And you know that, Nial. They are vermin! Vermin!'

'Ach! Not the hedgehog thing again!' exclaimed Alistair McKinley. 'Now they are real vermin and we'll soon be taking care of them.'

Megan Munro shot to her feet. 'They are not vermin. They are God's own creatures and you will not touch one of my hedgehogs.'

Nial held a hand out to appeal to Megan for calm, but she shrugged him off angrily.

'I'll not touch your wee hedgehog farm, don't worry, lassie,' returned Alistair, 'but I make no promises for all the other hedgehogs I find on the island.'

'It is not a farm, it's a sanctuary,' Megan snapped, and slumped petulantly back into her seat.

A background murmur of merriment ran round the hall and Calum gleefully made notes. It was just the sort of heated exchange that he had been looking for. Indeed, despite his fear of Miss Melville, he had been machinating for such a reaction. Bella Melville eyed him with displeasure, but he just kept his head down and continued jotting.

Vincent Gilfillan stood up. 'Are we not getting a bit off the track here? Let's be honest. The issue is about a wind farm being set up on the Wee Kingdom, is it not?'

Torquil noticed the two men who had been sitting on the back row, from time to time guffawing and mumbling to each other. Their faces had become serious as Vincent started to talk.

'What does this new laird plan? Do we know if he's got a significant wind farm plan in mind?'

Liam Sartori swiftly stamped to his feet. 'Mr McArdle, the new laird, is not prepared to comment on that.'

'And would you mind introducing yourself?' Miss Melville asked. 'Do you represent the laird?'

Liam grinned. 'I am in his employ. Sartori is the name. And yes, I represent his interests at this meeting, as does my colleague here, Mr Daniel Reid.'

'And can you enlighten us?'

Liam grinned and shook his head. 'No comment, that's all we are permitted to say.'

'Except,' added Danny, 'that Mr McArdle is a staunch believer in renewable energy. Surely that's a good thing in this day and age.'

The comment evoked a mixed reaction from the audience. Indeed it became obvious after a few moments that there was about a fifty-fifty balance, many people being in favour of anything that might increase the number of jobs and pump money into the island.

'We want to be the first!' yelled a young man in the middle of the hall.

'That's right; we need to get in before they build one on Lewis.'

Torquil looked over the audience and saw Alistair mumble something to Vincent, and gesture with a nod of his head towards Liam Sartori. Then he saw Calum raise a hand and take to his feet again.

'It seems that there are a lot of islanders who would welcome wind energy.'

The number of nodding heads and a chorus of assent left no doubt but that the audience was not as anti-wind farm as the SNWF committee had anticipated. It was immediately followed by a chorus of anti-windmill comments, then by a general murmur of disagreement, which prompted Miss Melville to take to her feet and try to subdue it. As she did so, Torquil stood aside as Liam Sartori and Danny Reid edged their way out of the hall with amused expressions on their faces. He looked over at Calum, who was scribbling away as if there was no tomorrow, clearly enjoying the melée.

He was unsure himself exactly how he felt.

From the meeting Torquil went to pay a visit to Jessie McPhee. A typical West Uist mist had descended suddenly from the Corlins, and its presence was enough to dampen his spirits. He smiled wistfully as he rode up to the shed at the back of the McPhee cottage. There were at least five holes in the shed roof, a result of Ewan's hammer-throwing practice. Torquil pictured the big red-haired constable winding himself up and hurling the Scottish hammer over the roof as he worked on getting the trajectory just right to get maximum distance. Getting around to repairing his 'low shots' had been a frequent bone of contention between Ewan and his mother.

'He was a strapping lad,' Jessie said, with tears in her eyes and a cup and saucer in her hand, as she and Torquil sat before a peat fire in the front parlour.

'We must not give up hope, Jessie.'

Torquil had known and respected Jessie McPhee all of his life. She had been widowed when Ewan was a child. Her husband, Balloch, had been a fisherman, like so many of the islanders of his generation. And in his spare time he had been a special constable, one of the stalwarts of the Hebridean Constabulary.

'You were always a good friend to Ewan,' Jessie replied, finishing her tea and laying the cup and saucer down on the basketwork tray on the coffee table. She sighed. 'But who are we trying to kid? First it was Balloch and now it's Ewan. Both drowned. It is something we islanders have to live with. You yourself lost your parents to the sea, and I am not the first West Uist woman to lose her menfolk, and I doubt if I will be the last. I just hope that his body will wash up on the shore someplace and then we can lay him to rest properly.'

Half an hour later as he rode his Royal Enfield Bullet along the snaking headland road, scattering countless gulls from the dunes, he had to agree with Jessie McPhee's pronouncement. He slowed up as the mist suddenly became thicker and he flicked on his full headbeam.

He just could not get his head round the loss of Ewan. He was so big, so strong and robust. He was not looking forward to the inevitable Fatal Accident Enquiry on his friend and colleague.

'Damn it!' he exclaimed, as he slowed and swung the Bullet off the road and through thick bracken onto a thin track through the heather towards the Corlins. It was a shortcut that he often took on his way back to the manse.

He heard a cacophony of dog barking ahead of him and a moment later the Bullet's headlamp beam caught the eyes of first one then two dogs advancing towards him through the mist. He slowed down as he saw a figure appear behind the dogs, frantically waving to him.

'Heel, Willie! Heel, Angus!'

Torquil immediately recognized the two West Highland terriers and their elderly owner, Annie McConville. The old woman's eyes were wide with alarm and she looked shocked.

'Annie, what are you doing out here?' he asked, as he cut the engine and dismounted. He pulled the machine onto its central pedestal and pulled off his gauntlets. Annie was well known throughout West Uist for her dog sanctuary in Kyleshiffin. She was breathless and, for a moment, unable to speak. She grabbed the sleeve of his leather jacket with shaking hands.

'We've found a body! Over there!'

Torquil looked to where she was pointing and, on the rocks at the foot of an almost sheer cliff-face, lay the broken body of Kenneth McKinley.

CHAPTER SIX

Annie McConville was a formidable lady. Some people thought of her as an old dog-loving woman who was losing her wits, while others were more generous and averred that she was simply a glorious eccentric. The longer Torquil had known her, the more he had become aware of the strong personality that lurked behind the façade of eccentricity. He was sure that she fostered the image, just as Miss Melville played up to her image as the retired local schoolmistress.

Yet there was one quality possessed by Annie that was now abundantly clear to Torquil. The old lady had a level head. She had discovered a body under tragic circumstances and had neither panicked nor gone hysterical. What she had done before Torquil arrived was to examine the body for any signs of life.

'The poor soul has been dead since yesterday, I would be betting,' she said, looking over his shoulder as Torquil squatted beside the body of the crofter as soon as he had telephoned to Kyleshiffin for assistance.

'He's had a fall, that's for sure. Dashed his brains out,' she said conversationally, as she clipped leads on the two West Highland terriers who were both cowering unhappily at her ankles, clearly anxious to get away from the disquieting dead body.

Annie sucked air between her teeth. 'Aye, it looks like an eagle killed him.'

Torquil had noticed the three long gashes on Kenneth's face, extending from above the left eye and running diagonally down across his cheek to the corner of his mouth. It was an obvious wound that stood out from the gashes and contusions that he seemed to have sustained in his fall.

Gingerly, and futilely he knew, he felt the neck for a carotid pulse. The cold skin was a shade somewhere between blue and purple and felt rock hard as rigor mortis had long set in.

'He'll have been after the eagle eggs up there, I'm thinking,' Annie went on.

'You may be right,' Torquil said, pursing his lips pensively. 'But perhaps he was after the eagles themselves?'

'Now why would you be saying that, Inspector McKinnon?' Annie asked in a voice that almost seemed indignant, as if she was irritated that he had come up with an alternative theory to her own.

Despite himself, Torquil answered automatically, for he was mentally trying to piece things together. 'Because you don't necessarily need a rifle to rob a nest of eggs.' He pointed mechanically to the bullet that lay beside the body, as if it had been thrown out of Kenneth's camouflage jacket pocket upon impact with the rocky ground. 'It looks like a .308 rifle bullet.' He straightened up and peered round in search of the rifle. When he saw no sign of it he looked up at the sheer rock face and the ledge high above. Perhaps it is still up there, he mused to himself.

Annie tugged the Westies' leads and the two dogs stood upright eagerly ready to retreat.

'I didn't see that,' she said coldly. 'We'll be away then, Inspector. You know where I am if you are requiring a statement.'

Torquil noted the angry tone that had suddenly entered her voice. 'Are you all right, Annie?' he asked concernedly.

'I am perfectly well, thank you. I just do not want to say something now that I might regret later on.'

Torquil eyed her quizzically. 'What do you mean? Why would you say something that you regret?'

In response, Annie zipped up her anorak to its limit and sniffed coldly. 'Oh don't worry, Inspector McKinnon, I didn't mean that I have anything to hide! I meant that I don't want to say or think anything ill of the dead. Especially not when someone has lost their life so young. It is just that I don't have a lot of sympathy for anyone who harms one of the Lord's creatures — be that animal, bird or man.'

Torquil watched her walk off with the two Westies tugging at their leads.

Her parting words had given him a strange feeling. 'Animal, bird or man.' He looked down at the bullet lying beside the body. He had left it there deliberately, since it would need to be photographed beside his body. It was certainly a calibre that would be enough to kill a man.

Doctor Ralph McLelland arrived in the Kyleshiffin Cottage Hospital ambulance about quarter of an hour later. It was not a purpose-built ambulance, but was in fact a fairly ancient camper van that had been donated to the cottage hospital by the late Angus Macleod. Sergeant Morag Driscoll arrived moments after him in the official police Ford Escort.

Torquil led them to the body and explained his findings before the GP-cum-police surgeon went to work, assisted by Morag, who was forensically trained.

Ralph McLelland was one of Torquil's oldest friends. He was the third generation of his family to minister to the local people of West Uist. He had trained at Glasgow University then embarked on a career in forensic medicine, having gained his diploma in medical jurisprudence as well as the first part of his membership of the Royal College of Pathologists. But then his father had fallen ill and he had felt the old strings of loyalty tug at him, so that he returned to the island to take over his father's practice and look after him in the last six months of his life. He had been in single-handed practice for six years.

As for Morag Driscoll, she was a thirty-something single parent of three children. She too had for a time striven to break loose from her island background and had undergone CID training in Dundee before returning to West Uist, marriage and parenthood. Her husband's early demise from a heart attack had given her a personal drive to keep healthy — which she managed in the main, except for a slight problem with her weight — so that she could provide for her 'three bairns,' as she called them.

Together, Morag and Ralph were a formidable team, forming as they did the unofficial forensic unit of the West Uist division of the Hebridean Constabulary. They knew unerringly what the other needed in terms of the examination of the body and the scene.

'Is it a straightforward accident, do you think?' Torquil asked, after the pair had spent about half an hour examining and photographing the body, the surrounding area, collecting bits and pieces and bagging them up in small polythene envelopes.

Ralph and Morag looked at each other. Ralph raised his eyebrows and Morag shook her head.

'Well, it looks like it could have been an accident,' said Ralph. 'But I don't like the look of that bullet you found.'

'That's my view as well,' agreed Morag. 'And where is the rifle?'

'That's what I thought,' replied Torquil. 'I took a walk up to that ledge and saw where he must have tumbled over. But there is no sign of a gun there. So either he didn't have one with him.' He paused and stroked his chin worriedly. 'Or he had one — and someone for some reason has removed it from the scene.'

Death has a galvanizing effect upon people. An hour and a half later Torquil stood beside Alistair McKinley in the mortuary of the Kyleshiffin Cottage Hospital. He could empathize with the old crofter as he pulled back the sheet to expose the corpse of Kenneth, for he himself had personal experience of having to identify the dead body of a loved one. He remembered that it was like being hit with a sledge hammer, then having your insides twisted like an elastic band. He recalled the scream that threatened to erupt from the depths of his being, the instantaneous dryness of mouth and the overwhelming sense of disbelief.

Alistair's normally ruddy complexion suddenly went pale, as if he had instantly haemorrhaged three pints of blood. And he teetered for a moment as if on the point of fainting. But he didn't. He immediately straightened up and swallowed hard, fighting down rising bile in his throat.

Then, 'That is my son, Kenneth McKinley,' the old man volunteered. 'As you know well enough, Inspector McKinnon.'

'I am truly sorry, Alistair. I am also afraid that —'

'That bastard McArdle is going to pay for this!'

'I'm sorry,' Torquil said quietly, with the intention of keeping Alistair calm. 'What connection is there between them?'

'This is his fault. The lad was as mad as a hatter after Gordon MacDonald's funeral. He was disappointed that the — *laird* — told him he couldn't have Gordon's croft. He went off in a foul mood. When he was in one of those dark moods you couldn't —' His face creased into a woeful expression of pain, '— you couldn't argue with him. He was capable of doing anything.' He shook his head. 'Only this time he went and got himself killed.'

'What did you mean about Mr McArdle, Alistair? About him paying?'

Alistair held Torquil's gaze for a moment, before shaking his head. 'I meant ... nothing, Inspector. It is not for me to say what will happen. But the good Lord may have designs on those with blood on their hands. That's all I have to say.'

Suddenly, his weather-beaten face creased and tears appeared in his eyes as a sobbing noise forced itself from his throat. He wiped his eyes with a pincer-like movement of his right finger and thumb. 'I should have stopped him. It's my fault.'

'How so?'

'I was cross with him. We had an argument as well. I told him he needed more backbone. I said I was fed up with his fantasies. When he went off with his rifle, I should have stopped him. I should have locked him in his room, the way I used to.'

'He had a rifle with him when he left, did he? You are sure about that?'

'Absolutely sure.'

Torquil did not think it an appropriate time to mention that the gun was missing.

The Padre was pulling into the Cottage Hospital carpark on his 1954 Ariel Red Hunter motor cycle on his way to visit Rhona when he saw his nephew come out of the back door of the little hospital with Alistair McKinley. The old crofter's demeanour and posture told him that some tragedy had occurred. The fact that they were coming out of that particular door immediately rang alarm bells since the door only opened from the inside, and he knew full well that it meant they had come from the mortuary.

He crossed the car-park to meet them. After seeking Alistair's permission, Torquil explained about the finding of Kenneth's body at the foot of the cliff.

'Do you need some company, Alistair?' asked the Padre.

The crofter scowled. 'If you are going to the Bonnie Prince Charlie, the answer is yes, but if you mean do I want God's company, the answer is definitely no!'

Lachlan glanced at his watch as Torquil retreated, but not before he had given him a look that meant 'look after him'.

The Padre sighed inwardly. He felt profoundly sad at the loss of a young islander. He put a comforting hand on Alistair's shoulder. 'No, it will just be me. The Lord never pushes Himself on folk, but He's there if you need Him later.' He squeezed the shoulder. 'Come on then, we'll drink to your lad's memory. Just the one drink, though. The whisky bottle can be a false comfort at a time like this.'

Alistair McKinley said nothing but allowed himself to be steered down Harbour Street to the Bonnie Prince Charlie Tavern. The aroma of freshly cooked seafood assailed their nostrils as they entered the bar, behind which the doughty landlady Mollie McFadden and her bar staff were busy pulling pints of Heather Ale and engaging in healthy banter with the clientele.

'And what can I be doing for you gentlemen?' Mollie asked, as she finished serving another customer and greeted them with a smile. She blinked myopically behind a pair of large bifocal spectacles perched on the end of her nose. She was a woman of almost sixty years with a well-developed right arm that had pumped a veritable sea of beer over the years.

'A drink in memory of my boy,' Alistair McKinley said; then raising his voice above the background of chatter, 'And a drink for anyone who will drink with me.'

Mollie's face registered a succession of emotions from shock to profound sadness. 'Oh Alistair, I am so sorry to hear that. An accident, was it?' she asked, as she signalled to her bar staff to begin dispensing whiskies from the row of optics above the bar to the assembled customers willing to join the crofter in a drink.

'A tragedy,' Alistair returned. 'He fell from a cliff at the base of the Corlins.'

Mollie paused momentarily from pouring a couple of large malt whiskies for Alistair and the Padre. 'Was he climbing in the Corlins?'

The crofter shook his head. 'He was after shooting the eagles, I'm thinking.' He picked up one of the ornamental Bonnie Prince Charlie jugs of water that lined the bar and added a dash to his whisky.

Mollie nodded sympathetically. Being well used to orchestrating toasts and all sorts of drinking ceremonies, both joyous and tragic, she clanged the bell above her head. As the bar went silent she drew attention to the crofter standing in front of her.

'To my lad, Kenneth McKinley,' called out Alistair, raising his glass.

A chorus followed, then about twenty glasses were raised, drained and then snapped down on the bar. Half a minute or so of silence ensued, then the customers dutifully and respectfully came up and offered their condolences to the bereaved father.

When the throng had passed Alistair McKinley fixed Lachlan with a steely gaze. 'You said just the one, but I have a mind to drink this place dry. Will you be staying with me?'

The Padre had charged his old briar pipe and was in the process of applying a match to the bowl. He blew smoke ceilingwards.

'My words were merely cautionary, Alistair,' he said. 'I will happily have one more drink with you, but then I will take you home myself. If it is your wish to drink more then I suggest that we get you a small bottle to take home. You need to keep the lid on it.'

'Padre, you mean well, I know. But at this moment I don't give a monkey's curse for anyone. I've lost my boy today and that means I've lost my whole damned reason for life.' He tapped his glass on the bar and nodded meaningfully at Mollie, for her to replenish their glasses.

Lachlan laid his pipe in an ashtray and put a hand on the crofter's arm. 'Alistair, I know you are hurting right now, which is only natural. But it would be best to deal with it naturally. Drinking will only make the hurt worse.'

Alistair did not bother with water this time. He drained his glass and immediately signalled for another. 'I'll find my own way home, Padre. And right now, the only person that needs to worry about me drinking isn't you — it's that bloody laird!'

One of the things that Torquil had not missed while he had been away was the twice weekly telephone call he was obliged to make to his superior officer, Superintendent Kenneth Lumsden.

'Time to phone the headmaster,' he said to Morag when he arrived back at the converted bungalow on Kirk Wynd, which served as the Kyleshiffin police station.

Morag had been engrossed with paperwork at the front desk. 'Rather you than me, boss,' she replied, laying her pen down and jumping down from her high stool to lift the counter flap. 'Would you like a wee fortifying cup of tea to set you up?'

Torquil sighed and shook his head. 'I've gone off tea for

now,' he shrugged his shoulders dejectedly. 'I'm sorry, Morag.'

Morag nodded, her own face dropping. They were both thinking of Ewan and his ever-willingness to make tea. 'That's OK, boss. I guess it wouldn't taste the same without being stewed!'

Despite themselves, they both grinned at the reference to Ewan's ineptitude at brewing tea.

'Do you think there's a still a chance, Torquil?'

He bit his thumb. 'Of finding him alive?' He gave a slight shake of the head. 'I can't see it. But I hope to God we can find his body, for Jessie's sake. I'm going to go out in the *Seaspray* first thing in the morning. Are the Drummond twins going to be about?'

'Aye. They said they'd be in to see you at nine-thirty. They've been a couple of stars while you've been away, but they still have to make their living.'

'Thank heaven for our special constables,' agreed Torquil, walking into his office. He dialled Superintendent Lumsden.

To say that there was a personality clash between Torquil and his superior officer would be an understatement, for they had clashed horns on several occasions, and on one it had even resulted in Torquil being suspended from duty for a short spell. The superintendent hailed from the lowlands of Scotland and seemed to loathe and despise the Hebridean way of life. He was a big man with a ruddy face, a walrus moustache and a chin that could have been carved out of wood. He was a widower and had applied for the post with the Hebridean Constabulary because his only daughter had married a teacher on Benbecula and he wanted to be close to her. A police officer of the rules-and-regulations variety, he had never found it easy to deal with the more laidback approach to life of the islanders. Although he lived on Benbecula and worked between offices on North and South Uist, his jurisdiction ran throughout the whole of the Outer Hebrides. The running of the West Uist division of the Hebridean Constabulary particularly incensed him. Although it only consisted of an inspector, a sergeant, a constable and two special constables, he considered it shambolic to the point of chaos. He disliked the disregard for uniform, schedules and rank. For this he held Torquil McKinnon personally responsible. He felt that twenty-eight was too young to achieve the rank of inspector, he himself having to wait until he was in his mid-thirties.

'I had been expecting your call yesterday, McKinnon,' his voice boomed down the phone as soon as Torquil was put through to him.

'I have been catching up, Superintendent Lumsden. Would you —'

'What's the latest on McPhee?'

Torquil bristled. Somehow to have his friend referred to by his surname, as if they were discussing a local crook rankled. Part of him felt he should remonstrate, but he choked back the feeling and replied calmly.

'He is still missing, sir. I am going out to look around the island myself first thing in the morning.'

There was a moment's silence, then a soft creaking noise from the other end of the phone. Torquil imagined the beefy superintendent shaking his head disdainfully, his stiff collar producing the creaking.

'Do what you have to do, McKinnon. But bear in mind it is five days now since he went missing. He is bound to be dead.'

'I know that, sir. I just want to find his body. He is — was, my friend. I'll be going out with the Drummonds.'

At the mention of the Drummond name Torquil imagined that he heard the same neck-creaking noise. Then, 'If there is no news by tomorrow, I feel that a first report to the Procurator Fiscal should be made. It looks as though there will have to be a Fatal Accident Enquiry.' There was a sigh. 'It would be better if we had a body, though.'

Torquil's hackles rose again, but he suppressed his ire. 'Speaking of a Fatal Accident Enquiry, Superintendent, I have to report that there has been another death. A climbing accident, I think. We found a body at the foot of a cliff at the base of the Corlins.' He declined to mention that Ralph McLelland, Morag and himself all had reservations about the death.

'Damn it, McKinnon. Are you some sort of jinx? You go away for a holiday then all hell breaks loose, people fall in the sea and go missing, or fall off cliffs.'

Torquil was about to reply, when his superior snapped, 'Fax me a full report by the end of the day.'

The line went dead and Torquil found himself staring at the receiver held in his white-knuckled fist. 'Thank you for your usual support, Superintendent Lumsden,' he said.

CHAPTER SEVEN

Wallace and Douglas Drummond, the two West Uist Police special constables, were only fifteen minutes late, which was actually pretty reasonable for them. They had been out fishing from the early hours and were still dressed in their yellow oilskins and smelled strongly of fish with just a hint of tobacco. They were drinking tea from thick mugs and chatting with Morag when Torquil came out of his office. They both shuffled awkwardly and shook hands with their inspector, whom they had known since their childhood.

'It is a sad business, Piper,' said Douglas.

'And it will never be the same without Ewan,' agreed Wallace. There was a tear in his eye and a rueful smile on his lips as he held up his mug. 'He liked a strong cup of tea.'

Torquil nodded. Although six foot tall himself, he had always felt small in comparison with Ewan and the two Drummond twins, who towered over him.

They were like peas in a pod, both about six foot five inches in height and with lithe, strong bodies that had seen much toil on the seas and fought many a battle with the elements. Although both were fond of Heather Ale, which was well known across the island, their liking for marijuana was known only to the cognoscenti. As a member of that order, as well as being their superior officer, Torquil turned a blind eye. As long as they were discreet and did not allow it to interfere with their duties, he thought it not unreasonable to take a liberal view about it.

'Well, we'd better be going,' Torquil said, pulling on his waterproof jacket. 'Wish us luck, Morag.'

Five minutes later the *Seaspray* coasted out of Kyleshiffin's crescent-shaped harbour, which was replete with small fishing vessels, yachts and cruisers, as it usually was in the summer months. When they hit open water, Wallace opened her up and they scudded across the waves as they headed north to do a circuit around the island.

It was a hazy day with patches of mist. As they cut a swathe through the water, parallel to the stacks and skerries of the coast, they attracted a following of gulls. Eventually, when they sensed that there would be no food forthcoming, they dispersed and rejoined the swarms of birds that seemed to eternally circle the great basalt columns. It took about twenty minutes to round the northern tip of the island, during which time Torquil had been scanning the shores with binoculars for any signs of a body. As they coasted down the west coast towards the curious star-shaped peninsula of the Wee Kingdom, the songs of the fulmar and gannets rose above the winds as adult birds zigzagged back and forth to countless nests in the cracks and hollows of the steep sea cliffs.

Torquil scanned the rocks and sea caves on the shoreline. 'It would be on these rocks that a body would most likely be swept up,' he said aloud to the twins.

'And thank God he hasn't been,' replied Wallace. 'It would be awful to find his body churned and hacked up like that.'

They skirted the three great basalt stacks, each a virtual islet, atop the last of which was the ruins of the old West Uist lighthouse and the derelict shell of the keeper's cottage. Then they rounded the south-west shore with the machair stretching to the lush undulating hills and gullies, beyond which was the small central Loch Linne. On the hills above the McKinley croft they saw the black-coated Soay sheep that old Alistair McKinley was so proud of.

As they headed south, passing the oyster beds and the little jetty alongside which the crofters' boats were moored, Douglas pointed towards the Wind's Eye croft where a large container lorry was parked beside the old thatched cottage. A tall metal tower had been newly erected and a couple of figures could be seen working on scaffolding around it.

'Well bloody hell! There's the first of those monstrosities on old Gordon MacDonald's croft. They haven't wasted much time.'

Wallace whistled. 'Just two men, as well. I must say though that I thought those windmills would be taller than that. It only looks to be about thirty or forty feet high.'

'It may just be an experimental one,' said Torquil. 'I guess they will have to put up all sorts of wind-measuring anemometers and things before they put up permanent structures.'

'Well I don't like it,' Douglas said gloomily. 'And nor would Ewan. When we last had a pint together, he was having a real go about them.'

And at mention of the big PC, they brought their minds back to the task in hand. Torquil shaded his eyes and peered seawards, towards the distant Cruadalach isles, an archipelago of about a dozen machair and gorse-covered islets.

'We'll go and check out the Cruadalachs now,' he said. 'It was beyond there that you found the *Seaspray* drifting wasn't it?'

'It was,' replied Douglas. 'But we checked them out already.'

'And the helicopters went over them, too,' agreed Wallace.

'I know, I read the reports. But I want to see for myself. And when we've done that we'll come back and do a full sweep round the east of the island.'

Wallace swung the catamaran around and they headed off

towards the mist-swathed Cruadalach isles.

Approaching the little islets, Torquil raised his binoculars as Wallace cut their speed. Then he picked up the microphone and clicked on the loudhailer. 'This is the West Uist Police,' his voice boomed out through the mist. 'Is there anyone on the island?'

There was silence except for the motor of the *Seaspray* and the wind.

'Are you expecting anyone to be here, Piper?' Wallace asked.

Torquil shook his head. 'No. But there's something odd about the atmosphere of the place, don't you think? I think there's something wrong.'

The twins looked at him blankly. 'Like what?'

'There is the smell of death in the air,' Torquil replied softly.

Wallace sighed. 'If you are after trying to freak us out, you're succeeding.'

Torquil smiled at his friends. 'I'm sorry, lads, but does it not just strike you as odd that there is no sign of life here?' He raised his eyes to the sky. 'No gulls. No seals.'

'Bloody hell, Wallace!' Douglas exclaimed. 'He's right. And there should be, there is rich fishing round here, as we well know.'

'Come on then,' said Torquil pointing towards the nearest isle. 'Let's take a look at them one by one.'

It took them the better part of an hour to land and have a look at all of the Cruadalach isles. And it was not until they landed on the last one, a long undulating beach and machair islet with tall, coarse marram grass and yellow-blossomed gorse bushes, that they heaved a sigh of relief.

'Ewan's body isn't here, thank God,' said Wallace.

'But someone has been here,' Torquil announced, after a few moments study of the beach. He pointed to a piece of driftwood that lay some feet away. 'Look at the pattern of sand on it. It looks as if it was used as a kind of rake, maybe to eradicate footsteps.'

And, as the twins watched him, he crouched down and started examining the machair. 'Bird watchers, do you think?' Wallace suggested. Torquil seemed to be on some sort of a trail, slowly working up the beach onto the machair. Finally, he disappeared behind a large clump of tall marram grass.

'Or maybe not just wanting to watch birds.' Torquil said, rising to his feet and coming out of the grass holding his cupped hand out. 'Maybe whoever it was had killing them in mind. Look at this. An empty cartridge.'

The twins joined him and examined the cartridge. 'That's a .308. That's more firepower than you need to pot a few gulls. That'd be enough to kill —' His face suddenly drained of colour and he looked aghast at his inspector. 'You don't think —?'

But Torquil didn't say anything for a moment. He was busy studying the cartridge. 'I don't know what to think yet,' he said at last. 'Except that maybe we had better check all the firearm licence holders on the island. Kenneth McKinley had a live .308 lying beside his body.' He took out a small plastic bag from a pocket and dropped the cartridge case carefully inside.

'Come on then, we need to get back.' Neither of the twins thought that a bad idea.

The Padre had played four holes before propping his bag in the porch of St Ninian's Church, which bounded the green of the hole called *Creideamh*, meaning 'Faith'. On the other side of the green was the cemetery, where his brother and sister-in-law, Torquil's parents, were buried. It had been his intention to go into the church to pray, but a thought struck him and he turned and strode over the green, filling his pipe on the way. He struck a light to the bowl and let himself through the wrought-iron gate into the graveyard.

'Well, brother,' he said, a few moments later as he stood over his brother's grave. 'A lot has been happening here lately.' He took his pipe from his mouth and stared at the bowl. 'But I suppose you know all that already. I just wish you could give us a hand and find Ewan's body. Torquil is fairly chewing himself up over it.' He leaned forward and ran a hand over the smooth marble face. 'You would have been proud of him, you know. He's made a fine officer — Inspector McKinnon, the youngest inspector in the west of Scotland.' He grinned to himself. 'But his friends all call him Piper —because he's the champion piper of the isles now. In fact —'

He was interrupted in his reverie when he heard a noise from the road on the far side of the cemetery and looked round.

Jessie McPhee was dismounting from an ancient bicycle. 'I am glad to catch you, Padre,' she said, letting herself in by the little iron gate, a bunch of pink carnations in her hand. 'I'm just coming to tidy Balloch's grave and lay a few flowers. I hoped that he'd — you know, look out for Ewan.'

Lachlan put his arm about her shoulders. 'I was going into the Kirk, Jessie. Would you care to come with me? We can say a prayer together if you like.'

Jessie nodded with a sad smile. 'That would be good, right enough. But another part of the reason I hoped that I'd see you was so that you could give Torquil this.' And she held up a small black book. 'Ewan was no great writer, but lately he'd taken to jotting things down at night. I think he was in love. I've not read it myself, I didn't think it was right. But maybe Torquil as his friend and Inspector could. I only thought about it after he had gone yesterday.'

The Kyleshiffin market was in full swing as the *Seaspray* cruised into its mooring. Holidaymakers and locals were milling around the market stalls that were clustered along the harbour wall, or bobbing in and out of the half moon of multi-coloured shops that gave Kyleshiffin a strange sort of kasbah atmosphere. Calum Steele was sitting on the harbour wall, eating a mutton pie, obviously waiting for them.

'*Latha math!* Good morning,' he called in both Gaelic and English as Torquil hopped off the catamaran while the Drummonds tied her up. He wiped a trickle of grease from the first of his two chins and raised his eyebrows hopefully. 'Any news, Piper?'

'Nothing, Calum,' Torquil replied with practised guardedness. Everyone on the island knew that Calum took his role as a newspaperman very seriously. He saw himself as a man of letters, an investigative journalist with a duty to keep the good folk of West Uist up to date with the news. He virtually produced the daily *West Uist Chronicle* by himself, which was how he liked it because it meant that he had no one to please except himself. And although most of the time the paper consisted mainly of local gossip, advertising, and exchange and barter columns, yet it managed enough of a circulation to keep a roof over Calum's head and enough in his expense account for Heather Ale and petrol for his Lambretta scooter. The truth was that the islanders liked local gossip as much as anyone else, and Calum was an avid peddler of it. Consequently, everyone was wary of him, especially if they might end up in the *Chronicle* the next day.

'Is that the truth, Piper, or is it the official response?'

Torquil raised his eyebrows and touched his own chin. Calum reflexively wiped another errant trickle of pie grease from his face and then rolled the paper bag that he had been using to collect pastry crumbs between his palms.

'I'm hoping that you're not thinking of littering, Calum Steele,' Wallace Drummond jibed as he jumped down onto the harbour.

'It's an offence, you know,' agreed Douglas, joining him. 'You don't want to be committing an offence in front of officers of the law.'

Calum spluttered. 'Officers of the law! You two are a couple of fishing teuchters. I've a good mind to write something up in the *Chronicle* about harassment of the press.'

'Is it a threat of defamation now, then?' asked Wallace.

'That's an offence too,' Douglas said. 'And you've got crumbs on your anorak now. You want to watch all those calories, you know.'

Calum flushed. 'You pair of malnourished, long-limbed Neanderthals, I'll give you calories — where they hurt!'

The twins looked at each other and nodded their heads. 'Oh, he's good with words, isn't he? No wonder he's the editor of the local rag.'

'A rag! You two should learn to read and then you'd know if it was a rag or not!' But then, as they both burst into laughter, and even Torquil grinned, he shook his head resignedly. 'One day I'll sort the pair of you out.' And then he said to Torquil, 'I saw Ralph McLelland. He told me about Kenneth McKinley. That's a sad accident, so it is.'

'Aye, I don't know what old Alistair will do without him,' Torquil returned.

'I'm going to go over and see him. Do a proper obituary.' He pulled out a small camera from his anorak. 'I thought I'd take a few pictures of the Wee Kingdom while I'm up there. Give it a bit of colour and link it up with the piece I'm doing about the wind farm.'

'Aye, there's some sort of wind tower being put up on Gordon MacDonald's croft now,' Torquil informed him. 'We saw it from the sea.'

'This new laird could change the whole nature of the island if he gets his way,' Calum said. 'I'm going to see if I can get an interview with him. It would be a good thing to introduce the folk of the island to the new laird with a photo-feature. What do you think, boys?'

'I'm wondering if you've got a licence for that digital camera, Calum?' Douglas Drummond said with a twinkle in his eye.

Jock McArdle was at that moment standing on the shore of Loch Hynish, tossing sticks as far as he could in the direction of the crannog with its ancient ruined tower. His two Rottweilers, Dallas and Tulsa, launched themselves in and swam powerfully to retrieve them, depositing them on the pebble shore with much barking as they pleaded for more.

McArdle was a dog lover. He especially loved big powerful animals like these. He appreciated their strong muscles, their loyalty and the verve with which they attacked life. They were both bitches; mother and daughter. Dallas was the youngest and seemed capable of swimming forever. Tulsa had been just the same when she was young, and, even now, amazed McArdle by being able to keep up with her daughter. Especially on this late afternoon, after she had seemed so off colour in the morning and had vomited up her morning meal. He had thought she was coming down with a bug.

'Fetch, girls! Fetch!' he yelled, lobbing a large stick as far as he could.

The dogs charged in together and after a couple of lolloping splashes were soon out of their depth and were swimming in pursuit of the stick. The laird of Dunshiffin watched the progress of the big black and tan heads, yelling encouragement to them both. He delighted in the fact that they were both revelling in the competition. They reached the stick together and turned, each with an end in their mouth as they started to swim for shore.

Then the younger Dallas growled and managed to wrench the stick from her mother.

'G'wan, Tulsa, don't let her get away with that!' McArdle shouted.

Dallas edged away and Tulsa seemed to put on a spurt as well. Then she gave a strange yelping bark and stopped. Dallas swam on, growling and working the stick into her mouth, her powerful teeth biting into the wood.

Tulsa's head momentarily disappeared beneath the surface of the loch.

'Tulsa!' McArdle cried, as Dallas reached the shallows and bounded out of the water with the stick.

Tulsa's head resurfaced again and McArdle began to heave a sigh of relief. Then her head started to sink again, but she spluttered and started to swim on weakly. Dallas, confused, stood in the water and barked continuously.

'Come on, you stupid bitch!' the laird screeched. 'Come on!'

Once again, her head started to sink and McArdle finally realized that his beloved dog was in real danger of drowning. He peeled off his jacket and tugged off his shoes, then went racing into the water, launching himself into a dive. As a youngster in Govan, he had learned to swim competently. Now with a powerful crawl, he swam as he had never done before, intent on saving one of the few living creatures that he actually felt anything for.

Ahead of him, he saw the dog's head spluttering as she

attempted to swim on. And then he was on her. He grabbed her thick studded collar and immediately turned onto his back and began hauling her back towards the shore. A part of his mind reflected upon those life-saving classes that he had taken as a youngster, but never expected to use. And certainly not on saving a dog.

Tulsa was a dead weight by the time he reached the shore, and he himself was in a state of near panic.

'Shut the hell up!' he cried at Dallas, who was barking and running around in the shallow water in a frenzy.

He manhandled Tulsa through the shallows, immediately conscious of her weight increasing dramatically as they arrived on solid ground. He pulled her onto the pebble beach and stared, unsure of what to do next.

Then Tulsa began to convulse.

CHAPTER EIGHT

Katrina Tulloch bit her lip and rose from the dead body. She removed the earpieces of her stethoscope from her ears and coiled the instrument in her hand. 'I'm sorry, Mr McArdle, but she's gone.'

McArdle stared at her through tears. He swallowed back a lump in his throat. 'How the hell? She was only eight, for God's sake?' Katrina looked down at the Rottweiler's corpse lying in its own excrement, aware of the howling of Dallas in the back of the nearby 4x4. She had been in the vicinity when the laird's call had come through via her automatic redirect to her mobile.

'She was a powerful animal,' she said. 'Looked healthy enough and no obvious signs of death. Had she shown any symptoms in the last day or two?'

'She'd been off her food a bit. She puked up food this morning.'

'Anything else. Cough, weeing more? Any diarrhoea?'

McArdle shivered slightly as he stood in his sodden clothing. 'Aye, as a matter of fact she's had a bit of diarrhoea lately and seemed thirstier than usual. Oh, and Jesmond, the butler, was complaining about her slobbering on his precious hall floor.'

Katrina bent down and pulled open the dog's lower jaw. She sniffed, then rose looking puzzled.

'What's wrong?' McArdle snapped.

'I thought I smelled garlic. Dogs don't usually like that.'

'Tulsa would eat anything,' McArdle replied dismissively. 'But what killed her?'

'I won't be able to tell anything else without doing a post-mortem.'

The laird shook his head. 'No! You are not cutting up my Tulsa.'

Katrina shook her head sympathetically. 'I can understand that, but what about some blood tests? I can run a screen and might be able to come up with an answer.' She pointed to his wet clothes as involuntarily he shivered again. 'And I think you'd better get home and get into some dry clothes, Mr McArdle. You don't want to go down with something yourself.'

'I'll be OK. I've phoned for my boys to come and bring me some clothes. Can you take the blood here and now?'

Katrina hesitated. 'I suppose so; it's just that it might be easier if I took her body back to my surgery. If you want I could arrange for her to be cremated.'

McArdle shuddered rather than shivered this time. 'I'm taking her back to the castle. She didn't know it for long, but she seemed to like it well enough. Besides, I know that Dallas there will be feeling it, so burying her in the grounds seems right.'

Katrina went back to her van and got out her venepuncture kit and a few specimen bottles. She bent down by Tulsa's body. 'Did she have any different food in the last few days?'

'She always has the best, and whatever extra scraps the boys give her. Why, what are you thinking?'

'Just wondering if she could have taken something bad into her system.'

He glared at her. 'Do you mean poison?'

'I meant food poisoning, actually. But I suppose we'd need to consider if she could have eaten anything else. You don't have rat poison down at the castle, do you?'

He turned away as she sank the needle into a vessel and

pulled back on the syringe, dark purple blood oozing back into the plastic cylinder.

'Are you a wee bit squeamish, Mr McArdle?' she asked matter-of-factly.

His reply was curt. 'I'm squeamish about nothing! And I'm scared of nothing.'

'I didn't mean anything,' she replied apologetically. 'You've had a shock, what with having to pull her out and everything.'

'Never mind that,' he replied. 'What you were just saying though? About poison. Could someone have poisoned my dog?'

'I can't say without the results.'

'But it is possible?'

'Yes. If she was convulsing, like you said.'

The noise of a fast car coming along the road was followed by a screech of brakes and a skidding of wheels on gravel as a black Porsche Boxster ground to a halt. Liam Sartori and Danny Reid jumped out.

'You OK, boss?' cried Liam, as they jogged down to the loch side.

'God! Is that Tulsa?' Danny asked. 'Crikes, I'm sorry to see that, boss.'

'And is this the vet?' asked Liam, eyeing Katrina admiringly. 'Do you need a hand, dear?'

'I'd rather you didn't call me "dear",' Katrina returned, frostily. 'And yes, I am the vet — and no, I don't need any help.'

Sartori held his hands up in mock defence. 'No offence meant.'

'What are we going to do with Tulsa, boss?' Danny Reid asked. 'Dallas sounds upset.'

'We'll take her back to the castle,' McArdle replied sourly.

'Or rather you boys will in the 4x4. I've got an appointment in the town. Did you bring me fresh togs?'

Liam was returning from the Boxter with a holdall of fresh clothes when the characteristic whine of a scooter was followed by the appearance round the bend of Calum Steele. The *Chronicle* editor-in-chief parked behind the Boxter and came jauntily down the slope to join them.

'Hello, Katrina, what have you there? A drowned dog, is it?'

With the dexterity of a seasoned conjuror, his camera had appeared in his hand and he had taken a couple of shots before he even reached a standstill beside the group. He nodded at Jock McArdle. 'It's not the usual attire for swimming, so I deduce that you went in and brought the beast out?' He grinned and held out his hand. 'You must be Mr McArdle, the new owner of Dunshiffin castle? I was meaning to make an appointment with you and see how you're settling in. Get your comments on the wind farm and all.'

'I don't give interviews to the newspapers,' McArdle replied emphatically, ignoring Calum's outstretched hand.

Calum continued to grin good-humouredly. 'Ah, but maybe you don't know about the *Chronicle*. My paper is the epitome of responsible journalism. You ask anyone on West Uist. You see, it's the best PR you could have on the island.' He raised his camera and took a photograph of the new laird and his two employees. 'How about a more smiling one this time? Then we could maybe go and have a chat and a drink —'

'I don't do photographs either.'

'Och, as the new laird you are news, whether you like it or not,' Calum persisted bullishly. 'The public have a right and a desire to know all about you.'

Katrina had put her blood specimen containers away in her bag and now stood up. She felt uneasy at the hard expression that had come over McArdle's face. 'I'll — er — be away now then, Mr McArdle. I should have the blood results in a couple of hours and I'll be in touch if I find anything odd.'

Calum's head swivelled quickly on his stocky neck. 'Odd? Is there something odd about this dead dog?'

'This dead dog, as you so politely put it, was my dearly beloved pet. If there is anything odd about her death then it is nobody's business except mine and the vet's here.'

Calum was not renowned for his sensitivity. He pointed the camera at the dead animal and snapped another picture. 'You're not thinking that it was poisoned, are you?'

'Why did you ask that?' McArdle snapped. 'Why use the word poison?'

For the first time Calum discerned the hostility that Katrina had found almost palpable. 'Well, I suppose I meant polluted rather than poisoned. Blue-green algae in Loch Hynish, that sort of thing. But I'm sure it wasn't. Everything is pure and fresh on West Uist.' He smiled placatingly. 'I am sure there is no reason to be concerned.'

'But I am concerned about infringement on my privacy,' McArdle returned drily. 'Especially when I'm so recently bereaved.' He nodded at his employees and immediately Calum found his right arm pinioned in a vice-like grip by Liam, while Danny prised the camera from his hand.

Calum watched dumbfounded as the Glaswegian hurled the camera as far as he could into the waters of Loch Hynish.

'What the hell did you do that for?' he demanded. 'That's criminal! That was an expensive camera. I'll have the law on you.'

'I told you no interviews and no photographs,' McArdle said coldly, through gritted teeth.

Katrina saw Calum's face turn puce, just as she noted the

belligerent and insolent grins on the faces of Reid and Sartori. And she was all too aware that the young Rottweiler was howling anew and throwing herself against the closed door of the 4x4.

She caught Calum by the arm and pulled him away. 'Come on, Calum. Leave it for now.'

Dr Ralph McLelland had gone out on his rounds after his morning surgery and, as luck would have it, was just leaving the house of one of his elderly patients on the easternmost point of the island when Agnes Calanish, the wife of the local postmaster, went into labour. It was her fifth child and she wasted no time about it. The baby was delivered, her episiotomy was stitched up and the baby attached to the breast by the time Helen McNab, the midwife, arrived.

'A fine busy man you have been here, Dr McLelland,' cooed Helen, as she took over. 'And such a shame about Kenneth McKinley.'

'However will old Alistair manage the croft without him,' agreed Agnes, as her newborn babe suckled away contentedly. 'And what with all these windmills that they say are going up.'

'Windmills?' Ralph queried.

Guthrie Calanish came in with a tray of tea to celebrate his latest offspring. 'Aye, the first of them is up now and they are busy setting up a second. I was over at the Wee Kingdom this morning. There are two men and they seem to be setting them up like dandelion clocks.' He looked regretfully at the local GP. 'Are you sure you'll not stay for a cup, Doctor?'

'No. I'll be back in tomorrow. But I'm afraid I have work to complete after Kenneth McKinley's death.'

'Paperwork, eh,' sighed Guthrie. 'The bane of a doctor's existence, I'm thinking.'

Ralph smiled and left. He had work to do all right, but it was not nearly as pleasant as filling out a few papers.

Kenneth McKinley's body was waiting for him in the refrigerator of the Kyleshiffin Cottage Hospital mortuary. He had promised to do the post-mortem before lunch, and then let Inspector McKinnon have a report first thing afterwards.

While Ralph was carrying out the post-mortem on Kenneth, Katrina was back in her laboratory working with reagents on the blood tests she had taken from Tulsa. When she was at veterinary school, she had taken an intercalated BSc degree in toxicology and was well able to do the lab work herself.

The garlic smell had worried her, and her preliminary test had shown that she was right to be worried. She packaged up the specimens for later despatch and full analysis at the department of veterinary toxicology at the University of Glasgow, and put them in the fridge. Yet in her own mind, she had enough information. She phoned the mobile number that Jock McArdle had given her.

She hadn't felt at all comfortable about the way McArdle and his heavies had treated Calum Steele. The man was a bully, that was clear. Yet she felt sorry for anyone who lost their pet under such circumstances.

Arsenic was a particularly nasty poison.

Calum Steele was leaning against the front desk recounting his experience on the shore of Loch Hynish to Morag when Torquil came in. So deep into his diatribe was the journalist that he did not hear the Inspector come in.

'Thugs! They're just bloody thugs!' Calum exclaimed, hammering his fist on the counter.

'Who are thugs?' Torquil asked, clapping Calum on the shoulder.

'That new laird and his henchmen.' He recounted his meeting with them all over again, much to Morag's chagrin. 'One of them threw my camera into the loch. It was brand new. *Chronicle* property! I want to charge them with criminal damage.'

'Are you sure about that? He's a powerful man, I hear.'

Calum's face went beetroot red. 'The press will not be intimidated by a bunch of Glasgow bullyboys. I'm going to do an exposé on him.'

'An exposé?' Morag asked. 'And what are you going to expose about him?'

'His thuggery! His insensitivity. His intention to suppress the mouthpiece of the people.'

'Do you have a witness to all this?' Torquil asked, trying hard to suppress a grin. The newspaperman was well known for losing his rag.

'Katrina Tulloch. She saw it all. And she whisked me away just in time, or — or — I'd have shown them.'

'In that case I'm glad that she did. It's best to avoid physicality, as you well know.'

'Huh. I'm not afraid of anyone. I'm from West Uist, born and bred, just like you. I'll not be intimidated by Glasgow bullies.' Torquil put an arm about Calum's shoulders and gently moved him towards the door. 'Calum, I'll look into this, I promise. I'll have a word with this new laird and get his side of the story.'

'Aye, well, have a word with Katrina Tulloch, too. She'll tell you exactly what happened.'

'I'll do that, don't worry. I'm needing to have a word with her in any case.'

Calum nodded. 'Well I'm off to write a piece on thuggery right now. Just tell that laird to start buying the *Chronicle* from now on. If he wants to take on the might of the fourth estate, he's got a fight on his hands.'

Once he had gone Morag shook her head and frowned. 'Let's just hope Calum doesn't go over the top. You know what he can be like when he gets a bee in his bonnet.'

'Aye, he gets a sore head,' replied Torquil with a grin. 'And then we get a pain in the neck. He was like that when we were in school. But his heart is in the right place.'

Ralph McLelland was not happy. He had walked up to the police station with the manila folder containing his report on the post-mortem, and accepted Morag's offer of tea and biscuits in Torquil's office.

'There's something wrong, Torquil,' he said at last, as he dunked a shortbread in the tea.

'About Kenneth McKinley's cause of death?' Torquil asked.

'No, it's clear enough that he died as a result of the injuries he sustained in the fall. He had multiple contusions and fractures of his skull, spine, pelvis and all four limbs. His rib cage was smashed to pieces and he had a ruptured liver and spleen and a torn right kidney. No, he died instantaneously, there is no doubt.'

'Is it those marks on his face?' Torquil asked. 'Those scratches?'

'Aye, partly that. There were three ugly gashes on his face.'

Morag swallowed a mouthful of tea. 'Do you think someone scratched him?'

'Something, I think. They were vicious raking wounds, like a claw of some sort.'

'Or a talon,' Torquil suggested. He told them of his conversation with Annie McConville when she found his body.

'Aye, well, that would fit right enough. But eagles don't

attack people, do they?'

Morag interjected. 'There have been reports about the Corlin eagles attacking animals. Megan Munro telephoned in a complaint about them. She said they've been killing hedgehogs in her sanctuary.'

Torquil eyed her with amusement. 'And what does she want us to do about it? Arrest them?'

'Och, you know what some of the folk say about eagles attacking small animals. It's possible, I suppose.' said Megan.

'But not a man,' returned Ralph, pushing his mug across the table and smiling benignly, in the expectation that it would be refilled.

Torquil blew out a puff of air between pursed lips. 'What about if an eagle thought it was being attacked? If he'd been out there with a rifle, for example.'

Ralph and Morag considered the suggestion for a moment. 'That would be possible, I think,' said Ralph. 'But I'm no expert on birds. Maybe you need to ask someone who knows.'

'Nial Urquart might know,' Morag suggested, pulling out her notebook and jotting a reminder to herself.

'But he had no gun with him, did he?' went on Torquil. 'And I went back later and didn't find anything either at the foot of the cliffs, or up on the ledge that he looks to have fallen from. There were a few scuffs, but no sign of anyone else being there.' He shook his head and reached into his pocket. 'But strangely, this morning when the twins and I were out checking the Cruadalach isles, I found this.' He held out his hand to reveal the plastic bag with the empty cartridge. He laid it on the desk and opened his drawer, from which he took out another plastic bag containing a live bullet. 'This was the .308 that we found beside his body. The question is, if they were from a rifle owned by Kenneth McKinley, what was he doing out there on the Cruadalach isles?'

'Maybe we'd better be asking Alistair McKinley a few questions,' Morag said. 'But we'll have to be easy with him. He'll be in a pretty fragile shape.'

'He said he felt guilty about letting Kenneth go off on his own,' Torquil said. 'And he told me that he had taken a rifle with him. The thing is — where is it now?'

Ralph clicked his tongue and drew the file towards him. He turned a page and tapped it with his middle finger. 'I said there were a couple of things. One was the presence of those wounds. The other was the contents of his stomach. It was full of a strange goo, half-digested of course. I had a look with the microscope and I'm pretty sure his last meal consisted of worms, slugs and a few snails. All raw!' He waited as Morag curled up her nose and covered her mouth to indicate her revulsion at the idea. Then said, 'Washed down with a few drams of whisky, judging by his blood alcohol level.'

'All in all, not normal behaviour,' said Torquil. He nodded at Morag. 'You're right, we need to ask Alistair a few questions. I'll go over and see him first thing tomorrow morning.'

After Ralph left, Torquil spent the following half-hour writing up his report for Superintendent Lumsden. He duly faxed it through and was just preparing to head off to the Corlins for another look around near the eagle nest and the point where Kenneth McKinley had met his death, when the telephone rang and Morag informed him that the superintendent was on the line.

'Good afternoon, Superintendent Lumsden, did you get my —'

'What the hell is it with you, McKinnon? Do you have to be antagonistic?'

'Antagonistic to whom, Superintendent?'

'To your superiors!'

Torquil's hackles rose immediately. 'Are you suggesting that I have been antagonistic to a superior officer, Superintendent Lumsden?'

'Christ, McKinnon, you're at it again right now! But no, that wasn't what I was meaning. I meant being antagonistic to your social superiors. This is the second laird who has come up against you and —'

'Hold on a minute, Superintendent Lumsden. For one thing I have no idea what you are talking about. I have had no dealings at all with the present laird of Dunshiffin. And as for him being a social superior, that is balderdash! I have not even met the man, but I do know that he has simply bought an estate on West Uist. That gives him no rights over anyone. He is a landowner, pure and simple.'

'Well, I've just had him on the phone for ten minutes ranting about the attitude of the people of some place called the Wee Kingdom, and the antagonism of the people in general and the uselessness of the local constabulary!'

'I repeat,' said Torquil as civilly as he could, 'I have had no dealings with him at all.'

'He says one of his dogs has been poisoned and he wants action. I want you to give it to him, McKinnon. We have to maintain a good rapport with important people like him.'

Torquil took a deep breath and forced himself not to lose his cool any more than he was doing. 'We will investigate his claims, sir.'

'Good. And what about that report I wanted faxing through?'

'It should be with you already, Superintendent.'

'Well it hasn't arrived. Send it again!'

There was a click, as of the receiver being slammed down on a telephone in Bara, and Torquil once again found himself staring at his dead receiver.

After sharing his frustration with Morag, Torquil telephoned Dunshiffin Castle and spoke to Jesmond.

'The laird is not available, Inspector McKinnon. He has left instructions not to be disturbed. He is upset about the death of one of his dogs.'

Torquil thought he detected a slight tone of irreverence as the butler mentioned the death of the dog. 'Well, tell the laird when he is available, that if he wishes to make a report about his dog's death he can jolly well come into the station and file one — personally. Goodbye, Jesmond.'

'I shall tell him exactly that, Inspector. Goodbye.'

Torquil thought he detected a note of glee in the crusty old butler's voice.

When Torquil arrived home that evening, he opened the front door of the manse and was immediately assailed by the aroma of devilled rabbit, one of Lachlan's specialities, and by the sight of his uncle on his hands and knees in the hall, leaning over the carburettor of the classic Excelsior Talisman that the two of them had been gradually restoring over the past umpteen years. Bits and pieces of the bike lay on oil-soaked newspapers along the side of the long hall.

'Have you a problem, Uncle?' Torquil asked, knowing all too well that when the Padre had something he needed to work out, he either went and hit golf balls or started tinkering with the Excelsior Talisman.

The Padre raised his eyes heavenwards and exhaled forcefully. Then he gave a wan smile, wiped his hands on an old rag and stood up. 'You might say that, laddie. But I'll solve it one day.' And giving the carburettor a mock kick, he pointed to the sitting-room with his chin. 'You look as if you've had a tough day. Why don't you pour a couple of drams while I check on the supper?'

And five minutes later, with a whisky in their hands, they sat on each side of the old fireplace and exchanged news of the day. Lachlan listened with a deepening frown as he heard about the superintendent's attitude over the telephone.

'That man is nothing but a boor, Torquil! An obsequious boor at that. I think he kow-tows to the gentry.'

Torquil sipped his whisky. 'I haven't met this McArdle yet, but I don't like the way he's taking on the mantle of "the laird" as if it gives him rights over the island.'

'But he has land ownership rights. The Dunshiffin estate is pretty big, and, of course, he has substantial rights apparently over the Wee Kingdom.'

'Well, I'm thinking that I'll be locking horns with him before too long.'

The Padre nodded sympathetically, then, 'I saw Jessie McPhee this afternoon. She was visiting her husband's grave.' He omitted to tell his nephew that at the time he had been paying his own respects at Torquil's parents' graveside. 'She's making peace with herself over Ewan, the poor woman.' He pulled out his pipe and was reaching into his pocket for his tobacco pouch when his hand touched the little black notebook that Jessie had given him. 'Oh, you'd better have a look at this. It's Ewan's. Jessie said that he'd taken to making lots of wee notes. She particularly wanted you as his friend and senior officer to have a look.'

Torquil laid down his whisky glass and reached out for the notebook. He skimmed it, immediately recognizing the big constable's untidy handwriting. It seemed to be quite shambolic, having no set order; quite typical of Ewan, Torquil thought. There were bits and pieces of observations, things he'd highlighted to do, to say to various people, including Torquil. But interspersed among it there were personal thoughts.

The Padre noticed his nephew's change of posture, his expression of studied concentration. Slowly Torquil's head came up, his eyes sharp. 'He had a lot on his mind. It looks like he was feeling pretty desperate.'

CHAPTER NINE

Morag was looking bleary-eyed next morning after spending half the night looking after her youngest daughter Ailsa, who was subject to the croup. Sitting on the other side of Torquil's desk she read his summary of Ewan's notebook, which he had divided into three brief sections, respectively dealing with his feelings about Katrina Tulloch, his suspicions about something he suspected Kenneth McKinley of being up to, but which he hadn't been altogether clear about, and things that he was planning to discuss with Torquil and others.

'He seemed to have lost his heart to Katrina,' Morag said with a sigh. 'She's a bonnie girl, but — ' She shook her head and stopped in mid sentence.

'But what?' Torquil queried.

Morag yawned as she thought. 'I don't suppose it is fair of me to say it, but she's a bonnie girl and she knows it. There's something ... sensual about her. I think she would not be a one-man woman.'

'But I understand that she's been upset since he disappeared. Lachlan told me about Gordon MacDonald's wake.'

'Oh yes. Just as we all have been upset. And she's been spotted wandering around the coast roads and the skerries. The Drummonds have seen her van parked overlooking St Ninian's Bay and Calum Steele says she burst into tears when he saw her in the Bonnie Prince Charlie the other lunchtime.'

Torquil nodded and pushed the latest edition of the *West Uist Chronicle* across the desk for her to see. 'Speaking of our esteemed journalist, I think he's well and truly peeved.'

Morag read the headline:

THE LAIRD, THE CAMERA AND THE LOCH

There followed a piece of Calum's most purple prose describing his encounter with the Laird of Dunshiffin, the dead dog, the Glaswegian bodyguards and the hurling of his digital camera into Loch Hynish. Morag smiled as she read it.

'So he's considering a claim for damages,' she mused, as she read that Calum had been forced to buy a very expensive substitute so that the *Chronicle* photographer would still be able to illustrate the articles in the paper.

'He's not planning to make friends with the new laird, then?'

Torquil frowned. 'And he's in danger of losing credibility as well. Look at the next page. He's written a piece about Kenneth McKinley.'

Morag turned the page to find a photograph of a golden eagle in flight, with an insert photograph of Kenneth McKinley above a headline reading:

DID A GOLDEN EAGLE MARK CROFTER OUT AS PREY?

Morag stared at the article with wide eyed disbelief, and then slowly read it out loud:

While out walking her dog at the foot of the Corlins yesterday, Miss Annie McConville, the well-known proprietor of the Kyleshiffin Dog Sanctuary, discovered the body of Mr Kenneth McKinley of Sea's Edge Croft. It seems that Kenneth had been climbing and tragically lost his footing.

But upon his face were the unmistakable marks of a bird's talons.

'No doubt at all, he was struck down by one of the eagle's,' Miss

McConville told our chief reporter.

Miss McConville told us that she had discovered the body minutes before the arrival of our local Inspector Torquil McKinnon. Miss McConville reports that she pointed out the talon marks to the inspector, who seemed perplexed. A post-mortem examination is awaited at the time of writing.

Kenneth McKinley was the only son of ...

Morag slapped the pages together. 'That's typical of the wee ferret. He's wheedled gossip out of Annie McConville and speculated like crazy.'

'Aye, just like he usually does. But I think he's done it half on purpose. He knows that the golden eagles have caused mixed feelings on the island. There are the superstitious brigade and the bird lovers.'

'And the bird lovers are all up in arms about the proposed windmills,' agreed Morag. 'Calum will be loving all this.'

Torquil sipped his tea. 'Well, let's get back to Ewan's notebook. What do you make of the next section? What do you think he suspected Kenneth of? It is not clear from his notes.'

Morag looked at the notes then picked up Ewan's actual notebook. 'May I?'

Torquil nodded and watched her expression as she skimmed through it.

Suddenly, tears welled up in her eyes and she bit her lip. 'Oh my God! This bit makes me feel so guilty.' She read: *'Morag has her hands full, ask Torquil.* He must mean that I was so preoccupied about Ailsa and her schoolwork. She's missed so much school lately with this croup that she keeps getting. And Ewan didn't feel he could burden me with his worries!' And, despite herself, she sobbed anew.

In a trice, Torquil was around the desk and slipping a

comforting arm about her shoulder. 'Now that is the last thing that you should be thinking, Morag. We don't know whether any of this is of the slightest relevance. Ewan was a good police officer. If he thought it was something you ought to know about then he would have asked. We mustn't get ahead of ourselves here.'

And pulling a tissue from the box on his desk she quickly controlled herself and resumed her customary visage of solid professionalism. She returned to the diary and flicked through the pages with barely a sniff or two.

Eventually she said, 'I think he's got two trains of thought going. On the one had it seems a bit personal, like he thinks Kenneth was watching him and Katrina. There's a hint there that he doesn't like the way that he caught him looking at Katrina and him when they were out having dinner at Fauld's Hotel one evening. And the other thing seems to be a suspicion that Kenneth was up to something. Look, there are times and dates when he's noted down when he saw him. And there are a few words in capital letters that he's boxed round — GUNS and BOND and FAIR FANCIES HIMSELF. I don't think he liked young Kenneth McKinley much. Maybe he saw him as a rival?'

Torquil clicked his tongue pensively. 'Aye, possibly. He was always a tad insecure, for all his great size. But with the word GUNS we come back to the missing rifle again, don't we.' He drummed his fingers on the desk. 'And what did he mean by BOND?'

'Beats me.'

'OK then, what do you think about those things he wanted to ask me about?'

The first was simply the name KATRINA, followed by a question mark.

'That's easy,' said Morag with a smile. 'You know he's always looked up to you as a friend, an older brother even, as well as his senior officer. He wanted to know your opinion about what he should do.' She shook her head and added wistfully, 'And the big darling thought I was too busy.'

Torquil frowned. 'Me, with my track record?' He shook his head, dismissively. 'What about FAMILY?'

'I don't know about that one.'

'We can come back to it. That leaves the last word, WIND?'

'I think everyone on the island has that word on their mind at the moment,' said Morag. 'What with windmills and wind farms.'

'Aye, and the more I think about it, the more I think it's an ill wind that's been blowing lately,' Torquil mused.

Sister Lizzie Lamb was busy, which was not at all unusual for her. No matter how many patients she had under her care, she was always busy. She could have six extremely ill patients in the cottage hospital and cope admirably, or just the one and be run off her feet. But patient care never suffered, or was in any way compromised. She just liked people to know that a nursing life was a busy life.

With Rhona McIvor as the only patient, her business extended to getting all of her administrative chores done, as well as overseeing a good spring-clean of the sluice, the supplies room and then an inventory of the mortuary equipment.

When the new laird presented himself at the reception desk, Maggie Crouch, the hospital clerk, scuttled off and found Sister Lamb in the supplies room. After a few words of exasperation, Lizzie left Giselle Anderson, her irreplaceable nursing assistant, to carry on with the spring-clean while she went to attend on the visitor.

'Rhona McIvor has had a heart attack and still must not be over-tired,' she said, leading the way into the side room where they had moved Rhona. 'Doctor McLelland was quite precise in his instructions.'

'Don't you worry, Sister,' returned Jock McArdle. 'I just want to pay my respects — I'll only be a couple of minutes.'

Sister Lamb was plump, forty-five, with an old-fashioned neatly starched uniform and an over-developed sense of the romantic.

'You sent her all those beautiful flowers, didn't you, Mr McArdle?' She smiled knowingly. 'She's a lucky lady.'

McArdle grinned affably, as he divined the real question that lay behind her remark. 'Ah no, Sister! You think that we —' He made a to-and-fro gesture with his hand. 'Nah. Nothing like that.'

Sister Lamb turned the corner and stood outside Rhona's room, her face betraying a slight disappointment that the romance she had speculated about was no such thing. She gave a little professional cough. 'I wasn't thinking anything, Mr McArdle. I was just looking out for my patient. Mind what I said now, she's not to be over-tired or over-excited.'

'I'll be two minutes with my friend. Sister. That's all.'

Torquil had to wait at the end of the causeway over to the Wee Kingdom, as the large container lorry edged across. It had emblazoned on its sides a picture of a row of windmills linked by lightning bolts and the words NATURE'S OWN ENERGY underneath it. The driver, a large man with a pony-tail and heavily tattooed arms, gave him a thumbs-up sign as he inched past. His companion, a younger man in a red baseball cap, was smoking a cigarette. Almost languidly, he flicked the dog-end out of the cab window so that it bounced off the front wheel of the Bullet. Immediately Torquil's hackles rose and he held up a hand for the driver to stop.

'Dropping litter is just as illegal on West Uist as it is on the mainland,' he said, turning off the Bullet's engine and hauling it up on its central stand. He ground the cigarette end under the heel of his heavy buckled Ashman boot then bent down and picked it up. 'I am Inspector McKinnon of the Hebridean Constabulary, and I am willing to overlook this — just this once!' He held up his hand to the open window. 'Take your litter home please and dispose of it appropriately.'

The youth glowered at him, but, after a dig in the ribs from the driver, he took the dog-end from Torquil and deposited it in the ashtray in the cab.

'Sorry about the boy here, Inspector,' said the driver, leaning towards the window. 'He's from the city and he doesn't know how tae handle himself at times.'

'I ken fine how to handle myself,' the youth returned sourly.

Torquil eyed him dispassionately. 'That's OK then. But just don't overstep the letter of the law while you're visiting this island, or you'll find that we enforce it pretty strictly here.' And then ignoring the youth he pointed to the two wind towers that had been erected on either side of the Wind's Eye croft cottage. Both of them were surrounded by scaffolding with ladders leading up to wooden platforms near the top. One had a slowly revolving three-bladed propeller and the other had a series of spinning anemometers at various heights above the platform.

'You didn't waste a lot of time putting them up. But they're a bit smaller than I imagined they would be. What are they, about forty or fifty feet tall?'

'That's right, Inspector. They're our standard fifty-foot

towers. They are just basic ones to gather information. We measure wind speeds and directions with the anemometer one and the propeller has no turbine, it is just to record likely operating patterns. They're all recording data which the boffins back at the head office will work out later. We've done our work for now and are just off to bring the next lot over.'

'How many are you putting up?' Torquil asked.

'Ten more on this piece of land.' He said, indicating the Wee Kingdom. 'Then assuming everybody's happy with the estimates they get, who knows. It may be that we'll be putting up the real McCoys, the big turbines.' He grinned. 'Then it'll be proper wind farm here we come. And for that we'll have a whole gang of workers, not just gangers like me and the lad here.'

He turned and looked at the youth beside him, as if he had received a kick. The youth held up his watch and the driver pursed his lips. 'Would you excuse us then, Inspector? We need to catch the ferry.'

Torquil nodded and waved them on. 'Just watch your speed on these narrow roads,' he instructed.

'We'll go easy, Inspector,' returned the driver. He grinned as he nudged his companion. 'And maybe your wee ticking off will do the lad a bit of good, eh? I keep telling him to give up these coffin nails of his.'

When they had gone Torquil started up the Bullet and made his way over the causeway towards the McKinley croft. As he rode past Wind's Eye with its incongruous wind towers, he found himself mentally recoiling from them. These flimsy looking windmills were bad enough, but a wind farm with giant turbines would change the whole face of the island.

Rhona blinked myopically at Jock McArdle with ill-concealed

disdain. 'What, no flowers for me today?' she asked coldly.

'No flowers,' he replied casually. 'Just a message.' His lips twisted into a smile that was curiously devoid of warmth. 'See, I'm here as a sort of postman.' He made a theatrical adjustment to the knot of his paisley pattern tie then reached into the inside breast pocket of his Harris Tweed jacket, and drew out a long envelope. 'Maybe I'm a wee bit over-dressed for the part, but I thought I'd deliver it myself. You'll be interested to know that it is all entirely legitimate.'

'Do you think I am remotely interested in anything you have to tell me, Mr McArdle?'

His mouth again curved into his mirthless smile and he smirked. 'And do you really think that I don't know who you are, or what you used to do for a living — Rhona McIvor? I've got the memory of an elephant, so I have. But you don't, it seems.' He tossed his head back and laughed, a cold sinister laugh. 'Have I changed all that much?'

A look approaching fear flashed across her face and she reached for her spectacles. When she put them on, McArdle quickly recognized that he had rattled her. And that she had recognized him. He grinned maliciously as he laid the envelope between a vase of flowers and a pile of cards on her bedside cabinet.

'Enjoy your reading,' he said, before turning and letting himself out. For a moment Rhona stared at the closed door with a look of horror, then she turned her attention to the waiting envelope. Her heart seemed to have speeded up.

Torquil found Alistair McKinley in one of his outhouses, vigorously working his handloom. Working out his grief and frustration, Torquil guessed.

'I've brought you a copy of the post-mortem report, Alistair,'

Torquil said, as he pulled off his gauntlets. 'It's just a preliminary report, mind you, that we'll be submitting to the Procurator Fiscal for the Fatal Accident Enquiry.'

The old crofter sighed and laid down his shuttle. He heaved himself out of his high chair and held out his hand for the letter, which he immediately stuffed in the front pocket of his dungarees. 'I'll read it later, although I'm thinking that I already know what it will be saying.'

Torquil nodded grimly. 'Death from catastrophic head injury, multiple internal contusions and ruptures, and multiple fractures.'

'Aye! And I know well what it won't say. It won't say a thing about the culprits.'

'Meaning what?'

'Meaning the man who caused him to go off like he did. And the devil bird that made him fall.'

'You've read the *Chronicle* then?'

The crofter nodded. 'But I knew it anyway. I saw his bonnie face myself, remember? You were there when I identified his body. I recognized those scars as talon marks when I saw them.' He swallowed hard and tears formed in the corners of his eyes. 'But there will be justice coming.'

Before Torquil could follow up on the remark, Alistair straightened up and gestured towards the door. 'It's time for a cup of tea. Will you join me, Inspector?'

A few minutes later, as they waited for the kettle to boil, Torquil looked around the kitchen. It was surprisingly clean and functional. A row of basic cookery books were ranged along one half of the solitary shelf, the other half being home to a row of pots containing various herbs and condiments. Pans hung on the wall, crockery was stacked neatly in a dresser, and the old stove was in pristine condition.

'You have the eye of a policeman, Torquil McKinnon,' said Alistair. 'You are wondering how two men managed to keep their kitchen so tidy. Well, it is respect for my late wife, God rest her soul.'

Torquil nodded politely and made no comment about his own home, the manse, which he shared with his uncle. Many of the nooks and crannies of the manse were filled with golf clubs, sets of bagpipes or bits and pieces of classic motorbike engines. Their home was not as neat as the McKinleys'.

With the teapot filled and the tray loaded, Alistair led the way through to the sitting-room. In ways, it mirrored the kitchen in its Spartan tidiness. The walls were painted a pale green and the brown carpet, although clean, had three or four frayed patches. There was little in the way of luxury in the room. No modern hi-fi system or computer, just an oldish television set, a box radio, two armchairs, a dining-table with three plain chairs around it, a few pictures and photographs on the mantelpiece. A bottle of whisky with two empty glasses beside it stood on one of those tall thin tables that looked as though it had once supported an aspidistra. Torquil noted the photograph of Kenneth McKinley propped against the bottle and imagined that the old crofter had been drinking a toast or two to his departed son the night before.

As Alistair poured tea, Torquil asked, 'You told me that Kenneth had gone out with a rifle. Are you absolutely sure about that?'

A thin smile floated across the crofter's lips. 'I wondered when you would get round to asking that. As you know from your records, we have licenses for all our guns.' And picking up his cup he crossed the room to the bottom of the wooden staircase. 'Come up and I'll show you our gun cupboard. It's all as it should be. We always keep the guns up here under lock and key.'

The gun cupboard was made of heavy oak and stood on an upstairs landing outside the bathroom. It was heavily padlocked and had been bolted to both the wall and the floor. 'There you are,' said Alistair, as he unlocked the padlock and opened the cupboard door. Inside, in wooden partitions, there were three guns: two shotguns — one 12-gauge and one 20-gauge — and a .22 Hornet rifle. The end partition was empty. At the top of the cupboard, above the partitions, was a locked metal cabinet that was also bolted to the back of the cupboard. 'The guns are just as you have them recorded on our firearm certificates, which I assume you have checked out.'

Torquil nodded, and pulling out his notebook opened it at his last entry. 'So it is the Steyr-Mannlicher Scout that Kenneth took with him?'

'It was. When can I have it back?'

'That's just it. We haven't found the gun!'

The crofter looked aghast. 'You haven't found it? That's not possible.'

'No sign of it at all. And that is serious. Were there any distinguishing features about the rifle?'

Alistair McKinley swallowed a mouthful of tea. 'I can let you have a photograph of it.' He went along the landing and opened a bedroom door. 'This was Kenneth's room,' he said, almost forlornly, standing aside for Torquil to enter.

The posters on the wall attracted Torquil's attention. They were recruitment posters for the marines: men in combat clothes charging through jungles, or wearing heavy camouflage gear stalking through woodland, guns at the ready. Then he noted the bookcase, neatly stacked with books about guns and weaponry, the SAS, and various manuals on hunting. On the bed was a scattered pile of clothing: dungarees, various camouflage jackets, rolls of thick socks. Beside the bed was a series of photographs of Alistair, Kenneth himself and his dead mother. Alistair leaned past him and picked up the framed photograph at the back.

'He liked this one. He got me to take it one day when we were up in the Corlins.'

Torquil took it. It was a carefully posed photograph of Kenneth with a rifle aimed at some distant target. 'It looks as though he's modified his rifle a bit,' he commented.

'Aye, he made his own sound modifier.'

Torquil looked him straight in the eye. 'Why did he need a silencer?'

Alistair shrugged the question away. 'If you are trying to take out half-a-dozen rabbits before they make it to their burrows then muffling the sound makes a good deal of sense.'

'What might also help,' Torquil said, as they made their way back along the landing, 'is a sample of the bullets he used.'

Alistair eyed him curiously then shrugged and unlocked the metal cabinet at the top of the gun cupboard. He opened a box and drew out a bullet. 'There you are. Just standard .308 cartridges. And the other box has .22s.'

He reached into the cupboard and unlocked the partition with the 12-bore shotgun. 'I might as well get this ready for tomorrow.'

'For the hedgehog cull?' Torquil asked.

Alistair McKinley nodded curtly. 'Aye, and I tell you one thing, Inspector McKinnon, I'm in a killing mood.'

CHAPTER TEN

Vincent had been working himself up into a rare temper as he fed Geordie Morrison's chickens and collected their eggs. He felt that he alone of the Wee Kingdom community actually saw through Geordie's façade as the jolly carefree eccentric, the natural father and perfect husband. Oh, he was affable enough, charismatic even, but he had them all eating out of his hand. No one carped when he just took off with his family, generally leaving Vincent or the late Gordon MacDonald to tidy up after him and cover for his chores. Rhona had always been smitten by him, of course, and the McKinleys never really bothered. They had always tended to be pretty self-sufficient.

Only now, in amidst the irritation, was Vincent starting to worry. This time the family had been away longer than expected. It was usually just a day or two on some joy-ride or whim of Geordie's. He wouldn't have thought too much about it, except that they seemed to have suddenly run into death and tragedy everywhere. Gordon had suddenly died of a stroke or heart attack. Young Kenneth had killed himself on some foolish climbing accident in the Corlins. Ewan McPhee was missing, presumed dead. And then Rhona had almost died from a heart attack. There were too many things going on.

Why didn't Geordie Morrison have a mobile like everyone else? But oh no, him and his bloody 'green' lifestyle!

The germ of anxiety had become heated on the flames of the irritation that he was feeling about having to do all these extra chores. He began to wonder whether Geordie really had taken his family and gone off in their boat. The boat had gone, right enough, but were they all OK? Could they be stranded somewhere — or even worse! He tried to shove the thought from his head, but he couldn't help thinking that Sallie would usually send one of the kids around with a note.

Except when Geordie pre-empted her and just took them off, of course. He had done it before, the big galoot, and only given Sallie time to write a note, which Rhona had found on the mantelpiece.

That'll be it! Vincent thought. For goodness sake, I'll have it out with the dim-witted pair of them if I find a note just waiting there. Putting us through all this!

With the basket of eggs in one hand he let himself into the unlocked back door of their cottage. The whole place smacked of family life. The smell of children, their toys, paintings, crudely written messages to their parents were everywhere — on the floor, the walls, attached to the fridge.

Entering the equally children-dominated sitting-room filled him with sudden dread. What if they had had an accident and no one had known about it?

Bugger! Ewan McPhee had died out there somewhere and his body hadn't been found yet. He cursed himself for a fool and ran up the bare wooden stairs to see if he could find some clue: a map, a book, anything that might point to where they had gone.

But there was nothing. Their beds had all been made, the bathroom was neat and tidy, the towels neatly folded and hanging from the rails. No toothbrushes! That meant that they had gone off somewhere, but that was all.

He was on the point of taking the liberty of checking drawers to see if he could elicit some information, although for the life of him he didn't know what sort of thing to look for, when he heard footsteps downstairs.

'Geordie? Sallie?' he cried, turning and descending the stairs two steps at a time.

Megan Munro was standing in the middle of the room, wringing her hands in agitation.

She was dressed in a baggy pink sweater with matching pink bobble hat, with her jeans tucked into pink patterned Wellingtons. He could see that she was trembling so much that her large hoop earrings were actually shaking slightly. When she recognized Vincent her lower lip started to tremble and she began to move towards him.

'Megan, what's wrong?'

He was silenced as she threw herself into his arms and buried her face against his chest. He felt her rhythmic sobbing.

'Is it ... Nial?'

She moved her head in answer back and forth and mumbled between sobs, 'We — we had a row! About ... birds ... and hedgehogs. And her!'

'Her?'

'Katrina Tulloch. He says he's worried about her.' She made a choking noise. 'I said he was more worried about her than he is about me! And he went off.'

Vincent stood patting her back, just letting her get rid of her emotions.

She looked up at him. 'I went for a walk, just to straighten my head out and I saw movement in the upstairs window here. I thought the Morrisons must be back. I thought I'd be able to chat to Sallie. I thought she'd understand.'

Ignoring an unexpected pang of disappointment and resentment, Vincent continued to make supportive, soothing movements on her back. 'There, there,' he said softly.

The sudden bang on the doorframe made him snap his head up to see Liam Sartori standing in the doorway, an insolent grin on his face.

'Well, well! What a cosy scene,' he said, holding up a hand with a number of envelopes. 'Listen, don't let me interrupt anything here. I've just come to deliver some letters. You two are crofters, aren't you? I met the lady at the — er — party, the other day.'

'You mean at the wake!' Vincent returned sharply. 'You know that you were not welcome.'

Liam smirked. 'Ah well, that's me. Thick-skinned I am. Anyway, here's a wee letter for each of you,' he said, looking at the names on the envelopes and reading them out. 'Miss Megan Munro of Linne Croft, and Mr Vincent Fitzpatrick of Prince's Croft. And there's one for Mr and Mrs George Morrison of Tweed Croft, wherever they are.' He eyed the two of them, still standing with their arms about each other. 'Convenient that they're not here though, eh? It means that folk like you can have a wee tryst here when —'

Vincent freed himself from Megan's embrace and took two swift steps towards Liam, who immediately adopted a belligerent fighting pose. He grinned and Vincent noticed the strong smell of whisky on his breath.

'You fancy your chances with me, do you, old man?' he jibed, his words slightly slurred. 'Come on then. I'll show you, too.'

Vincent stood with his fists balled and his elbows bent. 'What do you mean, you'll show me too?'

But Liam merely shrugged. 'Nothing, pal. Just say I had a run in with one of your locals recently. Only he turned my offer of satisfaction down!' His face twisted into a sneer. 'But, of course, if you'd like to make something of it!'

Megan put a restraining hand on Vincent's arm. 'Leave it, Vincent. He's just a minion of the new laird. A bully boy. Just take the letters.' And then to Liam, 'Now just leave this property.'

'Oh, I will, missy. I've just one more letter to deliver to the old boy who lost his son then I'll be away.'

And with an insolent wink he turned and left them to open their letters.

Nial Urquart was flushed, bedraggled and slightly out of breath when he came across Katrina's van. It was parked by the side of the high coastal road. It was empty.

He spied her on the shingle beach below, wandering along the base of the cliffs where at low tide the sea-caves that typified the West Uist coastline became visible. He descended quickly and weaved his way between the rock pools, and the seaweed and limpet-covered rocks towards her.

'Katrina! What are you doing down here?'

She had turned at the sound of his voice, her face distraught. 'I'm looking for, for —'

He encircled her in his arms. 'You're looking for Ewan?' He put a gentle hand under her chin. 'It's no use, Katrina. You have to accept it. Ewan has gone.'

She shook her head emphatically. 'But I can't stop. I care —'

'And I care about you, Katrina.' He took a deep breath. 'I want you to let me care for you.'

She stared at him in disbelief. 'But you can't. There's Megan! You —' Then her eyes rolled upwards abruptly and he had to catch her as her body went limp and she fainted in his arms.

Sister Lamb called for Nurse Giselle Anderson as soon as she found Rhona McIvor collapsed on the floor beside her bed. After a cursory examination revealed that Rhona was not breathing and that she was pulseless, Sister Lamb began cardiopulmonary resuscitation while Nurse Anderson ran to get the portable defibrillator. By the time she had returned to Rhona's side, Maggie Crouch had sent out an emergency call for Dr McLelland.

Sister Lamb had already tried two defibrillation shocks to Rhona's chest when Ralph arrived. With three of them at work they wired her up to an ECG monitor, put up an intravenous line and injected some adrenaline, sodium bicarbonate and lidocaine into her, before applying two more shocks. But, despite their best efforts, it was in vain. After ten more minutes, Ralph declared her dead.

As Sister Lamb and Nurse Anderson started to lay out her body on the bed, they noticed that there was a letter screwed up in her left hand. Ralph prised open her already stiffening fingers and removed the letter. He smoothed it out on the bedside locker.

'Looks like she was trying to write something on the bottom of this letter,' he mused, bending and picking up a pen that had rolled under the bed, presumably when she had collapsed. 'Her heart was obviously pretty fragile. I wonder if this letter had anything to do with it?'

'I bet that the new laird brought her that,' Sister Lamb said over her shoulder. 'He was just in here before we found her.'

'Was he now?' Ralph murmured as he scanned the letter. His eyes widened. 'I'm only guessing, but I'd think this letter would have pushed her blood pressure through the roof. And I'd say that she collapsed before she could finish her note.'

'What does it say, Doctor?' Sister Lamb asked, as she and Nurse Anderson pulled the sheet up to Rhona's chin.

'Just two words in capital letters — CARD IN — then there is a squiggle, which I assume is when she arrested.'

'A card? Shall I check out her locker, Sister?' Nurse Anderson asked.

Sister Lamb smoothed the bedcover and stroked a stray wisp of hair from Rhona's face. 'That's a good idea. We'll need to get everything ready for her next of kin.' Having said that she put a hand over her mouth. 'Oh mercy me, she has no next of kin! She was all alone.'

There was a tap at the door and then it was pushed ajar to reveal a sad-faced Lachlan McKinnon. 'Is it OK to come in?' he asked. 'Maggie Crouch said that Rhona just passed away.'

Ralph opened the door fully and ushered Lachlan in. 'Come away in, Padre. I'm afraid that Rhona had just one strain too many.' He showed him the letter and explained about the visit from Jock McArdle. 'I'm thinking that she had a shock, then she arrested — and although we did our best, we lost her.'

Lachlan looked down sadly at the body of his old friend. 'I'll say a wee prayer for her then, if you don't mind. Who are you planning to tell?'

'We were just talking about that, Padre,' replied Ralph. 'She was on her own, wasn't she? I suppose it must be the other crofters on the Wee Kingdom.'

'Aye, they'll all take it badly. I was heading over there after I'd seen Rhona anyway. Would you like me to do the needful?'

'It would be a great help if you would,' replied Sister Lamb. 'And if you tell them we've got her things here. The letter and cards and all.'

Morag had logged all the messages and enquiries that had come in throughout the morning and duly gave Torquil an update upon his return from the Wee Kingdom.

'Calum Steele called in for his usual snoop around. He said to tell you that he'll be going up to photograph the windmills.'

'There are two towers up already. I had a wee run-in with the chaps that were putting them up. They're not as big as I

128

imagined, but they are just experimental ones to gather information about the wind. The foreman said that they are planning to put up about ten. If all goes according to plan, then they may start building the big ones and that means a real wind farm.'

Morag grimaced. 'That new laird seems set to put the Wee Kingdom crofters' backs up, that's for sure.' She tapped the book with her pencil. 'And talking about him — the Laird of Dunshiffin as he likes to call himself — he phoned up too. He wanted to see you straight away, but I told him you were out on official business. He put the phone down on me, the ignoramus!'

'Well, he can go and boil his head!' exclaimed Torquil with exasperation.

Morag laughed. 'May I tell him that myself if he rings again?'

'Actually, Morag, I rather think I'll enjoy doing it myself. I'm not over-keen on his diplomacy skills, especially when he's a newcomer to the island.'

Morag ran through the rest of the messages then went through to the kitchen to make tea while Torquil began work on his report.

When Morag came back through with the tea-tray, she found him comparing the empty cartridge he had found on the Cruadalach isles with the two live cartridges — one that had been found beside Kenneth's body and the other that he had obtained from the McKinley house.

'These certainly look to me as if they're from the same batch,' he explained. 'And from my chat with Alistair it is clear that Kenneth had a thing about guns. He had a bookcase full of books about weapons, the SAS and hunting.'

He shoved the photograph that Alistair had given him across the desk. Morag swivelled it round and frowned.

'I see what you mean. And it makes you think about Ewan's entry about GUNS in his diary.'

'Aye, and his gun is nowhere to be found.'

'Is it a dangerous gun?'

'They all are potentially deadly, Morag. And this one is a .308. It could easily take down a stag.' He shook his head. 'Superintendent Lumsden is going to love this. And I have to say that I have a bad feeling about it all.'

Torquil was just about to go off to meet the Drummond twins at the harbour when his mobile phone rang. It was Lachlan.

'I think you had better come out to the Wee Kingdom. I have just found a body.' His voice hesitated for a moment. 'It looks nasty, Torquil. Somehow I don't think this was a natural death.'

CHAPTER ELEVEN

Morag had phoned through to the cottage hospital and managed to get hold of Ralph McLelland, who collected her from the station in the West Uist ambulance. Torquil had gone on ahead on his Bullet and parked alongside the Padre's Red Hunter on the island side of the Wee Kingdom causeway. Ralph parked behind them and he and Morag got out and looked over the edge of the causeway.

There was a fifteen-foot drop to a small shingle shelf covered in swards of slimy kelp with a couple of rock pools before the shelf disappeared into the sea. Torquil and the Padre were kneeling beside one of the pools looking at the body of Liam Sartori.

'He's dead all right, Ralph,' said Torquil, looking up when he heard their arrival on the causeway.

'He was lying face down in this rock pool when I found him,' said Lachlan. 'I was on my way to tell the crofters about Rhona's death and I saw him from the top of the rise. I pulled him out and turned him over to see if I could do anything for him. I assumed that he'd drowned. I tried CPR for a few minutes, but —' He shook his head despondently. 'Then I realized that things weren't what they seemed.'

Morag and Ralph scrambled down to them.

'What do you mean, Lachlan?' Morag asked. 'He must have fallen off the edge of the causeway, and knocked himself out when he fell in the pool. Isn't that what happened?'

Torquil shook his head. 'I agree with Lachlan. There's something that doesn't fit here. You can see where he must have landed. The shingle is all disturbed over there. I can't see how he would have ended with his face down in that pool. It is too far away.'

'Maybe he stunned himself, then got up and staggered about a bit before collapsing in the pool,' Morag suggested.

'It's possible,' said Ralph, kneeling beside the body, 'but look at those gashes on his face. They're like talon marks. Like the ones on Kenneth McKinley's face.' There were three ugly slashes running across the bridge of Liam's nose. His face and hair were damp and blood oozed from the wounds.

'That's what worried me,' said Lachlan. 'I am not sure that I —'

There was the click and flash of a camera and they all looked up to see Calum Steele standing on the causeway, a new camera in his hand.

'Looks like the eagles have been busy again,' he said. 'He's the one who threw my last camera in Loch Hynish, by the way, Torquil.'

Calum Steele had already been up to Wind's Eye croft to photograph the wind towers and he insisted on accompanying Lachlan, despite the minister's protestations, as he went to break the news about Rhona's death to the crofters of the Wee Kingdom. As expected, they were all devastated, and all rushed in to the Kyleshiffin cottage hospital to pay their respects.

Calum rode back on his Lambretta along the Dunshiffin road with the aim of getting a surreptitious photograph of the new laird and his other minion to illustrate his article on the windmills, and to link up with the piece he was planning to write about Liam Sartori's death and the ongoing 'Birds of prey' series that he was developing in his mind. The thought of a 'killer eagle' had raised visions of him making it into the national news, where in his heart he felt that he belonged. And maybe, he thought as he rode along, he might drop in at the castle if the laird was out and pump Jesmond for a titbit of news about that dead dog.

Turning a corner he had to swerve suddenly as a Porsche hurtled towards him in the middle of the road. As a result, he skewed off the road into a patch of bracken and fell sideways. By the time he got to his feet, with the intention of haranguing the driver, whom he assumed would stop and come to his assistance, he was dismayed, then outright furious, to find that the car was out of sight. And he had recognized the car, the driver and the passenger.

'That bloody laird! I'll have him!' he cursed.

He rode straight back to Kyleshiffin, along Harbour Street then up Kirk Wynd to the police station. He saw red when his eye fell on the Porsche parked directly outside the station.

He dismounted and made for the door, fully intent upon giving them a good ticking off, West Uist style, but he stopped on the threshold as he heard raised Glaswegian voices followed by Sergeant Morag Driscoll's calm remonstrance.

'Look, police-girlie, I had a call to say that one of my boys has been taken by the police. Now I want to see him and I want to see your head honcho, right now!'

Morag stared at Jock McArdle with steely eyes and tight lips, then, still maintaining her calm, said, 'Firstly, Mr McArdle, don't you ever call me a police-girlie again, or I'll be on your case so tightly that you won't even dare to drop dandruff in public. And secondly, I am not obliged to discuss whether anyone has been taken into custody with a member of the public.'

'Damn it — *woman* — has my boy been arrested?'

'You can call me Sergeant Driscoll, not woman,' Morag returned firmly, indicating the three stripes on her Arran jumper. 'And the answer is no, we do not have anyone in custody at this moment.'

McArdle frowned. 'Then why did someone call me and say he'd been taken away?'

Morag drew her ledger closer and picked up a pencil. 'Who called you, Mr McArdle?'

McArdle looked at Danny Reid. 'Did Jesmond say who called?'

Danny shook his head. 'Just a message to say he'd been taken away.'

'That message did not come from here,' said Morag, looking puzzled. She tapped the pencil on the ledger. 'What I can tell you is that there has been an incident involving a young man and we are trying to determine if he has any next of kin.'

Jock McArdle stared at her in shock, then he thumped his fist on the desk, 'Incident? Next of kin? What gives here?'

Calum Steele had come in silently. He coughed and advanced towards the duty desk, drawing his portly body up to his full five foot six. 'Do you need any help, Morag?' he queried.

Danny put a hand on his chest and prodded him back. 'Just get out, chubby,' he snarled.

Morag laid her pencil down. 'No, there's no problem, thank you, Calum.' Then sternly to Danny, 'And you — don't touch the him again. If you do, then maybe there will be someone under arrest today!'

Danny glared at her then shrugged and took a step backwards.

'There was an incident earlier today,' Morag went on. 'A fatal accident, I am afraid. That is why we are trying to locate next of kin.'

'For Christ's sake! Why didn't you tell me this straight away?' Jock McArdle demanded, his face purpling with rage. 'Liam's dead, is that what you're saying? How? Who did it?'

'I think you should calm down a bit,' said Calum.

'And I told you to get away from me,' said Danny. 'If my friend's been killed somebody's going to pay.' His eyes had murder in them. 'Don't you tempt me, pal.'

The door opened and Torquil came in. He quickly took in the situation. 'Mr McArdle, I am Inspector McKinnon.'

'At last, the organ-grinder!' said McArdle. 'There are a few things I want to ask you, but for now just tell me, where is my boy?'

'Are you related to Liam Sartori?' Torquil asked. 'We have found the body of a young man and we have a name from his driving licence.'

'Naw, I am not related. But Danny here and me are as close as any family to him. Apart from us, he is alone in the world. All three of us are alone.'

'In that case perhaps you'd care to come with me and identify the body. It looks as if he had a tragic accident.'

Alistair McKinley, Vincent Gilfillan and Megan Munro stood disconsolately about the bed and looked down at Rhona, their neighbour and friend. They all had tears in their eyes.

'Goodbye Rhona,' said Vincent and he bent down and kissed her on the forehead.

'It is a black day. I didn't think it could get any worse than it was when my boy died, but it just has.'

'It's like a plague,' sobbed Megan. 'Like the Black Death. One person after another. Gordon, Kenneth and now Rhona.'

'And Ewan McPhee,' Alistair McKinley added, as he made the sign of the cross and kissed Rhona's forehead.

Sister Lamb and Nurse Anderson had been standing respectfully by the door.

'I don't think she would have had much pain,' said Sister Lamb. 'She must have just collapsed. We found her on the floor there and tried to resuscitate her, but it was too late.'

Nurse Anderson pointed to the carry-all beside the bed. 'We packed all her things for you to take away. The letter she was reading is on the top.'

'Let's see that letter?' Megan said, drying her eyes and crossing the room to pick up the letter.

'It was a bit crumpled up in her hand and we smoothed it out,' Sister Lamb explained. 'We think she was trying to write something on it when she collapsed.'

'The swine!' cursed Vincent. 'It is the same letter that we all had. From the new laird about erecting those windmills on the Wee Kingdom.'

'What's that she was writing, Vincent?' Alistair McKinley asked. He looked over Megan's shoulder. 'It's shaky writing. Looks like CARD IN.'

'We thought she must have been trying to write something else when her heart stopped and she collapsed,' said Sister Lamb. 'See the squiggle.'

'Maybe there is something in one of her Get Well cards? They are all in the bag.' Nurse Anderson suggested.

'Or maybe it's a card at the cottage,' suggested Megan.

'Who knows?' said Vincent. 'One thing about it all is clear though, that laird killed her as good as if he put a gun to her head.'

'Aye, and he was responsible for my boy getting himself killed.'

Megan suddenly stiffened and pointed out of the window. 'Speak of the devil. There he is with one of his bully-boys. Where are they going with Inspector McKinnon?'

Alistair made to leave the room. 'I'm going to give him a

piece of my mind.'

But Vincent restrained him. 'No, Alistair, not now. Not while we're here seeing Rhona.' He bit his lip. 'We're all too shocked to start something now.'

Sister Lamb leaned over to see the three men entering the back door of the hospital. 'Hadn't you heard? About the young man, one of his employees? I thought you would all know, what with it happening at the Wee Kingdom.'

'What happened, Sister?' Vincent asked.

'There was an accident. He fell off the causeway and he's dead.'

Megan took a sharp intake of breath and threw herself into Vincent's arms.

'Inspector McKinnon will be taking him to see the body.'

There was a heavy footfall from the corridor then Nial Urquart came in. 'I came as soon as I heard,' he said, looking first at Rhona's body and then at Megan in Vincent's arms. 'I'm here now, Megan,' he said, giving Vincent a frosty stare as he held out his arms.

'And just where have you been?' Megan demanded. She sniffed disdainfully. 'You've been drinking!'

'Just the one at the Bonnie Prince Charlie,' he returned. 'I found Katrina. She fainted and I thought she needed a brandy.'

'I needed you, too, Nial!' exclaimed Megan, brushing past him and breaking into a run down the corridor.

Nial looked at the others then hung his head. 'I'd better go after her,' he said sheepishly.

Katrina was feeling confused. Everything was collapsing around her and she was finding it hard to maintain any clinical focus. It was fortunate that her surgery had been particularly quiet and the visits had been few. That had given her a chance to search.

But again she heard Nial's words, and although she knew that he was probably right, still she felt that she couldn't give up. Not until his body was found. She shivered at the thought of that, and of how her life had changed since she had come back to West Uist. In debt up to her chin, she had been finding it hard to cope with the small island practice. And then Ewan had changed everything — forever.

She looked in the mirror above the sink in her consulting-room. Although her eyes were bleary from crying, and she felt a bit heady from the double brandy that Nial had made her drink, the face that looked back at her was still pretty. She grimaced at herself.

Damn that face! Her looks had gotten her in trouble again and again. Men! Ewan with his insatiable jealousy, Kenneth with his puppy-dog drooling over her, despite her being quite firm in trying to shrug off his attentions. And now Nial.

Damn them all!

She rinsed her face and dabbed it dry with a paper towel.

Come on, Katrina, she chided herself. *Get a grip. You've work to do. Got to get those specimens off to the lab in Glasgow. And that means make the ferry within half an hour.*

And the courier would be waiting for the special package.

She donned her lab coat and pulled on protective gloves. Then she went to the fridge and pulled out all of the blood and urine specimens and the tissue samples that were awaiting despatch and wrote out the necessary lab request forms for each one. She knew that McArdle would soon be pressing her for the full results on his dog.

Then she packaged up the special tissue sample and laid it in the collection bag. It looked just like all the rest.

When she had finished she stripped off the gloves, rinsed her hands again and stared in the mirror. Despite herself, her thoughts returned again to Nial and she felt a tremble of excitement.

Then she chided herself again.

'What a mess, Katrina, you bloody fool! How do you get yourself into such messes?'

Once Jock McArdle and Danny Reid had left the cottage hospital, Torquil sat and drank a cup of tea with Ralph and the Padre in Ralph's out-patient consulting-room.

'That McArdle is an unpleasant fellow,' said Ralph. 'I know he was upset, but he's not going to win any prizes for politeness.'

'Calum Steele said something like that, too,' agreed Torquil. 'And Calum isn't himself renowned for that attribute.'

'I thought that you handled him rather well though, laddie,' said Lachlan.

Torquil gave a wan smile and sipped his tea. 'For now. But he's wanting to come back and talk to me about his dog. Apparently Katrina Tulloch says it may have been poisoned.'

'The world doesn't seem to be with Mr Jock McArdle at the moment,' mused the Padre. 'What do you think he meant when he said he'd deal with things?'

Torquil shook his head. 'I think he believes that Sartori was murdered. He saw the scratches on the face, but he didn't buy them being done by an eagle.'

Ralph McLelland stood up. 'Well, it's only speculation at the moment. The post-mortem may tell us more. Can I go ahead?'

Torquil took a final swig of tea and stood up. 'Absolutely. He's been formally identified. Let's see what you find.'

Jesmond was looking nervous when Jock McArdle stormed

into the hall with Danny Reid at his heel.

'I have bad news sir,' Jesmond said. 'I tried your mobile but there was no answer. It's Dallas, sir. I called the vet, and she's on her way. But I think it's too late.'

'What's happened?' McArdle snapped.

'I heard her howling, sir. I found her lying in the billiard-room, shaking and frothing at the mouth. Then she just — died! I think she may have been poisoned too, sir.'

Ralph called Torquil at home that evening, as he and the Padre sat sipping pre-dinner drams of whisky.

The Padre watched his nephew speaking to the GP-cum-police surgeon over the phone, then replace the receiver, looking grim-faced.

'It looks as though you were right, Lachlan. There's no doubt in Ralph's mind. He's pretty sure that it was murder. And he thinks he has strong evidence to prove it.'

CHAPTER TWELVE

The mouth-watering aroma of fried kippers greeted Torquil as he came down to breakfast the following morning. The Padre was standing by the Aga reading the latest edition of the *Chronicle*. He sighed and handed the paper to his nephew.

'Calum has been busy,' he announced. 'He sails close to the wind a lot of the time, but he may find himself in a spot of trouble with this.'

Torquil sat down and spread the newspaper on the table beside his place setting. There was a large photograph of the two wind towers on the Wee Kingdom and the headline: WIND OF DISCONTENT.

The article that followed it was one of Calum's rants:

The threat of wind farms in the Hebrides is now a reality. The self-styled 'laird of Dunshiffin', Mr Jock McArdle, has steam-rolled the local crofting community on the Wee Kingdom. These ugly wind towers are each about fifty feet tall and have been erected on the common grazing ground adjoining the late Gordon MacDonald's Wind's Eye croft. The new owner of the Dunshiffin estate, of which the Wee Kingdom is a part, has gone against the local wishes and put his ill-conceived plan into action.

The West Uist Chronicle *states that the plan is ill-conceived as the legality of erecting these wind towers on common grazing ground is in doubt.*

Torquil lifted the paper as his uncle handed him a plate and put the skillet of kippers on a cooling board in the centre of the table.

'It's not too bad as an article,' Torquil said. 'I guess he's just echoing local opinion.'

'Ah, but he then goes on to get a bit personal about McArdle and he calls his employees "henchmen". Not content with that he accuses them of intimidation tactics, and mentions again about them throwing his camera into Loch Hynish.'

Torquil picked up his knife and fork and began to eat as he continued to read.

'It's the article on the next page that I meant though,' Lachlan added, as he poured tea.

Torquil turned to the inside page and saw the photograph of the body of Liam Sartori lying below the causeway. The face had been digitally blurred, but beneath the photograph was the headline: HAVE THE KILLER EAGLES STRUCK AGAIN?

There was a blown up insert at the bottom left of the photograph, featuring a golden eagle swooping on some prey.

'Good grief, he's gone mad!' Torquil exclaimed. And he read:

The body of a man, believed to be in the employ of Mr Jock McArdle, the new owner of Dunshiffin estate, was found face down in a rock pool yesterday below the causeway to the Wee Kingdom. Our reporter saw the body and informed us that there was unmistakable talon marks across the dead man's face. He was able to confirm that these were identical to those found on the body of Mr Kenneth McKinley, who died in a climbing accident in the Corlins last week.

Two deaths! Both with talon marks! Isn't it time that someone did something?

'The bloody fool!' Torquil exclaimed. 'What's he playing at? It's bad enough that he's published a photograph of the poor chap's body but to write that drivel. It is as if he is inciting some idiot to go hunting for eagles.' He shook his head in exasperation. 'Blast Calum and his inflated ego. Why does he feel he has to sensationalize everything?'

'And there are a lot of hotheads around,' agreed Lachlan. 'But he'll get flak from people like Nial Urquart and the bird lovers.'

'Damn!' Torquil cursed, as he pushed his plate aside. 'That's all I need with a murder investigation on my hands.'

No sooner had he said it, than his mobile went off. Morag's name flashed on the view screen.

'Torquil have you seen —?'

'Aye, Morag. I've got the *Chronicle* in front of me. Calum is a prize idiot.'

'He is that,' Morag agreed. 'But I didn't mean that, I've just been watching the tail end of the early morning Scottish TV news before I take the kids to the minders. Kirstie Macroon has just done a piece on the *"Killer Eagles of West Uist"* and she had a tele-interview with Calum. We may be in for an influx of reporters and sensation seekers.'

Torquil groaned.

'I've got everything teed up for first thing though,' Morag went on. 'The Drummonds and Ralph McLelland are coming in. I thought we'd have the briefing in the recreation-room at the station. I'll have it all ready for when you get in.'

Superintendent Lumsden had left a message with Morag for Torquil to telephone him as soon as he set foot in the building.

'I think his gout must still be playing him up,' Morag said with a grimace that told Torquil exactly the sort of reception he could expect when his superior officer answered the telephone. And indeed there were no pleasantries or preliminary banter: the superintendent just went straight for the jugular.

'Why the hell is it always the same with you, McKinnon? Do you set out to embarrass me with the chief constable? Why do I always seem to hear about what's happening on West Uist when I look at the TV news? Killer eagles for goodness sake! Have you no control over that numskull reporter Calum Steele?'

'The freedom of the press, Superintendent Lumsden,' Torquil returned.

'Bollocks! Why didn't you let me know about this?'

'I was going to contact you this morning, sir. I knew nothing about this story until I read the newspaper just now. In fact, it may be more complex than the report on the TV.'

There was a moment's silence on the other end of the telephone, and then slowly, Superintendent Lumsden growled, 'Go on, McKinnon, surprise me.'

Torquil took a deep breath. 'I was going to contact you this morning, sir, after my meeting with the police surgeon. Doctor McLelland did a post-mortem last night.'

'And?'

'We haven't had the meeting yet, sir. But there is a strong possibility that the man's death was more suspicious than we thought.' There was an interruption on the other end of the line and Torquil heard someone else talking in the background, and then Lumsden replying to them.

'Right, McKinnon, spit it out, I'm going to have to go. I'm about to take a call from the Laird of Dunshiffin.'

'It may have been murder, sir.'

Torquil winced as the superintendent howled down the other end of the line.

'Right! What a bloody fiasco! Have your meetings Inspector, then report back to me straight away. Meanwhile I'll see what your laird wants.'

'He isn't my laird, Superintendent —' But the line had gone dead.

When she heard the phone being replaced, Morag popped her head round Torquil's office door. She sympathetically smiled at him. 'Everyone is here. Are you ready to start? I've got the tea and biscuits ready.'

The atmosphere was subdued in the recreation-room, because everyone was conscious that Ewan was no longer with them.

Torquil began by informing them all about the Scottish TV early news programme and about Calum Steele's piece in the *Chronicle*.

'Aye, but what I can't understand is that anyone would listen to the wee windbag's theories,' said Douglas Drummond.

'Och, it's because he is a man of letters and not an ignorant fisherman like you,' replied his brother. 'Or like me, for that matter — even though we both beat him in the Gaelic spelling contests when we were all at school. You remember them, don't you, Piper?'

Torquil grunted assent and brought the twins to order by clapping his hands and standing up. 'What Calum has done is done!' he said. 'But although he has made the national news with his talk about killer eagles, it actually looks as if there is a more sinister killer abroad than an eagle. It looks as if there is a murderer on West Uist.'

He gestured to the local doctor. 'Ralph, would you give us a summary of your post-mortem findings on the body of Liam Sartori?'

While Torquil had been speaking, Ralph had been plugging his laptop into the station projector.

'I've done this as a Power-Point presentation,' he explained. 'That way I can show you each stage of my examination, from the initial finding of the body by the causeway, through my preliminary external examination of the corpse, the post-mortem dissection, and the pathological and microscopic specimens that resulted from it.' He looked at Morag. 'Can we pull the blinds?'

And a few moments later with the room in partial darkness, he pressed the home button on his laptop and a photograph of Liam Sartori lying on the rocks by the causeway flashed onto the wall.

'As Torquil has just told us, the media have drawn attention to the so-called talon marks on the face of the dead man.' He pointed a laser pen at the wall and indicated the livid lines on the face with the little luminous red arrow. 'Quite clearly, if these are talon slashes then they lead us to think that they are the same marks that we so recently saw on the face of Kenneth McKinley.'

'And are they, Ralph?' Torquil asked.

'I'm not sure,' the doctor returned, changing the slide with the touch of a finger, to reveal the body of Kenneth McKinley and the deep gashes on his face. 'What do you think?'

The others all craned forward to look.

'I am not sure,' said Wallace.

'Isn't there some test that will tell?' Morag answered.

'I honestly don't know — yet,' replied Ralph. 'I've never come across a death as the result of an attack by a bird of prey. But the point is, it could have been. And we also have to ask several questions. First, could he have fallen off the causeway after being attacked by a bird, and then risen stunned from a knock on the head? Could he have then staggered forward to fall face first into a rock pool and drown?'

'What makes you doubt that?' Torquil asked, already aware of Ralph's findings.

Ralph moved to the next slide.

'This!' he said emphatically.

And they found themselves looking at the naked back of Liam Sartori, as he lay on the metal post-mortem table in the cottage hospital mortuary. Ralph directed the luminous arrow of his laser pen to a discoloured area that started between the dead man's shoulder blades and ran up to his neck.

'In my opinion this mark was caused by a foot.' Ralph said. 'You can see petechiae, tiny pinpoint haemorrhages dotted around and the spreading purple discolouration. This would be consistent with a foot having been stomped down hard on him — and maintaining pressure for some time. Possibly holding him underneath the water surface of that rock pool.'

'You mean after he had staggered there?' Wallace asked.

'Except that we think he was dragged there, rather than staggered there,' said Torquil. And he described the position of the dead man's collar, the disturbed shingle where he had fallen.

'Here's a photograph of how we found him,' said Ralph. 'Bearing in mind that the Padre had pulled him out of the pool, yet the position of his collar would be hard to explain.'

He then ran through a number of slides detailing the morbid anatomical dissection. Despite herself Morag felt decidedly queasy and had to look away. The Drummonds, well used to gutting fish and removing vast amounts of entrails, nodded with interest and sipped tea.

'As you can see there, I am squeezing water from the lungs. But the question is, did that water get there before or after he died?'

'What does that mean?' asked Douglas.

'Well, the presence of water in the lungs doesn't by itself tell us a lot. It could have got into his lungs after he was dead.'

Wallace slapped his hand on the table. 'Gosh, I see what you mean. It could have been made to look like he was drowned.' Then he eyed the police surgeon doubtfully. 'But how else could he have died?'

'From this,' said Ralph moving the slide to a photograph of a human brain resting in a large stainless-steel dish. Once again he manoeuvred the luminous red arrow of his laser pen to highlight a large clot of blood that had formed over the left temporal area. 'That could have killed him, although I think it may have just been enough to stun or knock him out. He could have sustained it in a fall, but equally, he could have been hit and then fallen.'

'Did you do a diatom test, Ralph?' Torquil asked.

'I did, and here it is.' And with a press of the button the wall was illuminated with a microscopic section of what looked like bubbles in a mush of red pulp. All over the field were small dots of a greenish hue. 'Those bubble-like structures are alveoli, the air pockets in the lungs, and those little dots are tiny unicellular organisms called diatoms. The water in the rock pool sample I took is full of them. This slide shows that they are present both inside and outside the alveoli. That implies that his heart was beating for some period of time after he was in the water. The diatoms have been inhaled and have entered the bloodstream. I have other samples that I have yet to analyse, but if I find them in other organs it is pretty conclusive that he drowned.'

'And with that strange bruise on his back it looks as if he may have been held under,' suggested Torquil. 'But he was a big bloke. Would it have needed a lot of strength to keep him under?'

'Not necessarily,' returned Ralph. 'His blood alcohol level was high enough to have anaesthetized half of the fishermen in West Uist.'

Torquil crossed to the whiteboard that was usually used to keep darts or table tennis scores and picked up the marker pen.

'All right, we have a suspected murder victim,' he said, writing the name Liam Sartori on the board and enclosing it in a box. 'What do we know about him?'

'He worked for the new laird,' Wallace suggested.

Torquil nodded, wrote the name Jock McArdle nearby and enclosed it in a circle. He joined the box and the circle with a line. 'What else?

'He was from Glasgow. Not much taste in clothes,' said Douglas.

'He had a run in with Calum Steele,' said Morag.

Torquil added Calum's name and circled it.

'And he had a run in with Ewan,' Morag added.

Torquil turned and stared at her in surprise. 'Did he now? When? I didn't know about that?'

Morag coloured. 'Sorry, Torquil. I thought I had told you. I've just — I mean I had — things on my mind. I'll get the report book.'

She got up and went through to the main office, returning after a few moments with the large loose-leaf ledger. She put the book down on the table in front of Torquil and thumbed back the pages.

'Here it is. Early last week, a couple of days before he ... was last seen. Ewan cautioned him and his companion, a Danny Reid, about messing about with a motorboat in the harbour. When he approached them, they didn't realize that he was a police officer and started giving him lip. You know what a gentle giant he is —' She bit her lip, and went on. 'Anyway, he

149

showed them his warrant card and they just kept on being abusive and derogatory about West Uist, and about being the new laird's right-hand men. Then one of them tossed a cigarette end into the gutter and Ewan gave him the option of picking it up and taking it home or being run in there and then.'

Morag grinned as she recalled the scene of him telling her about it. 'When he began rolling up his sleeves — to use Ewan's words — "he fair scuttled down and picked it up." But Ewan thinks they went off muttering about getting him back.'

Torquil tapped the marker pensively on the table then turned and added Ewan's name. He hesitated a moment, then enclosed it in a box. 'We will use a box to indicate that Ewan is ... also dead.' He sighed and drew a line between the names. Then he added the name Danny Reid, circled it and drew interconnecting lines with Liam Sartori, Ewan McPhee and Jock McArdle.

After a moment he wrote the word 'dog' near Jock McArdle's name and enclosed it in a box, and underneath it wrote the words 'suspected poison', followed by a question mark.

'Right, now let's focus on the Wee Kingdom for a minute,' he said. 'Liam Sartori had been there, delivering letters, as I understand it; Lachlan told me about it. And the letters were all legal documents on behalf of McArdle, informing the crofters that he was going to have wind towers erected on the common grazing land adjoining their crofts.'

Ralph had been quiet since his presentation. Now he interjected, 'I am guessing that it is the same letter that the laird himself delivered to Rhona at the hospital!' His normally calm visage turned stern. 'I have every reason to believe that was the trigger for her heart attack.'

Torquil nodded, then turned and under the heading of Wee Kingdom added Rhona McIvor's name, which he duly boxed. He turned to Morag. 'We'll need a copy of that letter.'

Morag had been making notes. 'And I expect we'll need to interview all of the crofters.'

Douglas snorted. 'Aye, the ones that are still alive.'

And Torquil wrote the names as prompted by Morag: Alistair McKinley, Megan Munro, Vincent Gilfillan, all of whom he enclosed in circles. And then Gordon MacDonald and Kenneth McKinley, who received boxes.

'What about the Morrisons?' Morag asked.

'Good question,' replied Torquil adding their names alongside the other members of the Wee Kingdom community. Instead of a box or a circle he drew a large question mark beside their names.

As Torquil began making notes about the respective post-mortem findings on Liam Sartori and Kenneth McKinley, and then linking their names with the word EAGLE followed by a question mark, Wallace verbalized the growing anxiety that they had all been feeling ever since his brother's earlier comment. 'There seem to be an awful lot of folk's names in boxes on that board!'

Torquil moved to another part of the board and made similar notes about the contents of Ewan's notebook. He wrote the words: GUNS, BOND, FAIR FANCIES HIMSELF, then on another column KATRINA, FAMILY and WIND.

'SAS, camouflage clothes and guns,' mused Torquil as he tapped various entries on the board with the marker pen. 'And all that slug goo that was found in Kenneth McKinley's stomach — it all adds up to a rich fantasy life, I think. So BOND may have been James Bond! He saw himself as some sort of secret agent, it seems.'

Morag snapped her fingers. 'Maybe that's another link with Katrina Tulloch? Maybe he fantasized about her?'

Torquil circled Katrina's name, adding lines to Ewan, Kenneth McKinley and the poisoned dog.

'That's a spider's web you have there, Piper,' said Wallace.

'You're right,' Torquil mused. 'But where's the spider?'

CHAPTER THIRTEEN

Guilt had been a constant companion to Katrina for several days, but never more so than now, as she lay half-naked next to Nial in the long grass of the machair.

'I love you; you know that, don't you, Katrina?' Nial murmured, his lips playing over her throat.

'Nial, I — I —' Abruptly she sat up and began reaching for her discarded jeans and knickers. 'I think this was a mistake. It shouldn't have happened.'

He caught her wrist and pulled her back down. 'It was inevitable!'

'It's just that I feel so bad, so guilty about —'

'About Megan? She's my problem.'

Katrina bit her lip. 'I meant about Ewan.'

'Ah yes, of course. But even so, I think this was bound to happen. There's chemistry between us.'

And despite herself she had to agree. She had felt it for some time as well, but had done her best to suppress the feelings.

'How did you manage to find me?' she asked, as his roaming hands began to work their way under her clothes again.

'I suppose I knew that you'd be checking out the coast again.'

'You were lucky then. I had been busy and had to get specimens off on the ferry.'

He chuckled softly as she straddled him. 'Right now I feel I'm the luckiest man alive.'

Alistair McKinley whistled for Shep, his collie, and patted the rear seat of his old jeep. Beside him was his large leather hunting bag full of shotgun cartridges and his old 12-bore shotgun. He started the engine and set off.

As he turned out of his drive he saw Megan Munro waiting for him, arms akimbo. He stopped alongside her, immediately aware of two things. Firstly, she had been crying, and secondly, she was in a belligerent mood.

'Alistair McKinley, where are you off to with that shotgun?'

'Megan, lassie, I know that you've had a bad time of it, what with Rhona and ... your man, yesterday, but —' he sighed with a hint of exasperation — 'I'm not feeling that great myself. And where I go with my shotgun, for which I have a licence, is entirely my own business.'

'It's my business as well, if you are planning to kill hedgehogs. I'll stop you.'

Alistair grunted. 'Don't even think of messing with me, lassie. I've lost my boy and today I'm in a killing mood. I'm going to do what I need to do to ease my own pain.' He gunned the engine and engaged first gear. 'Now get out of my way.'

Megan stood staring after him, her temper seething.

'So much pain, so much hurt,' she mused. 'I've got pain of my own, you stupid old man. And I know how I'm going to deal with it.'

'Shop! Anyone home?' Calum Steele slapped his hand on the counter of the Kyleshiffin police station.

Wallace Drummond came through, a mug of tea in his hand. At sight of the tubby editor in his yellow anorak, he shook his head as if in disbelief. 'Dear me, you have a nerve, Calum Steele! Behaving like a hooligan after all that you've been doing.'

The smile that had been on Calum's face was quickly

replaced by a look of injured pride, and then by one of puzzlement, and finally by one of pure irritation. 'What are you babbling about, you teuchter? I hope you are not referring to my article —' the smile momentarily resurfaced — 'or my television appearance?'

'I thought it was an interview over the telephone that you gave, not an appearance,' said Wallace. 'But I should be warning you, Inspector McKinnon is not pleased.'

'So it's *Inspector* McKinnon today, is it?' Calum returned sarcastically. 'Well, is Inspector McKinnon in to have a word with me?'

'I'm here, Calum,' said Torquil, coming out of the recreation-room at the sound of the *Chronicle* editor's voice. 'And I'm glad to see you.'

Calum beamed and looked disdainfully at Wallace.

'Because I was meaning to give you a right royal telling off!' exclaimed Torquil. 'Just what on earth did you think you were doing with that piece of drivel about killer eagles? And printing that photograph was just downright irresponsible.'

'Ir-irresponsible?' Calum repeated. 'Me? I'm the most responsible reporter on the island.'

'Calum, you are the only reporter on West Uist,' replied Torquil.

'Aye, reporter, editor, photographer and printer. I am the media on West Uist.'

'You're a windbag!' Wallace interjected.

Calum looked thunderstruck and raised his hands beseechingly to Torquil. 'Did you hear that? I am —'

'You are a nuisance at the moment,' said Torquil. 'And why did you go and spread this gossip to Scottish TV?'

'I am a newsman. The public have a right to know about what's happening on the island. Even the folk in Dundee and

Glasgow have a right to know what's happening in the real world.'

'Well you may have shot the gun this time, Calum. We are treating the death of that young man as highly suspicious.'

The telephone rang three times and then stopped as someone answered it in the recreation-room.

Calum's face registered instantaneous excitement. 'Suspicious, did you say? Are you talking about suspicion of death caused by an eagle attack — or something else? Come on, Piper. Give me a piece of —'

'Calum, it's a good piece of my mind that you are getting now. You need —'

Morag popped her head round the corner. 'Sorry, boss, it's Superintendent Lumsden on the line. He says he wants to talk to you straight away.' She grimaced helplessly. 'Like right now!'

Torquil gave a sigh of irritation. 'OK Morag. Could you take over with Calum here?'

Morag nodded and moved aside to let Torquil pass. Then advancing to the desk, she asked, 'Right then, Calum, where were you with Torquil?'

'The inspector was ticking him off. Sergeant Driscoll,' Wallace volunteered.

'Away with you,' returned Calum. He leaned conspiratorially on the counter. 'Actually, he was just telling me that you lot suspect murder. Tell me more, Sergeant Driscoll.'

Torquil took the call in his office. As soon as he lifted the receiver, Superintendent Lumsden snapped; 'I've just come off the phone with your new laird.'

'You mean the new landowner, Superintendent,' Torquil interrupted.

'Don't mince words with me, McKinnon! The thing is, he's

upset. Not only has one of his employees been involved in a fatal accident, but his dog has been poisoned.'

'I was aware that he suspects his dog was poisoned, sir.'

'This is his second dog. He's feeling angry and thinks there may be a conspiracy against him.'

'There certainly seems to be bad feeling against him on West Uist. He has hardly endeared himself to the residents of the Wee Kingdom. He has started erecting wind towers before the situation has been clarified.'

'He's also fuming about the newspaper and the piece on the news.'

'I was just having a word with Calum Steele when you telephoned, sir. I understood that you wanted me to telephone you after the meeting.'

'Well, what was the result?'

'I think it was almost certainly murder, Superintendent Lumsden. I will fax the report through to you shortly. I think, under the circumstances, we will have to seal the island off.'

'Of course. Any suspects.'

'Too early to say, Superintendent.'

'Any leads?'

'A few. They'll all be in my report.'

There was a sharp intake of breath from the other end of the line, and a wince of pain. Torquil imagined the big policeman in his crisp uniform, with his foot bandaged. He felt little sympathy for his superior officer.

'OK, get on with it. Let me have that report as soon as possible. Meanwhile, I'll call the laird and tell him that there is now a murder inquiry going on.'

'Of course, Superintendent. Shall —' But before he could finish, there was a click and he once more found himself staring at the dead receiver.

Morag tapped on the door. 'I gave Calum the official line. We have no information to divulge and we are making inquiries. And I told him to behave.'

Torquil gave a half smile. 'And we can be sure that he won't! Ah well, let's get on with this thing. First of all, we have to seal the island off.'

'I took the liberty of getting on with that. No more ferries until further notice.'

Torquil smiled. 'What would I do without you, Morag?'

She returned his smile. 'The same as I'd do without you, boss. Just don't think of going! I hate to think what would happen if it was me who had to speak to Superintendent Lumsden.'

After Katrina had left, Nial continued his round of the coast, stopping every now and then to get out of his car and check out the nesting birds on the machair dunes and the cliffs. He mechanically jotted his recordings in a small notebook which he would later transcribe onto his laptop. The truth was that his mind was not fully on the job. Even spotting one of the eagles wing its way towards its high eyrie in the Corlins did not fill him with his usual enthusiasm. Instead, he was preoccupied by the women in his life.

Until a few days ago he had thought that he was madly in love with Megan. Then she had almost gone potty over those dead hedgehogs, and done a Lady Macbeth thing. It had spooked him, he had to admit, and it was then that he had become aware of the emotional door standing ajar. And shining through that opening was Katrina and his feelings for her. He grinned and felt a deep inner warmth as he thought of how rapidly those feelings had heated up until they had reached boiling point, for both of them, culminating in the passionate love-making that they had just enjoyed in the long grass of the machair.

Except that Katrina had emotional baggage. That policeman, Ewan McPhee. She felt guilty about him and he would have to work on that.

He was feeling torn between the two women. Megan or Katrina? He felt bad about his betrayal of Megan, but seeing her freaking out had altered his image of her. That was a weakness on his part, he felt. Yet he couldn't help it and part of his mind rationalized it by thinking that she had pushed him towards Katrina.

He grinned as he put his binoculars to his eyes and scanned the distant stacks and skerries.

'West Uist is a beautiful island, all right. And she's a beautiful woman.'

He had made up his mind.

Danny Reid was perspiring profusely. He was stripped to the waist and a coating of moisture covered his torso as he started heaping soil onto the grave. He hated digging. He hated all manual work if the truth be known, but burying bodies was one thing he hated above all else. And it had been a heavy body.

He had patted the turned earth into a smooth mound and was just replacing the turf that he had cut on top of it when he heard Jock McArdle's footsteps crunch on the gravel path behind him. He was carrying a decanter of whisky and two glasses.

'That's a good job you've done, Danny. And it is a good spot for them both. They hadn't been here long, but Dallas and Tulsa both loved tearing about this old patch of lawn.' He sighed and Danny noted the tears in his boss's eyes. 'We'll be able to see them from the snooker-room upstairs.'

Danny laid his shovel down and pulled on his T-shirt. 'Liam was right upset about Tulsa.' He nodded at the whisky glasses in his employer's hand. 'Are we going to have a toast to the girls, boss?'

McArdle held out the crystal whisky glasses for Danny to hold while he poured two liberal measures of malt. 'Aye, but we're also going to toast Liam. That was Superintendent Lumsden on the phone again. He tells me that Liam was definitely murdered. They're starting an inquiry.'

Danny stared at McArdle, his hand clenching the glass so that his knuckles went white. 'The bastards! Who do you think did it, boss?'

McArdle ignored the question for a moment. He raised his glass. 'To the girls! And to Liam! May we always look after our family.'

They both swilled their drinks back in one.

'It has to be one of those bastards on the Wee Kingdom,' McArdle replied. 'And I'm guessing there is no chance on earth that the local flatfeet will be able to find the buggers. We're going to have to do it ourselves, Danny.'

'How's that, boss?'

McArdle smiled, 'I've got an idea to flush them out.' He hefted the cut crystal glass in his hand and nodded towards the ornamental fountain in the centre of the lawn. In unison, they threw their glasses at the fountain.

Jesmond had been watching from an upstairs landing window. He winced as he saw the hundred-year-old crystal smashing on the fountain.

'Peasants!' he exclaimed. He reached for his mobile phone.

The Corlins were shrouded in swirling mist by the time that Alistair left his jeep at the foot of the cliffs, just at the spot where a few days ago, they had found the broken body of his son. He pulled off his shoes and socks and wiggled his feet, flexing the well-developed toes that typified many of the outer islanders — especially those who were descended from the old cliff-scaling families of St Kilda's. Alistair was proud of his heritage and had tried to instil that pride into his son. He had taught him to hunt, to survive in the wild when the weather was at its worst, how to forage for food under rocks and in pools, and he had taught him how to climb.

And that was what had been eating away at him for days. How could Kenneth have fallen? He was as sure-footed as any of the old St Kildans who used to scale the sheer cliffs of Hirta, the larger of the isles, in order to snare the Culvers and take their eggs as they nested. Alistair felt sure that it had been an outside agent that had caused his fall and he intended to investigate for himself. His soul burned to find satisfaction.

'If your spirit is here, Kenneth — come with me.'

He swung his hunting bag over his shoulder and then swung the shoulder sling of his shotgun bag over his neck and right shoulder so that the bag hung across his back and would not impede him as he climbed.

And he began to scale the almost sheer face, his fingers and toes finding holds and clinging long enough to hoist and pull himself up. Despite his age, he climbed with the effortless ease of a monkey.

'You were a good lad, Kenneth. You didn't deserve to die so young,' he whispered to himself, as he swiftly ascended towards the shelf of rock from which it was reported that his son had fallen. 'I know why you were coming here.'

He pulled himself up over the ledge and lay for a few

moments waiting for his breathing to settle to normal. And as he lay there, his shrewd eyes pierced the swirling mists until he caught a glimpse of the eyrie some distance away.

'You devil birds!' he cursed under his breath, as he pulled off his shotgun bag and drew out his 12-bore. He reached into his hunting bag and drew out two cartridges. Breaking open the gun, he slid them into place and snapped it shut.

'Now we wait until you go hunting,' he mused. 'Take your time. I'm in no hurry. I'm a hunter, too. Just like my boy.'

There was the sound of a toe scuffing rock and Alistair spun round, his eyes wide with surprise.

'You! What are you doing here?' he challenged.

CHAPTER FOURTEEN

Vincent Gilfillan had been busy all morning. He had dealt with his own chores before going on to feed Rhona's goats and then do some work on her weaving quota. He knew that he and the others would have to get together and work out what they were going to do about her croft. But of course, the complication was the new laird. The possibility that he would repossess her croft and rescind the right of transfer seemed highly likely.

'Damn the man,' he muttered to himself. 'We should have been in contact with the Crofters Commission to find out exactly what rights we have.' He shook his head sadly as he tidied up and left Rhona's weaving shed. It was exactly the sort of thing that Rhona would have seen to. And she would have done if she hadn't died so suddenly.

At the thought of her death, he pictured the new laird and he felt his anger seethe to boiling point. In his mind he saw him going into the cottage hospital with Inspector McKinnon and he thought back to what he had wished he had done. Part of him wished that he had not stopped from going out to challenge him. But then he thought of Rhona lying there, her face alabaster white.

He pushed open the door of her cottage, went through to the main room, lined with bookcases, antiques and numerous handmade mats covering the polished wood floor. He slumped down on the settee beside the holdall containing the things he had brought back from the hospital. The smell of her perfume and the odour of her cigarettes was all around him and he felt slightly heady. He gave a deep sigh of despair and leaned forward, sinking his head in his hands as he began to sob.

He was still sobbing when Torquil found him there ten minutes later when he pushed open the door.

'I thought I heard someone in here,' Torquil said, coming in and pulling off his large leather gauntlets. 'And I am glad to find that it is you. We need to talk. But first, I have to tell you that we are investigating a murder.'

Vincent looked up and wiped the tears from his eyes with the back of his hand. 'Whose murder, Inspector?'

'One of Jock McArdle's employees. The tall flashily-dressed one with attitude. It was his body that we found by the Wee Kingdom causeway.'

'He had a bad attitude, right enough. I met him yesterday. In Geordie Morrison's croft. I was there with Megan Munro and he came in and gave us a letter each from the new laird.' He wrinkled his nose distastefully. 'I thought that he smelled of whisky.'

'What were the letters about?'

'I think you know already, Inspector,' Vincent returned. 'The same as the letter that McArdle devil gave Rhona.' His face twisted in distaste. 'You know — the one that killed her! The one about having wind towers put up on the common grazing ground by our crofts.'

'Have you got your letter?'

'Not here. I think I may have just screwed it up.' He chewed his lip reflectively. 'But Rhona's letter should be here in this holdall. I haven't had a chance, or the inclination, to unpack her stuff.' He unzipped the bag, opened the sides and pulled out the letter.

Torquil read it and nodded. 'Enough to give anyone a shock, let alone someone who had just had a heart attack.' He held out the letter for Vincent to see. 'I understand from Dr

McLelland that it looked as if she was trying to write a message when she collapsed. Any idea what she meant by this CARD IN?'

Vincent shook his head. 'No idea. It may mean one of those Get Well cards that she had. They are all in there as well. As I said, I haven't had time to check her things.'

Torquil put the letter back into the holdall. 'I think that I had better take the bag back to the station. There may be something of relevance. I'll give you a receipt for it all.'

Vincent looked at him with puzzled brows. 'I thought you were investigating the murder of that young thug. Why do you need Rhona's things?'

'There have been several deaths. Too many for comfort. We're keeping an open mind about them all.'

'That's just what I was thinking yesterday, Inspector. That's why I was in Geordie's cottage. I was looking to see if I could find some clue as to where he'd taken his family.'

'And what was Megan Munro doing there?'

'I think she had the same idea. But she was upset.'

'Tell me more.'

Vincent stood up and stretched the muscles of his back. 'I'm not sure that I should be saying anything about Megan's problems.'

Torquil eyed him sternly. 'I repeat, I'm investigating a murder. Why was she upset?'

Vincent sighed. 'I think she is having trouble with Nial Urquart. She was upset, I comforted her, that's all.' He held his hands palms up in a gesture of helplessness. 'She threw herself into my arms and I was giving her a friendly hug. There was nothing more.'

'And what did Sartori say?'

'Nothing much. Just a smart comment, then he gave us the

letters and said he was going on to see Alistair McKinley.'

'And that was the last you saw of him?'

'Yes. I had chores to do and Megan was desperate to find Nial. I had already taken care of Geordie's chickens and collected the eggs. And to tell you the truth I was bit peeved with him. He's always going off and taking his family with him, and he's never too good at telling us where he's gone.'

'Who does he usually tell?'

Vincent hesitated for a moment, his expression grim. 'Rhona.'

'And presumably she hadn't told you where they went?'

'No, but she wouldn't, would she?' he replied brusquely.

'Do I detect a touch of pique there, Vincent?' Torquil asked.

Vincent ran his hands across his face. 'Aye, maybe. Look, the truth is that Rhona liked younger men. She always had. Never anything deep. She liked to be in charge of her life.' He gestured round the room at the bookcases packed with books, the upright piano by the wall, the old manual typewriter and the reams of neatly stacked paper on an old roll-top desk, then, 'Geordie was the latest.'

'And does everyone on the Wee Kingdom know that?'

The crofter shook his head. 'I knew it, and I suspect that Alistair knew it too. But I'm pretty sure that Sallie, Geordie's wife doesn't.'

'Or perhaps she found out and that's why they've gone off somewhere.'

'Maybe,' Vincent returned doubtfully. 'Geordie is an unpredictable man. I am just not sure what to think.'

'And were you one of Rhona's lovers?' Torquil asked matter-of-factly.

Vincent gave a soft whistle, and then smiled winsomely. 'You don't pull punches, do you, Inspector?' He glanced at a photograph of all of the Wee Kingdom crofters on the mantelpiece. A smiling Rhona was in the middle. 'The answer is yes, years ago, for a few months. When I first came to the Wee Kingdom to take over my croft when my mother's cousin died. But not since then. I loved her then.'

Torquil nodded. 'The Padre tells me that you've been here about twenty years now.'

Vincent nodded. 'That's right.' He seemed to look into the distance, into the past. 'Twenty years, how time flies. Rhona was sort of playing at crofting back then. She was still commuting back and forth to the mainland, and working as a writer in Glasgow or Edinburgh.'

'She was a journalist, I believe,' said Torquil. And crossing to the roll-top desk he looked at the piles of neatly stacked papers and the documents in the pigeon holes of the desk. 'It looks as if she was still busy with writing.'

'Aye, she hadn't written anything for years, but she started again — just articles — a few months ago. Mainly about lifestyles and crofting.'

'She seems to have been very methodical.'

'Rhona was the administrator of all of the Wee Kingdom business outlets. She did all the paperwork for us.' He shook his head. 'God knows how we'll cope now. I'm helpless at that sort of thing.'

'And what about the wind towers that McArdle is having put up?'

Vincent snorted with derision. 'He's got a lot to answer for.'

'It looks as if one of his men has already paid for him, with his life.'

'Aye, maybe so.'

Calum Steele had been busy on the internet. In his own mind he was an investigative journalist par excellence. He felt born to the job, being by nature both curious about his fellow citizens, and having an almost pathological urge to gossip.

'Calum Steele! You would spear the inside out of a calm with your questions!' Miss Melville used to say upon being barraged with his questioning in school. 'You need to go and be a journalist.'

And indeed that was precisely what he had done, the only thing being that he had done it locally. Being somewhat thick-skinned, it had never occurred to him that it had been Miss Melville's hope that he would leave the island to seek his fortune.

Calum had grasped the new technology with both hands. Although he liked to cultivate the image of always having a spiral-bound notebook with him, he always carried a state-of-the-art Dictaphone in his anorak as well as his latest love, his digital camera. He was still rankling at the criminal loss of his last one, which had forced him to shell out £500 on the new one at his elbow.

To his credit, he single-handedly produced enough copy to fill the eight pages that made up the local paper six days a week. Admittedly, four pages were taken up with advertising, but anything on the island that was remotely newsworthy, whether that was the purchase of a new tractor, the number of overdue library books, or the belief that eagles were attacking people, Calum would investigate and write it up. And a murder investigation to him was like manna from heaven.

Not being of a naturally sentimental nature, Calum had found himself in a strange place lately. The loss of PC Ewan McPhee had affected him more than he had thought it would. He had become maudlin and he found himself valuing his friends more than usual. Torquil McKinnon and the Drummond twins, who had all been at school at the same time, and Morag Driscoll, whom he had secretly adored for years, they all seemed vitally important in his life. He had become patriotic, territorial, and he had taken a great dislike to the brazenness of the new laird and his bully-boy tactics. He had decided to take up a crusade against the wind towers that were being erected on the Wee Kingdom.

'So, Mr McArdle, it's not just the king of ice cream that you are, is it?' he grinned to himself as he printed out his findings. 'Let's see what Kirstie Macroon at Scottish TV makes of this.'

And he reached for his mobile telephone.

Alistair McKinley lowered his shotgun.

'Lachlan McKinnon, what in the blazes are you doing up here?' He flicked his eyes at his shotgun. 'You shouldn't sneak up on a man with a shotgun. Accidents have been known to happen.'

The Padre waved a finger. 'Alistair, I was not sneaking up on anyone. If you must know, I came up here for inspiration. I am having trouble writing sermons and eulogies lately and I was preparing one for Kenneth. I thought that if I came up here, where he had his accident, I might get a sense of how he died. I imagine that is pretty much the same reason that you are up here yourself.' Then he pointed to the shotgun. 'Or were you here in some misguided sense of revenge?' He looked up at the misty Corlins. 'Were you hoping to pot a golden eagle? That would be foolish, you know.'

'Ach, maybe it would strike you as foolish, Padre, but you haven't lost your son. And it is better than me taking my gun and doing away with the real villain of the piece. The man who caused Kenneth's death and now Rhona's — that bastard

McArdle!'

Lachlan put an arm about the old crofter's shoulder. 'You are an old fool. Look at you, up here in these conditions in your bare feet! Is that the action of a sober man? Come on now; let's get you back safe and sound to your croft. I'll come with you and we'll have a dram.'

Despite himself Alistair gave a short laugh. 'You are not the usual type of minister at all, are you? Always encouraging me to have a dram. But I'll come with you. Will you need a lift?'

'I have my Red Hunter down below,' replied the Padre. He looked at the cliff edge. 'And if you will take my advice you will take the path down with me, and not make any more foolish attempts to climb in your bare feet.'

He waited while Alistair unloaded his shotgun and slid it into his shotgun bag.

As they made their way down the path, Lachlan fancied that he heard the heavy flap of eagle wings overhead. He smiled to himself, for he had no doubt that he had at least saved one life that day.

Morag sent the Drummonds off and went back into Torquil's office where she had left Megan Munro with a cup of tea.

'I've sent my special constables onto the job,' she said, sitting in Torquil's chair opposite Megan.

'He's not safe, Sergeant. He says he's off to start that hedgehog cull, but I don't believe him. He said he was in a killing mood, and with that poor man falling and getting killed the other day, I thought that I should report him to the police.'

'Well, the Drummond twins will investigate and see if they can locate him. Just to be on the safe side.' She produced her silver pen and her notebook and laid them on the desk in front of her. She had only met Megan Munro once or twice before, but she knew all about her and her hedgehog-rescue operation. A pretty girl, she thought. Pity that she has to cover up her hair in those beanie hats and wear those mannish dungarees.

'I am afraid that I have to tell you, that death you just referred to — well, we are treating it as suspicious.'

Megan's eyes opened wide. 'Suicide, you mean?'

Morag shook her head. 'Possibly murder.'

Megan let out a gasp and covered her mouth with both hands. 'But it couldn't be. I saw him myself yesterday afternoon. He was delivering those awful letters from the new laird, about the wind towers. I didn't like him. He smelled of whisky and I had to stop Vincent from getting beaten up by him. I'm sure if I hadn't been there he would have been violent.' As she recounted the meeting in Geordie Morrison's cottage, Morag made notes.

'Where is Geordie Morrison and his family?' Morag asked.

'We don't know. I think with all the other tragedies that have been going on lately, we're all a bit worried that something might have happened to them.'

'What does Nial think of it all?'

At the question Megan suddenly burst into tears. Morag patted her hand and pushed a box of tissues across the desk to her. 'I am sorry, Megan. Is there something upsetting you?'

'It — it's Nial. We had a row yesterday. Two actually, one in the morning and one when he got home last night. And he's barely talked to me this morning. He was up and out before I woke.'

Morag made a note in her book. 'Are you worried about him?'

Megan nodded. 'Oh, I don't think anything bad has happened to him. In fact, I think I know where he is. And who he's with!' Morag said nothing; experience having long since told her that people will often volunteer their information. 'He will be with that Katrina Tulloch. He drools over her. I know that now. He's gone from my bed to hers.'

'That isn't something that I can do anything about, I'm afraid.'

'No, but perhaps you ought to know about him. He's not exactly the harmless bird officer that everyone thinks. He's opinionated and he gets a bee in his bonnet about things. When he does that he can be ... tenacious.'

'I don't follow?'

'We first met at an animal rights meeting.'

'Go on,' Morag urged.

'He used to be an activist. He —'

'Has he a record, Megan? Is that what you are saying?'

Megan bit her lip as if she was having an internal argument as to what she should divulge. Then, finally, 'He told me that he once fire-bombed the warehouse of a factory that was involved in supplying a laboratory with animals for animal experimentation.'

Lachlan stood looking out of the window of Alistair's cottage, a glass of whisky in his hand. 'It is a magnificent view that you have here. I hadn't realized that you had such a good sight of the old lighthouse.'

'Aye, and from the other side of the house we'll soon be able to see all these wind towers that fool of a laird is planning.'

'Are you sure that it is all legal, though, Alistair? Have you had it checked out? I am no expert, but I would have thought he would have at least needed planning permission rather than just hoiking them up.'

Alistair sipped his whisky. 'Rhona usually saw to all the business and legal side of the Wee Kingdom. I suppose one of us will have to see to it now.'

There was a knock on the open door and Wallace Drummond popped his head round the frame. 'Ah Padre, we weren't expecting to see you here.'

His brother appeared beside him. 'It is Alistair that we are needing to see.'

'Come away in lads,' the old crofter urged. 'We were having a dram. Will you have one too? In memory of my lad.'

Wallace shook his head with a pained expression. 'I am sorry. We would have loved to join you, but we are here on duty. Our sergeant sent us on an errand. It's a bit tricky.'

'Out with it then,' said Alistair.

Douglas pointed to the shotgun bag leaning against the wall. 'We have been told that we are to confiscate your guns. Until further notice, the West Uist Police have put a ban on any hedgehog cull on the island.'

Jock McArdle and Danny Reid were watching the evening Scottish TV news in the large sitting-room at Dunshiffin Castle while they waited for Jesmond to call them to dinner.

'See that Kirstie Macroon, boss,' Danny said with a slightly lascivious tone as he handed his employer a whisky and lemonade. 'Liam fair fancied her.'

The redheaded newsreader went through the headlines while they sat and drank. Then the backdrop behind her changed to a picture of Dunshiffin Castle.

'Here that's us!' exclaimed Danny. 'We're on the news!'

Jock waved his hand irritably and sat upright. 'Let's listen then.'

And now to West Uist and the revelation by the editor of the West Uist Chronicle that the death yesterday of Liam Sartori, one of the employees of the new owner of the Dunshiffin Castle estate was not due to an eagle attack, as we previously reported, but was in fact murder. The local editor, Calum Steele, is on the phone now.

Jock swallowed the rest of his whisky and lemonade and held the glass out to Danny for a refill.

Then Calum's voice came over the television:

The new owner of Dunshiffin Castle is himself causing quite a stir on the island. He has embarked on a programme of windmill erection, which is of questionable legality.

Jock McArdle cursed. 'Careful you wee bastard!' he said to the screen, which showed Kirstie Macroon nodding her head as she listened to Calum.

And our investigations have revealed that Mr McArdle has a cavalier approach to business. Today it can be revealed that whereas he is publicly proclaimed to be an ice cream and confectionary mogul, in fact he has many investments, most notably in a string of companies involved in animal research. He has previously been the target —

Jock McArdle shot to his feet. 'Get the Porsche. It's time that wee busybody learned not to meddle in my business.'

Nial Urquart had just walked into the sitting-room of Katrina's flat with a cup of coffee in his hand. He switched on the television and caught Calum Steele's piece on the news.

'Bastard!' he exclaimed.

'Who's a bastard?' Katrina called through from the kitchen.

Nial flicked the channel control to the BBC. 'Oh, no one. Sorry for my language. It's just my team. They lost in the league.'

Then he switched the television off.

The Bonnie Prince Charlie was busy, as usual. Mollie McFadden and her staff were occupied with pulling pints of Heather Ale and dispensing whiskies. At the centre of the bar,

Calum Steele was holding court, clearly enjoying his new-found celebrity status on Scottish TV.

He was just telling an eager group of listeners for the third time how he had winkled out the information from the internet, when he felt a tap on his shoulder and then felt himself being whirled round.

'I don't allow anyone to broadcast my business affairs,' Jock McArdle snapped.

'And I've warned you once before, chubby,' said Danny Reid, running a finger up and down the zip of Calum's anorak. He looked aside at his employer who nodded his head.

Calum swallowed hard and held his chin up. 'The press have a perfect right to keep the public informed.'

'Is that so?' Jock said, as Danny grasped the zip fastener of Calum's greasy yellow anorak. 'Well, let me give you a friendly warning, Mr Calum Steele. In future you will keep your nose out of my affairs and you will be ... respectful of my position.' He leaned forward and took the fastener out of Danny's hand. 'In other words — zip it!'

And he yanked the fastener all the way up and caught a tiny fold of Calum's double chin in the zip.

Calum howled in pain.

'Just a warning!' McArdle said. 'Good night everyone.'

As he and Danny Reid reached the door, Mollie's voice rang out. 'Aye, that's the door, Mr McArdle. Laird or no laird, you and your bodyguard are herewith banned! You are not welcome here again!'

McArdle turned and sneered. 'See, darling, that's OK. Why would anyone want to drink in this hovel anyway? Good night and God bless.'

It was ten o'clock by the old grandmother clock in her sitting-room and Megan Munro had cried all evening. She had sent three texts to Nial and tried to phone him half-a-dozen times, but without success. So desperate had she felt that she had even contemplated trying to drink a glass of wine, but the thought alone revolted her. But music usually helped her, loud music to try to lift her mood. Yet not even Queen nor the Red Hot Chili Peppers could help. She turned off the CD player and went to switch off the lights. It was then that she thought she heard the sound of crackling, and smelled smoke.

She looked out of the window and saw the glow from Gordon MacDonald's croft. The cottage was in flames and next to it, like a couple of beacons, the two wind towers were engulfed in flames.

CHAPTER FIFTEEN

The West Uist Volunteer Fire Brigade was scrambled upon receiving Megan's emergency call. They arrived within ten minutes in their 1995 Convoy van, which had been specially converted into a Light Fire Appliance. With its four-man team, lightweight pump and four fire extinguishers, it was doubtful that they would be able to deal with the inferno that was Gordon MacDonald's croft.

Torquil had been alerted as a matter of course and arrived moments after them on his Royal Enfield Bullet.

Alistair McKinley and Vincent Gilfillan had heard the crackling flames and had joined Megan Munro by the croft and all three had attempted to douse the flames with buckets of water from the nearby duck pond. It had been clear, however, that their efforts were in vain.

'Just thank the lord that there was nobody inside,' said Alistair.

'That we cannot be sure about, Alistair,' Torquil said, as they stood back to let Leading Fireman Fraser Mackintosh and his volunteers do the best that they could.

Vincent put a hand on Torquil's arm. 'You can't think that anyone is in there!'

Torquil bit his lip, his brow furrowed with anxiety. 'I doubt it, but one thing is clear — this is a case of arson. There is no way that the fire could have spread to the wind towers.'

Megan clapped a hand to her mouth. 'My God! Nial! Where is he?' She began to scream. And then she was running towards the cottage.

Vincent and Torquil both stopped her and drew her back.

Fraser Mackintosh came over. 'It is no use, Torquil. All we can do is contain it. It will have to burn itself out.' He pointed at the wind towers. 'At least those towers are metal and won't burn. The wood platforms we can probably put out, but it looks as if any equipment on them will have been destroyed.'

Vincent took Megan back to her cottage and the others watched and waited until the fire burned itself down and the roof collapsed. Fortunately, rain began to fall and helped to dowse the fire.

But even so, it was not until the first light of morning that they were able to enter the smouldering building. And it was then that they found the badly charred body of a man.

Doctor Ralph McLelland was doing an early morning call on Agnes Calanish's latest arrival, after her husband, Guthrie, had called him at five o'clock.

'We're right sorry, Dr McLelland,' said Guthrie, 'it is just that he seemed too young to be having the croup. We were worried that he might need to be admitted to the hospital.'

Ralph wound up his stethoscope and replaced it in his black Gladstone bag. 'No, there's no need,' he said, with a well-practised smile of reassurance. 'He's still getting rid of some of the secretions. His chest is as clear as a whistle. He'll be just fine where he is.'

The local doctor was well used to night visits, although the islanders by and large did their utmost to deal with problems until a respectable hour. For Guthrie Calanish who had to be up at four every morning to get down to the harbour for the early morning ferry, five o'clock seemed perfectly respectable.

'There might not be any post for some time, Dr McLelland,' said Guthrie. 'The ferries have been cancelled until further notice by order of the police. I was down at the harbour this morning just on the off chance, but nothing is doing.'

'It is all these deaths, isn't it, Doctor?' Agnes suggested, as she redressed the latest addition to the household on a changing mat.

'I am afraid so, Agnes. But the police will be making good headway.'

'Do you think so?' Guthrie asked. 'I heard from Wattie Dowel, the chandler, that they're pretty much in the dark. Could you —'

Ralph's mobile phone went off just then, which under normal circumstances would have caused him some alarm, since there was a good chance that it indicated another call and a receding opportunity to take breakfast before morning surgery. But he was well used to Guthrie Calanish's attempts to get gossip out of him, so he raised his hand for quiet as he answered the call.

He was not expecting it to be a call for him in his capacity as the police surgeon. His eyes widened as Torquil told him that they had found another body on the Wee Kingdom. He replied curtly, 'I'll be there in five minutes.'

'Something urgent?' Guthrie enquired, a tad too curiously for Ralph's liking.

He forced a smile. 'Just another call. A doctor's life is rarely dull, you know.'

Agnes smiled up at him. 'Oh, no one could ever accuse you of being dull, Dr McLelland.'

Guthrie gave her a withering look and showed Ralph to the door. He watched the doctor hurry up the path with shoulders hunched to protect his neck from the rain, then he nodded thoughtfully and reached for the telephone.

The rain stopped at about five o'clock. Morag and the

Drummond twins had arrived before Ralph. Once Fraser Mackintosh had satisfied himself that the site was safe from further fire, and he and Torquil had checked to make sure that there was no possibility that the charred body showed any signs of life, they had withdrawn to preserve the crime site. For that was what Torquil had deemed it to be, especially after Fraser had informed him that he believed there to be strong evidence of arson caused by some incendiary device.

'The place was petrol bombed, Piper,' he had said. 'The cottage and the wind towers.' And he had pointed out the shattered fragments of milk bottles and the empty blackened petrol can that lay in a corner of the burned-out sitting-room.

Both Torquil and Morag Driscoll were CID and forensic scene-of-crime qualified, having both been seconded for training a few years previously. It was the chief constable's view that the Hebridean Constabulary should be totally self-sufficient and able to deal with all situations, without recourse to the mainland force. Accordingly, together with their ever-willing special constables, they had cordoned off the crime site with posts and tape barriers and then donned protective white coverall suits, as dictated by the Serious Crimes Procedure, while they awaited the arrival of Ralph.

'My God, I can guess what you've got for me. I caught the characteristic smell half a mile off,' said the doctor as he closed the door of his car and came over to them with his bag in one hand and his forensic case in the other.

'It is nasty, Ralph,' said Torquil. 'There is a badly burned — unrecognizable — body, in the ruins of the cottage.'

He waited while Ralph opened his forensic case and from it drew out a white coverall suit. 'An accident?' Ralph asked suspiciously, as he climbed into his suit and zipped up.

Torquil shook his head. 'No, it is suspicious all right.'

'It's a sight that you would be better seeing without having had breakfast,' Wallace said.

'I nearly lost mine,' Douglas confessed.

Ralph nodded sanguinely and picked up his case. Then he followed Torquil and Morag along the designated access path into the ruins to view the body.

It was a grisly sight. The blackened, shrivelled body lay sprawled on the floor near the hearth in what had once been the sitting-room of Gordon's croft. Ralph sucked air between his lips with a pained expression and stood looking about him for somewhere to lay his bag down. Finding a spot he put the forensic case down and placed his bag on top. He knelt down, opened the bag and drew out his stethoscope and an ophthalmoscope. Torquil and Morag watched him admiringly as he painstakingly examined the body as best he could without disturbing its position. An absolute stickler for routine and precision in all matters medical and forensic, he checked to ensure that the body was truly dead, and that there was no activity in the heart or nervous system.

'Dead as a piece of coal,' he announced, coiling his stethoscope and replacing it and his ophthalmoscope in his Gladstone bag, his bag for the living. Then he reached for his forensic case, which contained the instruments he used for examining the dead.

'Can you tell us how long, Doctor?' Torquil asked, his tone moving to the official.

The inspector was rewarded with a look of scorn. 'You're kidding me, Inspector!' Ralph replied, with a touch of sarcasm. 'A body found badly burned in a burned-out ruin of a house! The normal post-mortem changes mean nothing.'

'Not even the body's position?' Torquil persisted.

Ralph allowed a grim smile. 'Ah, you noticed,' he said. 'The fact that he was not curled up is suggestive that the individual was dead before the fire started.'

Morag grimaced. 'Another murder?'

Torquil looked at her with a troubled frown on his forehead. 'It looks like it. But we have a more immediate question to ask.'

'Aye', said Wallace. 'Who the hell is he?'

Ralph looked up at the special constable and shook his head. 'That is going to be difficult, considering the fact that his features have been burned beyond recognition — except perhaps to someone very close to him. We may have to get hold of dental records.'

Torquil pointed to the blackened body piercings on the lips, ears and above the eyes. Then to the mouth, which seemed to have fixed into a charred look of agony. 'What do you make of that?'

And, as Ralph looked, so he noticed for the first time the gold chain about the body's neck, disappearing into the mouth.

'It looks like a chain, possibly with a medallion,' Ralph returned. 'I will know better once I have done a full examination back at the mortuary. But first do you want to get the scene properly photographed and documented?'

And for the better part of an hour Morag, the Drummonds and Torquil set about recording the scene in notes, photographs and diagrams. While they did so, Ralph drove back to Kyleshiffin and swapped his car for the Cottage Hospital Ambulance. On his way back he passed the familiar sight of Calum Steele on his Lambretta scooter. Despite Calum's wave to stop, Ralph merely acknowledged him with a nod of his head and drove on. He knew all too well that the *Chronicle* editor had somehow scented out a story, and that he would be trying his damnedest to winkle out whatever information he could. But, with a suspected murder on the cards, Ralph knew it was best to leave that to the official force.

Torquil was busy in the ruins, but heard the tell-tale Lambretta engine approaching.

'Shall I intercept the wee man himself?' Douglas asked.

Torquil sighed. 'No, but thank you for the offer. It would be as well to make this official and I need to make sure that he doesn't do his usual thing and expound his own theories to the public rather than the official line.'

'Good luck, boss,' Morag murmured, as she continued making a detailed diagram of the charred cottage ruin.

'Good morning, Inspector McKinnon,' Calum greeted from the other side of the tape barrier. 'Arson attack, is it? Is somebody dead?'

'What makes you ask those questions, Calum?'

The newspaperman gestured to the burned-out ruins and the blackened wind towers. 'A cottage can catch fire, but I can't see how fire would jump all that distance to catch those towers. And this is Gordon MacDonald's cottage, there was no one in here, was there? Those windmill riggers were using it I know, but they left the island on —'

'So why do you ask about a death?'

Calum tapped the side of his nose. 'Let's just say that as a journalist I have my sources. And I passed Dr McLelland on my way here, which rather implies that he was coming here on professional business. All that and the fact that he wouldn't stop when he passed me, meant that he had information that he didn't want to divulge.' He grinned. 'And you are all wearing those official white dungaree suits. So what's up, Piper? Tell your old schoolmate Calum.'

Torquil shook his head good humouredly. 'All right, Calum. This is the official statement, but don't go passing it on with any of your journalistic embellishments.'

'No, no, you can depend on me. I am a responsible journalist and there will be no poetic licence excuse from me. Just the facts.'

'And the facts are that the West Uist division of the Hebridean Constabulary are investigating a house fire on the Wee Kingdom, and the discovery of a badly burned body in the burned-out ruins of the cottage.'

Calum had clicked on the Dictaphone in his top pocket and for effect also jotted notes in his spiral-bound notebook. His eyebrows rose and he asked quizzically, 'Murder?'

'The fire and the death are being treated as suspicious,' Torquil replied.

Calum nodded sagely and wrote 'suspicious' in capital letters and underlined it emphatically. In his mind's eye he already saw the headline he would use for the piece. And more immediately, how he was going to deliver it by phone to Kirstie Macroon, the pretty red-headed newsreader with pert breasts that he frequently fantasized about, and whose voice melted his insides. Then, realizing that his mind was straying, he cleared his throat.

'The cause of death?'

'We are awaiting the post-mortem report. And that will be some time, since we have yet to remove the remains from the major incident scene.'

Calum leaned over and craned his neck to try to get a better view. Screwing up his eyes he could see the Drummond twins and Morag Driscoll inside, but that was all. 'And who is it?'

'We have not identified the body yet.'

'Any chance of a picture?' Calum asked, hopefully.

'Now you are pushing your luck, Calum. After that last stunt of yours down by the causeway?'

Calum was about to protest, but the noise of the West Uist ambulance crunching up the drive halted the words before he had formed them. 'Ah the doctor, maybe I'll —'

'Maybe you will leave Dr McLelland to get on with his police surgeon duties, Calum. And that isn't a request, by the way.'

Ralph got out of the ambulance and came towards them with a pile of plastic bags and a folded-up body bag. 'Morning, Calum,' he said as he passed. 'I'm sorry that I couldn't stop earlier, but I had urgent work to be doing. Excuse me.' And he passed back along the designated access path. Once inside the burned ruin, he carefully put plastic bags on the head, hands and feet of the body to ensure that no important pieces of evidence were lost, before he and a very green-looking Wallace lifted the body and placed it in a plastic body bag before gingerly moving it into the ambulance.

Torquil jotted down in his notebook, 'Unidentified body of man, badly burned, removed from the crime scene at 06.25 hours. Doctor McLelland, police surgeon, will perform post-mortem as soon as possible.' Douglas was looking over his superior officer's shoulder as he wrote. He prodded Torquil in the back. 'Is that official jargon, meaning, after the doctor has had his breakfast?'

His brother joined them as Ralph drove off in the converted ambulance. He was still looking green about the gills. 'Which is more than I can say for me. I don't think I'll ever be able to eat anything again.'

Calum grinned at them. 'What's that? Two strapping big hulks like you feeling a bit squeamish. What is the island coming to?'

And before they could retort, as they usually did, Calum left them with a wave as he ran over to his Lambretta.

'Is that what they mean about journalists following

ambulances?' Wallace asked.

Jesmond tapped on Jock McArdle's door at seven o'clock and received a firm and colourful rebuke for disturbing his employer's repose. Nevertheless, he persisted with a further knock, adding the words, 'An emergency call from the local constabulary, sir.'

There was a rustling noise from the other side of the door, the tread of bare feet then the bedroom door was hauled open.

Jesmond held out the cordless phone. 'Inspector McKinnon would like to talk to you, sir. He says it is urgent.'

Jock McArdle frowned and grabbed the phone. He snapped his name into the mouthpiece, then stood listening, his expression growing grimmer by the second. 'I'm on my way!'

'A problem, sir?' Jesmond queried, as dexterously he caught the phone again.

'You could say that! This could be the start of the next bloody war!'

And, as Jesmond caught the murderous look in his employer's eyes before the door was slammed shut, he knew that if there was a war involving Jock McArdle, no prisoners would be taken!

The Padre had been roused from a fitful sleep by the telephone at his bedside. Groggily, he reached for the receiver and mechanically answered, 'St Ninian's Manse.'

He heard harsh breathing on the other end of the line.

'Hello, St Ninian's Manse,' he repeated. 'This is Lachlan McKinnon here. Can I help you?'

No one said anything. All he could hear was the harsh breathing. Then there was a rasping laugh and the line went dead.

'Now who on earth could that be?' he asked himself, reaching for his horn-rimmed spectacles in the dark so that he could see the luminous hands on the clock.

It was just after seven. He sighed, then threw back the blankets and got up. As he pulled on his dressing-gown and prepared to go over to his little praying stool he couldn't but help feeling that the phone call held some significance.

Torquil led McArdle through to the mortuary suite and tapped on the outer door. Through the frosted glass panels they saw the dim green-gowned shape of Dr Ralph McLelland approach and unlock the door.

'This way please, gentlemen,' said Ralph, leading the way through a swing door to the white tiled mortuary where a plastic sheet covered a body.

'We have reason to believe that this could be the body of a Daniel Reid, lately from Bearsden in Glasgow and currently residing at Dunshiffin Castle.' Torquil stated. 'I am afraid that the body has been very badly burned, almost incinerated. Do you feel that you would be able to identify the body?'

McArdle's face was pale and there was a noticeable patina of perspiration on his brow, but he nodded. 'If it is Danny, I'll know him.' Torquil nodded to Ralph who slowly pulled back the sheet to reveal the head and neck of the corpse.

McArdle looked shocked, colour draining even more than before. He swallowed hard, his expression pained. 'Yes. I am pretty sure that is my boy.' Then he spotted the chain around the neck and the ends disappearing into the clenched mouth. 'That's his medallion, right enough! Where was he? How did it happen?'

While Ralph pulled the sheet back Torquil gestured for McArdle to follow him. 'I think we should go up to the station and have a talk, Mr McArdle. There are a number of questions that you will want to ask and also a whole lot that I need to ask you.'

'You're bloody well right there! And I'm going to have someone's head for this!' Torquil eyed the new laird dispassionately. 'As I said, we'll have a talk. But just so long as you know, Mr McArdle, this is police business now. We will deal with this and there will be no head-taking of any sort on my island.'

McArdle pulled out his car keys and stomped down the corridor. 'We'll see, Inspector. I'll meet you at your station.'

Ralph came out of the mortuary suite, bundling up his green gown. He deposited it in the wicker basket outside and reached for his jacket which was hanging on the peg above. I'm just away for a spot of breakfast, Torquil, and then I'll get on with the post-mortem. Is that OK?'

Torquil nodded assent. 'You must have a cast-iron stomach, Ralph.'

'Aye,' was the police surgeon's only reply.

'What do you mean, girlie?' Jock McArdle demanded of Morag. 'There are no ferries?'

Torquil heard the question as he came in the Kyleshiffin police station front door, in time to see Jock McArdle slam a fist down on the counter.

'I have just told you, Mr McArdle,' Morag returned, looking completely unflustered. 'All ferries to and from the island have been cancelled until further notice. The island has been sealed off pending investigations.'

'But I need to get some of my boys up here from Glasgow.'

Torquil intervened. 'As my sergeant just told you, Mr McArdle, there will be no comings and goings until our investigations have been completed. And remember what I said at the hospital: this is a police matter, not a personal one.'

'Whoever killed my boys made it personal.'

'And we will find whoever did it,' Torquil said, and lifting the counter flap he held it open. 'We'll continue this in my office, I think.'

Ralph McLelland had gone straight to Fingal's Cave, the cafe on Harbour Street that boasted the fastest, biggest and cheapest breakfast in town. He was in a hurry and felt in need of a good fry-up before he began his forensic work. He was sitting down enjoying a mug of sweet tea when the tinkly bell at the back of the cafe door heralded another customer.

'Ah, Dr McLelland,' said Calum Steele, picking up a menu. 'Mind if I join you?'

'Ah, Calum,' Ralph returned with a long suffering smile. 'Of course not. Grab a seat.'

Morag glanced at her watch and rubbed her eyes. She could hardly believe that it was still only eight o'clock. So much had happened since she received the call from Torquil and there had been so much to do. Before Torquil had put a call through to Dunshiffin Castle, they had taken a few minutes in the Incident Room to add a new box with the name Danny Reid, followed by a question mark. The other information that Morag had obtained from her questioning of Megan Munro had been added and they had agreed that they needed to follow up about Nial Urquart's involvement in the animal rights movement, and about Jock McArdle's interests in a company that supplied animals to laboratories involved in research. Now that Torquil was busy interviewing McArdle, she switched on her computer and logged onto the internet.

After half an hour, she had printed out several sheets of paper. Then rising she went through to make tea. A few minutes later, as she sat down to read the printed sheets, her eyes opened wider as she read through them.

'Torquil will certainly be interested in these,' she mused.

CHAPTER SIXTEEN

Torquil eyed the laird of Dunshiffin with interest. The man was rattled, he could see that. He seemed genuinely shocked and upset, but anger lurked close to the surface.

'How long will this post-mortem be?' McArdle demanded.

Torquil shrugged his shoulders. 'An hour maybe and then there will be all the other tests. I would be hoping for a preliminary result some time this morning.'

'What is it with this place, McKinnon? My two dogs and my two boys. All dead. All murdered. What are you doing about it?'

'I am interviewing you for a start, Mr McArdle,' Torquil replied evenly. 'For one thing, we are not sure if Danny Reid was murdered. His death is just suspicious.'

'Suspicious!' McArdle snapped, showing his temper for the first time in the interview. 'You saw the frazzled state he was in. Of course he was murdered.'

'What was he doing at the Wee Kingdom last night?' Torquil persisted.

'How should I know?'

'He is your employee — I mean he was your employee. I would have thought you might have known, especially after your other employee's death.'

McArdle sucked air noisily through his lips. 'My boys are not in my employ twenty-four hours a day. I don't know what he was doing last night. I expect he'd been for a few drinks. My boys liked a drink. And they were very close. I expect he went up there because he wanted to investigate Liam's death.' He leaned forward and clasped his hands together on the desk in front of him. 'You lot don't seem to have got very far. And that's why I take grave exception to this cock-eyed ban on the ferries. I want some of my boys to come over here.'

'The ban is necessary, Mr McArdle. We are investigating a murder, possibly two. There will be no movement on or off the island, neither by sea nor air. And there will be no exceptions.'

'I don't like your tone, lad! I've had whipper-snappers like you for breakfast.'

Torquil stared him hard in the eye. 'You would find me most indigestible, Mr McArdle. Now tell me, what were you doing last night?'

McArdle's cheek muscles twitched. 'I was at home, in my castle, working on papers. Ask my butler Jesmond.'

'I will be doing so, of course. But do you think it is possible that Danny Reid could have been trying to start a fire in the croft cottage and been overcome by the flames and the smoke?' He paused and rested his chin on his fist. 'Perhaps he had been drinking as you suggested, and maybe drank too much?'

'Naw!' McArdle replied emphatically. 'My boys could both handle their drink. And there is no way that Danny would have played with fire.'

'But that isn't so, is it, Mr McArdle?' said Torquil, reaching into a wire basket beside his left elbow. 'We ran a check on your employees.' He smoothed the paper in front of him. 'They both had records. Liam Sartori for burglary and possession of drugs and Danny Reid for arson!'

Jock McArdle leaned back and shrugged. 'So what?'

'So it is suggestive, isn't it? A man with a criminal record for arson is found dead in a burning building.'

'Don't be an idiot, McKinnon. Danny wouldn't have torched

my property.'

'That's *Inspector* McKinnon, by the way,' he corrected calmly. 'In that case, do you have any idea why anyone would want to set fire to your property? Especially with one of your employees in it?'

The new owner of Dunshiffin Castle clenched his teeth. 'I am a businessman. A bloody successful businessman. I have had enemies in the past and I seem to have enemies now.'

'Why is that, Mr McArdle? Could it be because of the way that you do business?'

'Now you are beginning to get my goat. I am a successful businessman. Say anything else and I'll have your guts for garters — I'll sue you and your tuppence ha'penny police outfit for defamation.'

Torquil stared back with his best poker face. 'There is no defamation in my questioning, Mr McArdle. But since you are so sensitive, let me rephrase the question. You have a robust way of conducting your affairs. People on West Uist have called it bullying. Take those wind towers of yours, for example.'

'All perfectly legal.'

'I understand that the legality is under question,' replied Torquil. 'And then there were those letters you sent to the Wee Kingdom crofters. And the one that you delivered yourself to Rhona McIvor — who collapsed and died immediately afterwards.'

McArdle frowned. 'I regret her death, of course, but I hope you are not suggesting a connection between my letter and the McIvor woman's death?'

'It has been suggested that there may be a connection.' Torquil returned, casually.

'Who suggested it?' McArdle snapped.

'Doctor McLelland, our local GP and police surgeon.'

Jock McArdle shrugged dismissively. 'A country quack!'

'Dr Ralph McLelland is a highly respected doctor.'

The new laird of Dunshiffin merely smirked.

Torquil eyed him coldly for a moment then glanced at the notes on the desk in front of him. 'Yes, I'll be in touch when I have more news, or if I have more questions for you.'

McArdle nodded curtly, stood up and crossed to the door.

'Oh yes,' Torquil said, as the laird put his hand on the door handle. 'You always referred to your employees as your *boys*. Were you actually related to either of them?'

McArdle shook his head. 'Neither of them had any family. It's just an expression. Glasgow talk. I've always looked out for my boys.'

'Is that so?' Torquil asked, innocently.

McArdle's eyes smouldered. 'I should have looked after them better, maybe. But I'll be looking after their memory, you mark my words — *Inspector* McKinnon.' He tugged the door handle and stomped out, almost knocking Lachlan over as he did so. 'Excuse me, Padre,' He snapped, then left.

Lachlan came in and stood in front of Torquil's desk. 'Our new laird seems in a hurry to leave,' he remarked.

'I wish people wouldn't call him the new laird,' Torquil replied, with a hint of irritation. Then, noticing his uncle's look of surprise, 'Sorry, Uncle. It was just a difficult interview. He was not in a good mood, understandably, after he had to identify his employee's body.'

Lachlan winced. 'I heard from Morag that it wasn't a pretty sight. Was he —'

Torquil's telephone interrupted him and Torquil picked it up straight away. 'Yes, Ralph,' he said, into the receiver. He nodded as he listened. Then said eventually, 'Aye, it would help if you could confirm it with the other tests. Half an hour, that would be great.' He replaced the receiver just as Morag tapped on the door and came in.

'I'm sorry. Uncle, what was your question?'

The Padre had plucked his pipe from his breast pocket and was in the process of charging it with tobacco. 'I was wondering if he was murdered?'

Torquil sighed. 'I'm afraid so. Ralph says it is definite.' He looked up at Morag and explained: 'That was Ralph just now with the preliminary findings. He thought that there were a couple of things that I ought to be aware of. Firstly, that there was enough alcohol in his system to sink a battleship.'

'And secondly?' Morag queried.

'His trachea was crushed and his neck was broken at the fifth cervical vertebra. It was murder all right. Someone throttled him and then snapped his neck like a chicken's.'

In the Incident Room half an hour later, Torquil stood by the white board with the Padre beside him, while Morag, the Drummond twins and Ralph McLelland sat around the table-tennis table that had been converted into the operations desk.

'I know it is irregular, but has anyone any objection to Lachlan sitting in with us? We're depleted in numbers and I think he could prove useful in our investigations.'

There was a chorus of approval, and Lachlan sat down, immediately laying his unlit pipe down on the table in front of him.

'We'll start with Ralph's preliminary report,' Torquil said.

As the police surgeon gave a brief synopsis of his post-mortem examination, Torquil added the name Danny Reid to the whiteboard. He drew a square around the name and added relevant notes underneath:

ALCOHOL. THREE TIMES LEGAL LIMIT
BODY BADLY BURNED
MEDALLION IN MOUTH
MULTIPLE BODY PIERCINGS
BROKEN NECK — FIFTH CERVICAL VERTEBRA

'Thanks, Ralph,' Torquil said, as the local doctor finished his report and sat down. 'So we have two definite murders here.' He tapped the boxed names on the whiteboard and went on, 'And a missing police officer — presumed dead, an entire family missing, an accidental death in a rock-climbing accident and a sudden death from a heart attack.'

'A tangled skein, right enough,' mused Wallace Drummond. 'And don't forget the two dead dogs, Piper.'

The Padre picked up his pipe and tapped the mouthpiece against his teeth. 'And it all seems to revolve around Jock McArdle.'

'Who can hardly be a suspect though, can he?' said Douglas Drummond. 'He wouldn't be killing his own boys, would he?'

Torquil nodded. 'Ah yes, his *boys*. Well, while I was interviewing him earlier this morning, Morag was busy doing some research and liaising with her contacts on the Glasgow force. She has made some interesting discoveries about the "laird of Dunshiffin". He isn't quite who he seems.' He nodded to his sergeant, and then sat down.

'He certainly isn't,' went on Morag. 'Mr Jock McArdle died ten years ago.'

There was a chorus of surprised murmurings.

'Do you mean identity theft?' Lachlan asked.

'Not exactly. There was a Jock McArdle in Glasgow, but he had nothing to do with our supposed laird. No, he quite legitimately changed his name by dead-poll ten years ago from Giuseppe Cardini.'

'The plot thickens,' said Wallace.

'But why did he change his name?' Douglas asked.

Morag stared back at him with raised eyebrows. 'Presumably it was because he had just come out of prison after five years — for culpable homicide.'

The first thing that Jock McArdle did when he arrived back at Dunshiffin Castle was to pour himself a large malt whisky, which he gulped down in one. Then he poured another and carried it through to the library which he used as an office. He sat down behind the leather-topped desk, cluttered with papers and gadgets, and unlocked the desk drawer. He stared inside for a moment then smiled and reached for the telephone.

Superintendent Lumsden answered almost immediately and the two men talked animatedly for a few minutes.

'McKinnon is a bit of a maverick, I know,' Superintendent Lumsden said eventually. 'But I'll make sure that he plays ball.'

'I appreciate it, Kenneth. We Glasgow boys have to stick together, especially in a situation like this.' And after a few pleasantries he replaced his phone on the hook.

He took another sip of whisky and smiled to himself. He was still grinning when there was a tap on the door and he looked up.

'May I offer you my most sincere condolences, Mr McArdle,' said his butler.

Jock leaned back and gestured for him to come in. He smiled wistfully. 'Thank you, Jesmond. Take a seat. Let's not be so formal. That's not my way, you see.'

'Thank you, sir. I realize that you like informality, sir,' he said, gingerly taking a seat on the other side of the desk from his employer.

'So from now on, I'm going to call you Norman. That's OK,

isn't it?'

Norman Jesmond smiled uncertainly. 'That's good of you, sir. It is a privilege, sir.'

Jock smiled. 'Well, Norman, there's something that I've been wanting to talk to you about. Something I found in the pantry.'

The butler swallowed hard, conscious that little beads of perspiration had begun to form on his brow. 'In ... in the pantry, sir?'

'Aye, in the pantry, sir!' Jock McArdle repeated abruptly; then leaning forward his hand dipped into the open drawer and came out again with a tin that he placed on the desk. 'And I wanted to talk about my dogs — and this tin of — arsenic, I think!'

'I — er — don't understand, sir.'

The butler's eyes widened as Jock McArdle's hand again dipped into the drawer and came out again, but this time with a short-barrelled revolver. He laid it carefully on the desk beside the tin.

'Aye, let's talk about my dogs and how they may have had some of this ... arsenic,' he said in an unnervingly quiet and calm voice.

Torquil groaned when Morag told him that Superintendent Lumsden was on the telephone again.

'Your laird is mightily displeased with your attitude, McKinnon, and I have to admit that I think he's got a point. He is thinking of lodging an official complaint. He feels that you were heavy-handed with him this morning when he identified his employee.'

Torquil had felt his temper rise as his superior officer used the word 'laird' again.

'We have information about McArdle, sir. He isn't what —'

'Inspector McKinnon,' Superintendent Lumsden interrupted, 'you seem to have a problem with Jock McArdle, I realize that. But just let me tell you, he is an influential man.'

'You mean he has a lot of money, Superintendent?'

The voice on the other end of the line sounded as if it now came through gritted teeth. 'I mean that he has powerful friends. You would do well to realize that, Inspector. Two of his employees have been killed and he wants police protection.'

'Protection?'

'That's right. And I said you would see to it. So see to it and keep me informed about the case.'

There was a click and Torquil found himself staring at a dead line again.

Moments later he relayed the superintendent's message to the Incident Room.

'The man is a fool,' said the Padre, voicing his disbelief.

'Didn't you tell him about Morag's information, Torquil?' Ralph asked.

Torquil shook his head. 'I didn't really have time. The superintendent rarely listens. Besides, I'm not sure that he needs to know just yet.'

'Be careful, laddie. Remember that the superintendent had it in for you in the past,' said his uncle.

Torquil nodded. 'I'll be careful.'

He looked at Morag. 'Go on now, Morag. Tell us about McArdle, or Cardini.'

'Well, my contacts at Glasgow told me that Giuseppe Cardini served five years in Barlinnie Prison in Glasgow for culpable homicide. But apparently it was touch and go as to whether he went down for the murder of Peter Mulholland, one of the twins who jointly ran one of the biggest gangs in the Glasgow area. They were into drugs, prostitution and extortion in the city. Giuseppe Cardini was thought to have murdered Peter Mulholland, although he claimed it was self-defence.'

Morag looked up at the assembled men in the room. 'And now comes the interesting bit. The police had been put onto him by an investigative journalist who had infiltrated the gang that Cardini worked for. Her name was Rhona McIvor.'

Ralph gasped. 'Well, I'm damned! I knew that she was a writer of sorts, but I didn't know she was into that sort of writing.'

'I thought I might be able to get a copy of her article off the internet, but I couldn't access it,' went on Morag. 'But I did manage to get a copy faxed from the records department. I have a cousin who works there. It was her first job of the day.' She opened a file and pushed a copy of the article across the desk for Torquil to see. 'I've highlighted a few interesting bits,' she pointed out. 'Matthew Mulholland, the other twin, had also claimed to have been attacked by someone, and a bullet-riddled car was pulled out of the River Clyde.

'So Cardini went to prison and while he was inside Luigi Dragonetti, the head of the gang, died of a heart attack. When Cardini was finally released, he just disappeared for a few months. It was then that he changed his name to Jock McArdle. And somehow he seemed to have been able to finance himself in the confectionary business, although the Glasgow police believe, and still believe but have been unable to prove, that he made his money through vice and extortion.'

'But what about the other gang?' Torquil asked, as he scanned Rhona's article.

'Matthew Mulholland died of a stroke on his way home from a Celtic match a week after Cardini reinvented himself as McArdle. Apparently he ran his Mercedes into a wall. Somehow the gang just disappeared — or rather a lot of the gang "went straight" and ended up on the new Jock McArdle's payroll. He just went from strength to strength, invested in several companies and became a millionaire.'

'And what about this animal rights thing?' the Padre asked.

'Ah yes, that was one of his companies. They bred mice, rats and guinea pigs and supplied them to several university and government laboratories. Highly lucrative, until they attracted the attention of animal rights activists. Unluckily for them!'

'What do you mean?' asked Torquil, raising his head from the article.

'There is nothing concrete to go on here, but apparently there was an active cell of animal rights activists operating in the south of Scotland. There were a couple of attacks on the homes of some of the McArdle company workers, and even a fire-bomb attack on Jock McArdle's house. A few weeks later, a couple of bodies turned up in the river. They were identified as being members of the animal rights cell.'

The Padre whistled softly. 'Not a nice chap, it seems. And now he says he wants police protection.' He shook his head in disbelief. 'Well, I should let him wait a while if I were you. What about Sartori and Reid? Where do they fit in?'

Torquil tapped the article in front of him. 'I'm thinking that they were what Rhona called enforcers or punishers. That is how she described Cardini when he was a young man. That would certainly fit with their bully-boy antics on West Uist.'

Wallace raised a hand. 'Excuse me, but what was the significance of the bullet-riddled car?'

Morag shrugged. 'I am not sure. Rhona made the point that the Mulhollands had probably killed whoever was in that car.'

'But was there no body?' Douglas asked.

'No body, so no charge against Matthew Mulholland. He denied any connection. It was only supposition that it was connected. False number plates and everything. But inside the glove pocket they found a gun, a Mauser, and a library book about guinea pigs.'

'Guinea pigs?' repeated Wallace.

'Could that be the animal rights folk again?' his brother asked.

'The police checked and the book had been taken out by someone called Enrico Mercanti, who was on the Dragonetti gang payroll. The police think that he was a fellow punisher with Cardini-McArdle.'

Torquil stood up and went over to the whiteboard, and added a few more notes under Jock McArdle's name.

CARDINI PUNISHER PRISON — 5 YEARS

ANIMAL RIGHTS CELL — BODIES FOUND

He drew a line between McArdle's name and Rhona and added a balloon with the word ARTICLE inside.

'Cardini to McArdle. Sounds similar, as if he wanted to retain the sound of his name. So does the Italian connection have more significance than we thought?' He suddenly snapped his fingers and added in capital letters the word FAMILY to the notes under McArdle's name. Then he drew a line from there to the notes relating to Ewan McPhee's diary, where the same word stood out prominently.

'Could Ewan have been meaning this family is McArdle's *family*?'

'Are you thinking about the mafia?' Ralph asked.

Everyone started speaking at once, as the possibility hit home. But Torquil had been scrutinizing the ever-more complex spider web diagram that had been gradually developing. 'There is something here,' he mused, tracing out lines in his mind.

'Look there!' he cried, tapping the board under Rhona's

name. 'CARD 1N! We've assumed she had written a message about a card. I reckon she was writing Cardini! But why? What else was she trying to write?'

The phone rang and Morag answered it. 'That was Calum,' she said a few moments later. 'He was wanting to tell us to turn on the television. Scottish TV have a bulletin scheduled for the next few minutes.' And as Wallace switched on the station television and found the channel, they found themselves confronted by Kirstie Macroon sitting at a desk behind which was a picture of the Kyleshiffin harbour. In a small square at the top of the picture was a smiling photograph of Calum Steele, to whom Kirstie was talking over a phone link.

'And have we any idea who the dead man was, Calum?'

'We have indeed, Kirstie. It was a man called Danny Reid, and he was in the employ of Jock McArdle, the Glaswegian millionaire who bought himself Dunshiffin Castle.'

'And you say that the wind towers around the house were burning, as well as the cottage?'

'It was awful. They were burning like beacons all night. It must have been a brighter sight from the sea than the old lighthouse itself. An inferno! And arson, without a shadow of doubt.'

'And are the police treating the death of Danny Reid as suspicious?'

'They have launched a murder investigation and Inspector Torquil McKinnon is leading the inquiry.'

'Thank you, Calum. I am sure we will be in touch again.'

'My pleasure, Kirstie.'

'Thank you again.'

Calum Steele's voice was heard again, but immediately cut off as Kirstie Macroon deftly continued with her bulletin.

'That was Calum Steele, the editor of the West Uist Chronicle who has been keeping us up to date on the current story about the windmills of West Uist. So now—' She stopped in mid-sentence and touched her earpiece. '*I am just informed that we have been able to contact Mr McArdle, the new laird of Dunshiffin, and the man at the heart of the wind farm scheme.*'

A picture of Jock McArdle on the day that he took possession of Dunshiffin Castle appeared, replacing that of Calum Steele.

'*Mr McArdle, we understand that tragedy has afflicted you twice lately and we offer our condolences. Regarding the wind towers —*'

She never finished her sentence. Jock McArdle's thick Glaswegian accent broke out and continued in a staccato barrage of anger.

'*My wind towers have been criminally burned down and two of my employees have been murdered. This island should be called the Wild West, not West Uist! I am under attack here, and I have a pretty damned good idea who is behind it all — and why! I have been on the telephone this morning to the highest police officer I could contact and I demand police protection straight away. Meanwhile I am locking myself away in Dunshiffin Castle, and then I'm going to put the police straight. I'll get justice for*

my boys.'

The phone went dead and Kirstie Macroon picked up again, as a photograph of Dunshiffin Castle now took up the backdrop behind her.

'*As you have just heard, Mr McArdle feels that the situation in West Uist is becoming highly dangerous and he has asked for police protection. This is Kirstie Macroon for Scottish TV. We hope to have more information on the lunchtime news.*'

Wallace turned the sound down.

'The wee fool,' cursed Douglas. 'What does Calum Steele think he's playing at, giving out information like that on national news?'

'Och, he's a journalist, Douglas. You know well enough what

204

he's like.'

'Well, I think he's a pain in the backside,' persisted Wallace.

'He's worse than that, I'm afraid,' said Torquil. 'He might not realize it, but he may have just signed someone's death warrant. Jock McArdle sounded as though he was preparing to pull up his drawbridge against a siege.'

Nial Urquart's hair was dripping wet from his shower as he came into Katrina's small sitting-room, a towel wrapped around his waist. Katrina was sitting in a silk dressing- gown with a mug of coffee in her hand as she watched the news flash on Scottish TV.

CHAPTER SEVENTEEN

'I thought you were going to make a great big fry-up after all our exertions of the night?' he asked with a grin, as he slumped down beside her and wrapped an arm about her shoulders. 'And right afterwards I'm going to sort things out with Megan.'

'Just a minute, Nial,' she said, raising a finger, her eyes wide with alarm, 'This is important. There was a fire on the Wee Kingdom last night — and a death.'

'A death? What? Who?'

Together they watched and listened to Kirstie Macroon's conversation with Calum.

'Thank God it was none of the Wee Kingdom folk,' whispered Katrina. She turned and looked at Nial. 'This isn't good. You ought to be there for Megan.'

But he was still watching the news as Kirstie Macroon talked to Jock McArdle, before signing off. 'The bastard!'

'Who?' Katrina asked, bemusedly. She noted the sudden gleam of anger in his eyes.

'McArdle! Him and his kind who profit out of suffering. It's all his fault. And now he's wanting police protection. Bastard!'

'It must have happened very late last night. I think you had better get in touch with Megan. She'll be frantic — as well as furious with us.' She bit her lip. 'It must have been awful. What did Calum Steele say, it was like a beacon, like the —' She suddenly stood up and switched off the television. 'Come on, we've got to get going. I've got a couple of visits to make then I have an operating session scheduled for this afternoon, and you need to go and talk to Megan.'

She disappeared into her room returning a few moments

later after having thrown on a jumper and pulled on jeans and trainers. Nial watched her gather her case, a water bottle and then open a cupboard under the stairs and pull out a rifle bag.

'Crikey, have you got to put some poor beast down?' he asked with a humourless grin.

She nodded. 'Always a possibility. Look Nial, could I borrow your boat?'

'Sure, the keys are on the bedside table. It's in the harbour, well-fuelled and ready.'

Katrina ducked back into the bedroom returning swiftly. She leaned over and kissed him on the lips. 'I need to rush. You talk to Megan. No, better still, you go and see her.'

He watched her through the window as she drove off in her van. He started humming as he flicked on the electric kettle and loaded a couple of slices of bread into the toaster.

'But first things first,' he mused to himself, as he reached for his phone.

Torquil finished his call then pocketed his mobile phone. 'That's Calum sorted,' he said with a scowl.

'How was he?' Morag asked.

'Peeved. He feels that he has pulled off a major coup and performed a public service, and he was surprised to hear me say that I may be pressing charges on him as a police nuisance.'

'And will you?' asked Lachlan.

'Of course not, but I just wanted to rattle him a bit, and get him off our case.'

Ralph had stood up and was packing his bag. 'I feel a bit guilty there actually, Torquil. He collared me at breakfast and pumped me for information. I didn't think he'd be straight on national news with it.' He shook his head guiltily. 'And I'm afraid I've got to be off. I have a surgery soon.'

Once he had gone, Torquil addressed the others. 'Right, we've got a number of leads to follow up. First —'

He was interrupted by the phone ringing on the station counter. Morag went through to answer it. They waited until she answered it and came back.

'That was Nial Urquart,' she volunteered. 'He says that he's worried about Katrina Tulloch. She's just left her flat in a hurry — he'd stayed the night, he told me — and she's taken some sort of a rifle. He says she looked preoccupied and went off as soon as she heard that news bulletin this morning.'

'Calum again!' said Torquil. And then after a moment's thought, 'But what could there be in that news bulletin to worry her?'

'There's more,' said Morag. 'She's taken the keys of his boat.'

'We'd better get after her and see what's going on,' said Torquil.

'We'll go,' said Wallace standing up. 'Shall we take the *Seaspray*?'

Morag stood in his way. 'No, with respect, I think I should go. I know her better than you. She's a woman and I've talked to her already. I know she's a bit confused at the moment.'

Torquil nodded. 'I agree; Morag should go.'

'And I'll keep her company, shall I?' suggested Lachlan. 'Better two people in the catamaran.' Then as she was about to remonstrate, he added, 'Remember that Ewan went missing after going off on his own.'

'Lachlan is right, Morag. Away you go. We'll sort out the rest of the tasks.'

Vincent was feeling exhausted and guilty after a sleepless night. After taking Megan back to her croft, he had listened to her rant about Nial's betrayal. He had wiped her tears away, and together they had speculated about the cause of the fire. At about five in the morning, they had drunk a couple of whiskies and each become aware of the chemistry that had been threatening to bubble to the surface for several months.

She kissed him and he recoiled.

'Megan, I'm old enough to be your —' She silenced him with another kiss. And then another. 'But what about you and Nial?'

'There is no me and Nial now.'

And then they moved to the bedroom where they stayed, cocooned from the world by their love-making, until the cockerel and the geese roused them back to reality, and the ever-increasing problems that surrounded them. But now the sex was like a drug and the hours seemed to drift by until Vincent finally heaved himself out of bed and started to pull on his clothes.

'I don't want you to go, Vincent,' Megan pleaded, and she insisted that he stay for breakfast. As she prepared food and boiled the kettle, Vincent settled down on the settee and turned on the television. As they ate, they watched the morning farming programme, which was interrupted by the news bulletin from Kirstie Macroon. They sat and watched in horrified silence.

'Oh my God,' gasped Megan. 'What is happening to this place? It is all falling apart.' She leaned forward and put her hand on his. 'But at least I have you now.'

Vincent shook his head. 'I don't know, Megan. It doesn't feel right.'

'It feels very right to me.'

'What should we do?'

She wiped her mouth with a napkin. 'We need time to talk and see where we're going here. But I have a job to do first. Wait a minute.'

And she disappeared into her bedroom, coming back after a few minutes with a large holdall and a rucksack. 'These are Nial's,' she said. 'Will you help me load them in the car?'

'I had better come too.'

'No, I have to do this myself.'

He helped her pack up the car and watched her drive off into the swirling mist. Then he purposefully strode back to his croft. He had an important job of his own to do.

Alistair McKinley had watched the firemen battle to contain the fire, then withdrew and watched the police go about their business after they discovered the body. After they had taken it away, Alistair went back to his croft and catnapped in his armchair before washing and breakfasting. Then, as usual, he went out and tended to his livestock and did some work on the loom. Half expecting a news report on the fire, he went in for a cup of tea and turned on the old television in time to see Kirstie Macroon's report. As he watched, he became more and more irate.

'So much death!' he whispered to himself. 'And all down to him!'

Methodically clearing up his breakfast things he set about doing the other chores that he felt could not wait, before going back to the outhouse that housed his loom. Pushing several boxes of wool aside, he prised up the flagstone in the corner, reached into the hollow beneath and drew out the rifle wrapped in polythene. He unwrapped it, gave it the once over, then reached into the hollow again and drew out his father's old hunting bag, which contained his spare ammunition.

'Just one more job to finish,' he mused. 'And this is in your memory, Kenneth my lad.'

Five minutes later his jeep disappeared into the mist, its red tail lights swiftly disappearing in the swirling yellow vapours.

Then a lone figure came round the side of the croft, heading swiftly across the ground towards the Morrison family croft. He sniffed the air as he went past it, heading up the rise towards Wind's Eye croft. He stood by the burned-out shell surrounded as it was by the plastic police tapes.

'Just one bloody great mess!' Geordie Morrison muttered to himself. 'Someone's going to pay for this. And I am going to see to that!'

Morag and Lachlan had arrived at the catamaran berth just in time to see Nial Urquart's motorboat disappear out of the harbour, heading northwards.

'It's a nippy little thing that she's got there,' said Morag, 'but we'll soon catch her.'

She donned a waterproof and life-jacket and started the *Seaspray* up while Lachlan untied the mooring ropes and then boarded beside her.

'Aye, as long as she doesn't disappear into the mists,' he said, as he donned waterproofs and life-jacket, while Morag went through preparations to leave harbour. 'Have you any idea where she may be headed?'

'None at all. But what worries me most is why she feels she might need a gun at sea.' As she expertly manoeuvred out of the harbour before accelerating northwards it looked as if Lachlan's fears might be correct. Already the boat had disappeared into the misty waters.

Morag switched on the radar and moments later she had a blipping image on the screen in front of her. 'We can't see her, but she's there right enough. And it looks as if she's heading around the coast.'

'Towards the Wee Kingdom, do you think?' Lachlan asked.

'Maybe,' Morag replied. 'Or possibly to Dunshiffin Castle.'

'Wallace, I want you to go to the Wee Kingdom and make sure that Vincent Gilfillan, Alistair McKinley and Megan Munro don't leave their crofts. We'll want to take statements from them later. Douglas, I want you to find Nial Urquart and bring him back here.'

'Are you going to question him, Piper?' Douglas asked.

'I am. But I'm going to go over things here first and get my thoughts in order. And I'd better give the superintendent a ring and put him in the picture.'

Once he was alone, Torquil went through to the kitchen and put the kettle on for a cup of tea.

Then, with his cup in his hand, he went through to the Incident Room and stared at the whiteboard.

Jock McArdle! And now he wanted police protection! He grinned. There was only him available to give that protection now. But protection against whom?

The answer came when the station telephone rang.

'Emergency!' The rasping whispered voice had an unmistakable Glaswegian twang. 'This is Jock McArdle at Dunshiffin Castle. I need help now! There's a nutter here — with a gun!'

There was the deafening noise of a gun being discharged, then a strangled cry, then silence.

'Bugger!' cursed Torquil. He dashed out, stopping only to pick up his helmet and his gauntlets. Moments later he was hurtling along the mist-filled Harbour Street on the Bullet.

Like many native West Uist people, Katrina had been used to handling boats since she was a youngster. She knew exactly where she was going and what she was doing. Her heart was racing and she felt more anxious than she thought possible.

She was unaware that she was being pursued.

It seemed to take an interminable time as she raced through the mist as fast as she dared go. And she was always conscious of getting too close to the coastline, with its innumerable stacks, skerries and hidden rocks. But at last she saw the Wee Kingdom loom out of the mists, and she steered a course parallel with it until she rounded the western tip, where three successive basalt stacks jutted out of the sea. On the top of the most westerly one, was the ruins of the old West Uist lighthouse and the derelict shell of the keeper's cottage. She headed straight for it, slowed the boat and manoeuvred to a stop by the aged jetty. Quickly tying up, she unsheathed her rifle from its bag and gathered her medical bag and water bottle. As she turned to look at the bleak ruins of the lighthouse, she felt a shiver of fear run up and down her spine.

She mounted the steps to the ruin, which was nowadays no more than the bare husk of a tower. The door had long since gone and the inside was full of collapsed masonry and years of guano from the gulls that even now were circling it, protesting noisily at a human presence. Then she turned her attention to the derelict lighthouse-keeper's cottage. She went along its frontage, trying to see through the wooden shutters that had been nailed in place years before. And then she was at the door, staring at the new looking padlock.

Another shiver ran up her spine as she tested her weight against the unyielding door. She listened with her ear at the door, but heard nothing.

Except the noise of an engine approaching through the mist.

Who the hell was this?

She had no time or inclination to find out. She dropped her bag and water bottle and taking careful aim with the Steyr-

Mannlicher rifle, she fired point blank at the lock.

Morag and Lachlan heard a popping noise as they approached.

'What was that?' Lachlan asked.

'It sounded like a muffled gunshot,' said Morag.

'You mean a shot from a gun with a silencer?' Lachlan queried. 'We'd best be careful here, Morag.'

And minutes later, having tied up beside the motorboat on the jetty, they made their way warily to the open door of the old lighthouse-keeper's cottage. Just inside the door a rifle was propped up against the wall, while inside they saw Katrina Tulloch sobbing her heart out and leaning over a body lying face down on the floor.

The turrets and battlements of Dunshiffin Castle, the thirteenth-century stronghold of the MacLeod family, were lost in the mist as Torquil approached. He stopped a hundred yards away and parked his machine by the side of the road and then advanced on foot. He had no intention of announcing his arrival, so he took to the grass verge and jogged along towards the bridge that crossed the moat. Unfortunately, there was no way of entering the castle by any other route, so he kept close to the walls of the gateway tower and thanked the mist for giving him some cover. Once in the gravel courtyard, he stepped carefully so as to avoid announcing his presence.

On the way there, he had stopped to call for back-up, but cursed when his phone failed to connect with any of his staff. He had thought of taking a detour to the phone box on the Arderlour road, but the sound of the gunshot when McArdle had called him had indicated the urgency of the matter. He knew that he would just have to use his wits and trust to the message he left in the voice box and his ingenuity.

There were no lights on, but one side of the large double front door was standing ajar. Torquil made his way towards it by following the courtyard wall and then climbing up the side of the steps to come at it from the side. He wrapped his goggles around the end of his baton and edged it into the doorway, using it like an angle mirror. Seeing nothing suspicious he crept through the door to stand in the hall as swirls of mist wisped through the door.

On the oak-panelled walls hung numerous stag heads, antlers, shields, with criss-crossed claymores and pikestaffs. On either side of the stairway leading up from the great hall stood empty suits of armour. Having been in the castle on numerous occasions over the years, as both guest and as a piper for formal occasions, he knew his way about the place. But the thing that led him at the moment in the chilly atmosphere was the unmistakable smell of a gun having been discharged. As he stealthily crept up the staircase, passed the larger than life size portrait of the Jacobite laird, Donal MacLeod, the odour became stronger. He reached the top of the stairs where twin galleries ran east and west with doors dotted along them and corridors at either end leading off into the interior of the castle. There the smell was very strong. Grasping his baton he headed for the west wing.

All of the curtains were closed and the long corridor was almost in pitch blackness, except for a line of light coming from a door at the end of the corridor. Torquil knew that this used to be the billiard-room in the previous laird's day. He stopped for a moment to take off his boots and then crept softly along the corridor in his stockinged feet. As he did so, he heard a click then a muffled thud, like the sound of a billiard cue striking a ball followed by it thumping into a pocket of a billiard table. It was then, as his eyes accustomed to the extra darkness of the long corridor that he was aware of a figure ahead of him, creeping along the wall towards the door.

He stopped to watch as the figure reached the door, seemed to peer through the crack, then gingerly push the door open. As they did, the smell of a gunshot mixed with cigar smoke seemed to grow even stronger.

Then a voice cried out from the room, 'Don't move a muscle, Cardini!'

Torquil moved swiftly on his tiptoes towards the door. Inside, he saw the back of a man dressed in a smoking jacket bent over the billiard-table, as if frozen in time having just played a shot. Just behind him, a man was standing with his feet wide apart, arms outstretched, both hands holding an automatic weapon, pointed directly at the back of the other's head.

There was no time for thought. Torquil was in the room in a couple of strides. With a swift upward strike of his baton, he knocked the man's gun upwards, where it discharged with a deafening explosion, shattering a window. Then, moving swiftly before the man gained control of the gun, he brought the baton down sharply on the back of his head.

As the assailant fell face down, Torquil kicked the gun under the table, and then leaned down to turn him over.

He was surprised to see himself looking down at the unconscious figure of Vincent Gilfillan.

'Thank God for the West Uist police!' came Jock McArdle's voice. 'You know, McKinnon, I think you've saved me a job.'

CHAPTER EIGHTEEN

Katrina looked round as a floorboard creaked as Morag and Lachlan entered the ruined lighthouse-keeper's cottage. Tears were streaming down her eyes, but her voice was instantly authoritative as she moved into clinical mode.

'He's alive! But only just. Phone for Dr McLelland and get him to drive his ambulance down to the Wee Kingdom jetty.'

'Who is it, Katrina?' asked Morag, screwing her eyes up as she entered the dimly lit ruin.

'My God, Morag, it's Ewan!' gasped the Padre. His look of amazement turned instantly to anger as he saw the stout ropes about his ankles and his wrists. 'Who could have done this?'

But Katrina was not listening. She had her bag open and was making a quick examination of the almost comatose police constable. He was in a state of collapse and utter squalor, having clearly soiled himself several times over the last few days.

Morag went outside for a moment and called Ralph. She returned with her emotions in a state of complete turmoil.

She was so relieved, yet like the Padre, so angry that anyone could have done such a thing to her friend.

A low groan escaped from Ewan's lips as Katrina went over his chest with her stethoscope.

'Oh Ewan, I am so sorry, so very sorry,' she sobbed, as she slung her stethoscope round her neck and reached into her bag for an intravenous giving set and a bag of saline.

'He's dehydrated and looks as if he's lost a couple of stone,' she volunteered. 'He needs intravenous fluids, cleaning up and a good work-up in hospital.' She wrapped a tourniquet about his arm, found a vein and adroitly threaded a needle and cannula into it. With her teeth she pulled off the seal on the saline bag and linked it up to the cannula. 'Hold that high would you, Sergeant?' she said, handing Morag the bag, while she taped the cannula in place then applied a bandage around the site.

'I'm so pleased to see him alive,' Morag said at last, tears streaming down her cheeks. She pointed to the large polythene water flagon on an old table with a tube that hung down near Ewan's head. The flagon was empty but for about a few millilitres of brackish water. 'Whoever tied him up here obviously left water, but nothing else.'

'And I guess they didn't intend to leave him here as long as this. The monster!' exclaimed the Padre. Then he turned to Katrina. 'But how did you know he was here? You have probably saved his life; you know that, don't you?'

Katrina bent down and kissed Ewan on the forehead. When she looked up her face was racked with guilt. 'I didn't save him, Padre. In fact it's my fault that he's here in the first place!'

Torquil looked up at the unmoving figure bent over the billiard table. He saw that although the figure was wearing a smoking jacket it was clearly not the stocky Jock McArdle. As he slowly straightened he saw that it was Jesmond, the butler.

A very dead Jesmond.

His cheek was actually lying on the table surface, his sightless eyes staring straight ahead. From his mouth a frothy trail of vomit had trickled over the green baize. Clearly he had not died a natural death, but his body had been arranged thus.

'I can see why you look a wee bit shocked, Inspector McKinnon,' came Jock McArdle's voice from behind him. 'He's not a pretty sight, is he?'

Torquil turned round and found himself looking down the barrel of a short-barrelled revolver. McArdle was standing behind the door with the gun in his outstretched right hand and a cigar clamped between his teeth. 'I never liked the little pip-squeak,' he went on conversationally. 'He didn't really hide the fact that he resented me and my boys.'

'And so you killed him?'

Jock McArdle shook his head. 'Oh no, I didn't! It wasn't me; he did it himself. He was showing me how he poisoned my dogs.'

'And he did this while he was playing billiards with you?' Torquil asked, sarcastically.

McArdle laughed. 'You're having a wee joke with me, is that right, Inspector? No, you are right. He croaked in my office and I carried him here to bait my wee trap. And it was working fine, until you came charging in like the seventh cavalry.'

'It looked as if you were about to be shot in the head,' Torquil said, equally conversationally. 'As a police officer I couldn't allow that.'

McArdle nodded. 'Oh yes, I should be grateful, shouldn't I? And if you had just hit him a wee bit harder you would have saved me a job.'

Vincent groaned and put a hand to his head.

'But you see what I mean,' McArdle went on with a deep sigh. 'I'll have to finish him myself.'

Torquil stood straight. 'I can't let you do that.'

McArdle sneered. 'You are hardly in a position to do anything about it, Inspector. In fact, I didn't expect any of you flatfeet to arrive so quickly. It would have been convenient if you had come along afterwards, but as it is, I'll have to dispose of you as well.'

Vincent was trying to roll over.

'Just stay where you are Mercanti!' he barked.

At the mention of the name, Vincent went rigid, as if a button had been pressed. He slowly turned to face the laird. 'Cardini! You murdering bastard. I almost had you!'

McArdle waved the revolver in the direction of the snooker table and the propped-up body of Jesmond, 'Actually, I'm afraid not, pal. You fell into my trap, hook, line and sinker.'

Torquil had edged slightly away from the table, but McArdle snapped at him, 'Stay exactly where you are — both of you. This is a Smith & Wesson 360. It has a light trigger —which you might remember, Enrico. A quick move from either of you and I'll cut you in half.'

Vincent looked up at Torquil. 'He means it, Inspector. Don't do anything stupid.'

McArdle guffawed. 'Aye, Inspector. You see Enrico here — not Vincent as you know him —knows his guns. We were partners, you see. Comrades and punishers together.' Then his semi-affable grin suddenly disappeared. 'Until the little bastard betrayed me!'

Torquil nodded. 'I know who you are, *Giuseppe Cardini*. I know all about you and the Dragonetti gang.'

Giuseppe Cardini stared at Torquil in amazement for a moment, then he laughed heartily again. 'So you lot are not as stupid as I thought.'

'And I know all about your prison stretch, your petty little gang war and your change of name.'

Cardini pointed the gun at Vincent. 'And how much do you know about Enrico here? He was supposed to be dead, you know?'

'I know about the car in the river,' Torquil replied. 'And I know that it was a piece of investigative journalism by Rhona McIvor that sent you to prison.'

'The bitch!' McArdle almost screamed. 'I've wanted to get even with her for years, but she disappeared. It was only a few months ago when she started writing articles for the magazines that I realized where she was. I wanted her to suffer. And I have the means to do these things legitimately these days. I wanted an estate in the islands and this place came up. A snip for me. It was as if it was all meant to be.'

'And this wind farm plan, that was all part of your way to get even with her?'

'Of course. The stupid old bitch didn't recognize me after all those years.' He touched his cheek. 'Not surprising maybe, since I've had a spot of cosmetic surgery, but she was going blind as a bat. That made it easier.' He laughed. 'A wind farm! I ask you, why would I be interested in anything like that? It's pathetic. Give me the National Grid any day.'

Vincent had eased himself into a sitting position on the floor. 'You killed Rhona?'

'Not me, pal. She killed herself all those years ago when she took you in. Tell us about it.'

'*You* killed her!'

There was a thunderous noise as Cardini took aim and shot Vincent in the foot. Blood immediately gushed out of a hole in his boot and he gasped as he writhed in agony. Torquil made a move to help him but the sound of Cardini tut-tutting halted him.

'I said — *tell* us!'

Vincent's face was covered in perspiration, but he gritted his teeth and tried to talk.

'You were always a sadistic bastard, Giuseppe. That was one of the reasons I needed to get away. Rhona gave me the means of escape.'

Cardini snorted disdainfully. 'Aye, she was a good-looking

woman and we never suspected she was a journalist, a spy.' He turned to Torquil. 'She got herself a job as a cashier in one of Luigi Dragonetti's betting shops, then gradually worked her way up to be a manager. That allowed her to get properly in the know of things. And that's when she started shagging Enrico there.' He spat on the floor by Vincent's feet. 'And that's when he betrayed his family!'

'Does family mean mafia?' Torquil asked.

Cardini guffawed. 'Naw! You've been watching too many Godfather films. Luigi Dragonetti was just a god. He was like a father to us — him and me. Before him we were just slum tinkers. He gave us respect and gave us lives.' He shook his head and took the cigar out of his mouth. 'Like I tried to be like a father to Liam and Danny.'

'That's rubbish!' Vincent snorted. 'Luigi Dragonetti was a sadistic bastard who modelled himself on Al Capone. He used folk like us to punish people. He didn't give a stuff whose lives we pissed on as long as he got what he wanted. Rhona taught me that.'

'Then that was another reason for her to die! I hated that bitch for the five years I lost in prison.'

'So was that your real reason for coming to West Uist?' Torquil asked. 'To arrange for her death.'

Cardini shrugged noncommittally. 'That was the ultimate aim. But first I planned to destroy her. And it was happening too — until this bastard started killing my boys.'

'Did you?' Torquil asked.

Vincent's face was fast draining of colour as blood oozed from the hole in his foot to form a gory puddle on the floor.

'No — and yes,' he replied in a rasping voice. 'I killed the first little sod, but I didn't mean to. I just got so angry over that letter and how he talked to Megan. Especially when we were getting close. When I left Megan, I waited for him to come back by the causeway. When I confronted him, man to man, he spat in my face.' He glared at Cardini. 'That was one of the things you used to do before you hurt people. Anyway, he tried to throw a punch but he was drunk and slow. I knocked him off the causeway, then I jumped down and dragged him to the pool.'

Cardini let out a howl of rage. 'My boy! You drowned my boy!'

Torquil realized that Cardini's temper was brewing up to volcanic proportions. He needed to keep things flowing for the present. 'So what about the other man, Danny Reid? Did you kill him too?'

'I did. But it was because Rhona warned me about Cardini.'

'That's what she meant by CARD IN?'

Vincent nodded. 'I knew that Cardini would have some sort of revenge planned for Sartori's death. I saw the bugger sneaking into Gordon MacDonald's cottage, planning to set it on fire. A warning to us. I recognized he was trying to provoke whoever killed the first piece of shit. So I stopped him and snapped his neck. And that's why I left that message for him.'

'Is that what the medallion in the mouth was all about?' Torquil asked.

'It was a sort of signature that we used in the old days,' Cardini volunteered. 'But that was when I realized that bloody Enrico Mercanti was alive and well on this piss-pot of an island!' He laughed. 'And that's when I laid my wee trap for you. It actually worked out a bit earlier than I planned, but that TV woman forced my hand by giving me the opportunity to send out a message to you.'

He raised the gun and Torquil slowly raised his own hand. 'OK, McArdle or Cardini, whichever you want to be known by, it is time to give me that gun. I am arresting you both.'

Giuseppe Cardini looked back at Torquil in mock amazement. 'You are arresting me?' He guffawed. 'I don't think you quite understand. I am defending my property here. That bastard killed my boys, then he came here and killed my butler and tried to kill me too. I struggled with him and you, our heroic local flatfoot, rushed to help me, only to get tragically killed in the line of duty.' He shook his head with mock sympathy. 'There have been too many police officers killed while doing their duty and I will arrange with Superintendent Lumsden, my good friend, for some sort of local monument to be erected.'

Torquil was aware of a patina of perspiration on his brow, but he managed to keep his voice calm. 'I said I will take that gun now. I have to get medical attention for Vincent here. And, by the way, thank you for your confession.'

Cardini scowled and pointed to the gun in his hand. 'I am the one in the driving seat, McKinnon. Now how about just saying your prayers?'

'I don't think there is a need for that,' Torquil said, deliberately looking past Cardini at the open door. 'You have got all that, haven't you, Constable Steele?'

Cardini sneered contemptuously. 'Nice try, flatfoot. Now say your prayers. Both of you!'

Calum Steele's voice came from the open doorway. 'I have it all on tape here, Inspector McKinnon.'

In a trice, Cardini spun round into a broad-based crouch, both arms outstretched and steadying the gun.

There was a sudden flash from waist height, followed by a burst of fire from Cardini's gun.

But his moment of surprise had given Torquil the time he needed. He flew across the room, kicked the gun upwards and, as he did so, grabbed Cardini's right wrist. They wrestled with the gun, and it scanned the room, spewing out two shots. Then Torquil managed to twist and bend Cardini's wrist back on itself. There was the snapping noise of bones crunching as the gangster's hand opened automatically and he screamed in pain as the gun fell to the floor.

Butt Cardini had been a street brawler and he immediately threw a left at Torquil's head. It was a shade too slow and he ducked and threw a straight left to Cardini's abdomen; then, as Cardini doubled over, he hammered an uppercut into his jaw. It lifted the laird off his feet and deposited him unconscious on the floor.

'And that's how we do things in West Uist.' Torquil said, blowing on his skinned knuckles. He turned to the door where Calum was climbing to his feet from the prone position he had adopted in order to hold up the digital camera and first dazzle then draw Cardini's fire.

'Well done, Calum. I've never been so happy to see anyone in my life. I thought that either you hadn't picked up my voice message or your Lambretta had finally packed in.'

'Never a bit of it, Piper. Mind you, that's the first time the West Uist investigative journalist has ever come under real live fire. And about that title "Constable Steele" — it has a certain ring —'

There was the sound of a click from the floor and they both turned to see Vincent propped against the leg of the snooker table, the crumpled body of Jesmond having tumbled into the bloody pool beside him. A rapidly spreading patch of blood was forming over Vincent's abdomen where one of the stray bullets had struck home.

'Just hold it where you are,' he rasped, his bloodied hands clenching a gun. 'Things are not — quite — finished!'

CHAPTER NINETEEN

Ralph McLelland broke just about every speed restriction on the island and arrived at the Wee Kingdom jetty within ten minutes of the Padre's call. Together with Katrina and Morag, he stretchered Ewan into the ambulance and drove straight to the cottage hospital. There, Sister Lamb and Nurse Anderson set about cleaning him up while Ralph took blood samples in order to determine his clinical state and electrolyte balance.

'He is dangerously dehydrated and still non-responsive,' Ralph told Katrina. 'I'll monitor him for a few hours to get him stable, but I have every faith that he will be on his feet in a week or so. Ewan McPhee is one of the strongest men I have ever known, but surviving this long on just sips of water has taken it out of his system.' He shook his head as he looked down at the haggard redheaded constable. 'I don't think many folk could have survived his ordeal.'

Katrina heaved an enormous sigh of relief then turned to Morag. 'And I think that you will want to have my account of all this?'

Morag's spirits had gone from rock bottom to sky high upon discovering that one of her best friends was still alive. Now, as an officer of the law, she snapped into professional mode. 'My thoughts exactly, Miss Tulloch. And I think it would be best if you accompanied me to the station to make your statement.'

Wallace Drummond had been on his way to the Wee Kingdom when he saw Alistair McKinley's jeep pulled off the road by the rough track that led up to the Corlins. He had a good idea of where he would find the crofter, so he coaxed the police

Ford Escort along the track and duly found him preparing to climb the cliff face.

'Alistair,' Wallace said, as he let the window down. 'I have already told you that you are not permitted to have a gun at the moment. You will give it to me now.'

The crofter shook his head, his face determined. 'Leave me alone, Wallace Drummond. I have something that needs to be done. I am going to shoot those bloody golden eagles.'

But Wallace was out of the car and, with a couple of quick strides, he caught hold of the bag carrying the gun that Alistair had about his shoulders. He slipped it off and held it behind him. 'And I am telling you that you will do nothing of the sort. There has been enough killing as it is. I am taking this gun and you back to the station with me. Inspector McKinnon says he wants to talk to you.'

'Put the gun down, Vincent,' Torquil said. 'You need medical treatment for that wound and you need it now.'

Blood was oozing from the wound in Vincent's abdomen and had soaked his trousers.

'I'm not worried about myself, Inspector,' he said, his voice losing power all the time. 'I am more concerned about that piece of excrement there.' He hesitated to gulp some air. 'He has a history of atrocities that you wouldn't believe. He liked to hurt people and watch them squirm. And he's murdered folk without batting an eyelid. I plan to be his judge, jury and executioner.'

'You can't do that, Vincent. That would make you a murderer, too.'

'I don't matter anymore,' he breathed. He gestured with the gun in his hand at Calum. 'Put those on the floor and switch them off.'

Torquil nodded to Calum, who acquiesced and laid down his camera and his Dictaphone.

'That's good, because I don't want any more of this being recorded,' Vincent said wheezily.

He stabbed the gun in the direction of the still unconscious Giuseppe Cardini. 'It is about him coming back into our lives. I thought that I had broken free from the Dragonetti gang and their ugly world of death and violence. Rhona helped to stage my disappearance and set me up with a croft here twenty years ago.' His eyes seemed to mist over. 'Clever woman, Rhona. She persuaded the old lady who owned it — she was ill and dying — to pass it on to me as if I was a relative. She sorted out my new identity, national insurance number, absolutely everything.'

Cardini began to stir as he made a slow return to consciousness.

Vincent rallied at the sight and aimed the gun at him. 'He deserves to die!' he exclaimed.

'The law will deal with him, Vincent. Don't do anything stupid.'

Cardini heaved himself up on his elbows, his eyes suddenly widening with alarm when he saw the gun in the hand of the blood-soaked Vincent. He gasped in horror as he realized he was staring death in the face.

The gun-hand began to waver and Vincent's eyes started to roll upwards. 'At ... at least ... I can now —'

Suddenly, as if every last ounce of energy had been used up, he slumped sideways and the gun fell from his hand.

Torquil swiftly produced handcuffs and cuffed Cardini. Then he and Calum turned their attention to Vincent. A quick examination failed to find a pulse and the enlarging pool of blood suggested that things were hopeless. Nevertheless, while

Calum called for medical assistance, Torquil attempted resuscitation.

By the time that Ralph had arrived, it was all too clear that the man they knew as Gilfillan was truly dead.

Giuseppe Cardini had been watching all that time, cursing them and making scathing comments. Now, he tossed his head back and began to roar with laughter. 'That serves —'

He suddenly went silent as Calum seemed accidentally to trip, and kicked him in the groin.

Neither Torquil nor Ralph McLelland saw it happen.

Katrina sipped the hot tea that Morag had brewed back at the station.

'I really liked him.' she explained. 'Ewan, I mean. But Kenneth McKinley just wouldn't leave me alone, and Ewan started to get jealous and suspicious. It is all my fault.'

'Why do you say that?' Morag asked, as she jotted things down with her silver pen.

Katrina put the mug down, her expression a mix of pain and guilt. 'Because Kenneth was working for me, and it all got out of hand. He was working ... clandestinely.'

Morag raised her eyebrows quizzically. 'Go on.'

'You have no idea how hard it is to make a living as a vet in the Hebrides. I was in debt up to my ears. I had a colossal student loan to pay back, and even working abroad in the East for a couple of years didn't make much inroad into it. When I took over my uncle's practice, I didn't realize that I'd be taking over his debt as well. He'd mismanaged things in a most appalling manner — as well as having a personal debt of several thousand with his gambling.' She looked beseechingly at Morag for some sign of sympathy. 'I was desperate and I had to make money as fast and as quickly as I could. There was no legal way I could do that.'

Morag made a conscious effort not to let her face register any sense of judgement. She had to let Katrina willingly offer the information. 'So what did you do?'

Katrina bent her head in embarrassment. 'I had contacts from my time in the East. Dodgy contacts with people working in the animal trafficking black market.'

Morag made notes and said nothing, merely encouraging the vet to continue with a nod of her head.

'In Thailand and China seal penises and genitalia are used to make virility medicines. In the Hebrides we have an almost limitless supply of them.'

Morag was unable to keep the revulsion out of her voice. 'But you are a vet! How could you contemplate such a thing?'

'I am a vet, but I eat meat. It is easy to judge me, but the seals were a rich source of revenue that I could tap into. I had a regular courier all lined up to take the stuff over on the ferry to the mainland along with my bona fide samples. From the mainland, he would arrange to ship them abroad. His exact route, I don't know.'

'We'll find out, don't worry,' Morag replied curtly. 'And what about Kenneth McKinley, how did he fit in?'

'He went out in his boat and shot them — procured their organs — then disposed of the bodies. He liked it, because he was a bit of a Walter Mitty. He liked to call himself the "assassin".' She leaned forward and pummelled her temples with her fists. 'I was such a manipulative cow. I fuelled his fantasy.'

'We know about his fixation with guns,' Morag said. 'And we are aware that Ewan McPhee suspected something about him.'

Katrina burst into tears. 'I know and I hate myself for it. That was how Ewan went missing. Kenneth told me that he had taken out — that was how he described it, as if he was a hit-man or something — a family group of seals. Ewan must have followed him and Kenneth jumped him or something. He said he had him holed up somewhere, and that he was teaching him — and me — a lesson. I think he had some idea that I would sleep with him to get Ewan free. He wore disguises when he was out shooting and I think he meant to frighten Ewan.' She bit her lip. 'Then it all went badly wrong. I met him up on the ledge in the Corlins and I tried to get him to tell me where Ewan was, but he was obsessed with shooting the golden eagles. Anyway, I didn't see it clearly in the mist, but I think one of them flew at him and seemed to hit him. He staggered over the edge and — fell to his death.'

She began sobbing again and Morag waited until she settled. Under other circumstances she would have made comforting noises, but she was feeling too angry and too revolted by the woman in front of her to do so.

'I went down to him,' Katrina went on at last, between sobs. 'He was dead, of course. Then I — I scratched his face, to make it look as if an eagle had struck him with its talons. I didn't know what else to do. I had to find Ewan, but I didn't know where he could be.'

'What about the rifle?'

'I took that and hid it. You've got it now.'

'And what made you go to the lighthouse-keeper's cottage?'

'I had scoured the whole island without luck over the last few days.' She looked up at Morag who was staring at her with her best poker face. 'I guess you probably know that I have just started an affair with Nial Urquart.'

Morag shrugged noncommittally. 'Go on.'

'Well it was this morning on the news. Calum Steele mentioned about those wind towers and the cottage burning like beacons — brighter than the old lighthouse. Then I thought that had to be it. Kenneth could have easily got to and from there from the Wee Kingdom. It is just below their croft. And, as you know, that's where he was. The poor man could have been dead, all because of me.'

'He could,' Morag replied coldly. 'And you can just thank your lucky stars that he isn't. Ewan McPhee is one of my best friends.'

Douglas Drummond pulled up outside the Morrisons' cottage just in time to see the family transporting bags from a huge wheelbarrow into the house.

'Ah, the police!' said Geordie, a well-built fellow with long hair and a full unkempt beard. 'I have a complaint to make. Someone has been into my house and made an almighty mess. Someone is going to have to pay!'

Douglas could hardly believe his ears, but rather than cause a scene with the youngsters about, he smiled and got out of the car. 'I was actually trying to find Nial Urquart, but there doesn't seem to be anyone left on the Wee Kingdom except yourselves. Maybe it would be as well if I took you down to the station to have a chat with Inspector McKinnon.'

'A good idea,' replied Geordie. 'I am not in a mood for shilly-shallying.'

'No, I can see that,' said Douglas. 'Neither is he.'

Megan Munro stood at the door of Katrina Tulloch's flat with the holdall and rucksack containing Nial Urquart's clothes. She had rehearsed the speech she was going to make, but when Nial answered the door with contrition written across his face, she merely dropped them on the mat.

'Megan, I'm an idiot!'

'You are.'

'I have made an awful mistake.'

'Me too.'

'Do you think we could —?'

In answer she flung her arms about his neck and he hugged her as if he would never let her go again.

'Of course we can!'

A week later, after an emotional rollercoaster trip, things started to settle down. The whole story about Jock McArdle came out and was duly written up by Calum Steele in the *Chronicle* and in interviews on Scottish TV with Kirstie Macroon. Giuseppe Cardini was transferred to a holding prison pending his trial, the windmills were taken down and the island saw a spate of funerals.

Vincent Gilfillan was buried in the St Ninian's cemetery next to Rhona McIvor, near to the grave of Kenneth McKinley.

Ewan McPhee slowly pulled through and was discharged from hospital into the doting care of his mother, Jessie. The entire division of the West Uist branch of the Hebridean Constabulary as well as the full staff of the *West Uist Chronicle* and the Padre descended on them and stayed far longer than they had intended, all eventually being ejected by Dr McLelland who gave them a lecture about over-tiring the patient.

Outside, Morag asked Torquil, 'So now that the big one is back safe and sound, have you given any more thought about leaving the Force?'

Torquil grinned. 'Of course I have. I am staying right where I am needed. With my friends.'

Calum was still nibbling one of Jessie's scones. 'About that roving commission we talked about, Piper? You know, me being a special sort of police assistant. I have been thinking and there could be mutual benefits —'

Torquil groaned and put an arm about the local editor's shoulder. 'Let's finish this at the Bonnie Prince Charlie, Calum. I'll even let you buy me a pint of Heather Ale.'

The Padre followed suit and put an arm about Morag's shoulders. 'Does Heather Ale sound good to you?' he asked.

'It does actually, Padre. And I think that we should drink to Superintendent Lumsden's fortune.'

'Why's that?' asked Wallace.

'Didn't you know?' Morag replied. 'He's been suspended, pending investigation of his association with McArdle.'

'Well, it couldn't happen to a nicer man, could it?' said Douglas.

'My sentiments exactly,' said Torquil with a laugh. Then, turning to Calum with a mock scowl, 'But don't quote me!'

A NOTE TO THE READER

Dear Reader,

Thank you for taking the time to read my novel, I hope that you enjoyed reading about the dark things that can happen on my idyllic little Scottish island on the edge of the world.

It is true that characters in a novel often take on a life of their own. That happened several times in this novel, when the story did not follow the path that I had imagined it would take. The characters felt so at home on the island of West Uist that they felt empowered to pay the piper to play their macabre tune.

I have been a lifelong fan of crime fiction, but to my mind the use of the laboratory and the revelations that DNA testing can instantly give, somehow rob many modern crime novels of their sense of romance. That was why I set my story on the remote Hebridean island of West Uist, so that it would be far removed from the modern forensic crime thriller. Also, because the island has the smallest police force in the country, it would not another gritty, urban police procedural. Crimes would have to be solved in a very old-fashioned manner.

I studied medicine at the University of Dundee and did some of my training in the highlands. I loved the sense of community in villages and determined that if I ever wrote a crime novel it would feature a Scottish detective working in a remote place, aided by friends, family and the local newspaper. Years later when Inspector Torquil McKinnon walked into my imagination I set about learning to play the bagpipes, although unlike Torquil, the winner of the Silver Quaich I have never been anything other than dire. Nonetheless, playing around with my pipes helps me as I am working out my plots.

Since golf is also a hobby and I had played on the remotest Hebridean courses, those sheep-nibbled links complete with dive bombing gulls had to appear in the stories. When I venture onto my local golf course I imagine the Padre, a steady 8 handicapper, playing alongside me, advising me on how to hit the green, sink a putt – or solve the newest clue.

If you have enjoyed the novel enough to leave a review on **Amazon** and **Goodreads**, then I would be truly grateful.

Keith Moray

https://keithmorayauthor.com

Sapere Books is an exciting new publisher of brilliant fiction and popular history.

To find out more about our latest releases and our monthly bargain books visit our website:
saperebooks.com

Printed in Great Britain
by Amazon